How to Survive a Ghost Story

Maddie Gudenkauf

Published by Dalygood Media, LLC, 2018.

While every precaution has been taken in the preparation of this book, the publisher assumes no responsibility for errors or omissions, or for damages resulting from the use of the information contained herein.

HOW TO SURVIVE A GHOST STORY

First edition. September 20, 2018.

Copyright © 2018 Maddie Gudenkauf.

Written by Maddie Gudenkauf.

To Kierra, my best enemy since 2011.

And to my family, for always supporting my weirdness.

Tip #1:
Keep your eyes open.

DESPITE THE ARTICLES and books her father made her read, Lucy Vitalis was not prepared for the alienating process of walking into her new school for the first time. She was aware nobody would want to be her friend — everyone already had their friends and Lucy was just an extra body. Everyone was supposed to treat her like what she was, an unnecessary addition to their already perfect social structure, and they would ignore her until she was forced into their attention. That was the conclusion she had drawn from all of her research and she was sticking to it. However, Sterben High School of Sterben, Kansas seemed to be the exception to all of the articles, books, and movies.

Everyone stared. All of the time.

As soon as Lucy got out of her father's truck, everyone's gaze settled on her and didn't look away. Perhaps Sterben was a small enough town that any new person not related to anyone was a shock to the system. Maybe it was her outfit; a vintage black dress with the matching flat brim hat that would've been considered cheap at her school in New York, but was now a luxury amongst the overwhelming wave of cheap graphic t-shirts and polyester polos at this school. Maybe they believed they were looking at a ghost, with Lucy's long blonde hair so fair it was practically white and her skin just as a pale. But Lucy knew what ghosts looked like and she was 95.6% sure she was not one.

Wait.

By the lockers near a water fountain, there was a boy.

Golden hair, dirty nose, scruffy shirt...the 70's style lukewarm orange lockers was the perfect backdrop.

As he stared at Lucy with gorgeous hazel eyes, she walked over and pulled her camera out from her black messenger bag. Everyone surrounding the boy had seen Lucy target him and they had all hurriedly ran away, hoping to not be included as victims to the new girl's weirdness. Now alone, the boy backed into the locker, a new look of fear resting in his eyes.

"Shush." Lucy whispered, bringing the camera to her eye. "Stay in frame."

Zooming the camera in, the lens would've touched the kid's nose if he moved even a hair. Before he could stutter another word, Lucy twitched on the button and a bright flash shined across the lockers. His pupils shrank and grew expansively.

"My eyes!" He exclaimed, grabbing his face.

Turning away, Lucy scrolled through her camera until she found the picture. An eyeball showcasing all the colors hazel can reflect with a pool of black dotting the middle. Freckles on tan skin with a wisp of golden hair and touch of pale orange metallic in the background. But...

"Angle." She decided. "We'll need to reshoot."

The boy screamed as soon as Lucy pointed the camera at him again. He tried to run off, but tripped over his own feet and slammed his shoulder into the lockers. With another shout of pain, he stumbled backwards and ran into one of the remaining bystanders that stuck around for the show. They laughed and shoved him back to Lucy. She brought the camera back to her eye. Screaming again, the boy ran forward, slamming his forehead into the lockers. He collapsed to the floor, causing all of the bystanders to laugh even harder.

The boy held himself by the elbows and groaned. Lucy ignored her new classmates' laughter and focused on his body. The glossy, pale multi-colored floor shone just enough for the boy's grubby shirt to reflect from it. She snapped the picture with another brilliant flash of light.

"What is going on here?" An elderly woman in a dress more appropriate for a box or a tablecloth came storming over. She shot an immediate glare at Lucy. "Who the hell are you and what did you do to the little Hunter boy?"

"Fascinating." Lucy held the camera back up to her eye. "I had heard that teachers like you still existed, but I thought it was an exaggeration."

"Teachers like me?!" The elderly woman said. "What do you mean teachers like me?"

"A poor sense of fashion matched with a bitter attitude from working in the most under-appreciated industry in our country," Lucy said as she focused her camera on the woman's apple broach. "I'm sure you were more optimistic at the beginning of your career, but after years of dealing with ungrateful, disrespectful students and the government overlooking the school's budget requests *again*, I'm sure it can make anyone grow apathetic for their wardrobe of the day." Lucy snapped a picture of the educator with a brilliant flash of light.

With no reaction to the sudden flash of light, the elderly teacher scowled.

"Get to Principal Hansen's office, both of you." She pulled the little Hunter boy off the floor by the collar of his scruffy shirt and shoved him toward Lucy. "*Now!* Everyone else, get to class!"

The onlookers scrambled, hastily attempting to look productive to appease the old woman.

"Excuse me, ma'am." Lucy raised her index finger. "In your misdirected anger, I think you've overlooked the fact that I'm a new student to this school and thus I don't know where the principal's office is located."

"Another word out of you and I'll transfer ya to Lebenville." The elderly teacher pointed a crooked finger at Lucy before turning to bark an order at someone who was fiddling with their locker. The student dropped the combination lock and sprinted down the hallway. The elderly woman hobbled after them in large strides.

Soon enough, the hallway was cleared. Only scattered papers and abandoned jackets remained. After a moment, Lucy put the camera to her eye and snapped another picture. The sound of the shutter echoed off the metal lockers and down the bricked hallway. She checked the picture. If the walls were brown, it would be an excellent photo to develop in black and white. Instead they were a pasty yellow, covered in hand-drawn posters and announcements, which made it delightful in color.

"Alright then, lead us to Principal Hansen," Lucy said, turning to the boy. "I'm assuming you know the way given the fact this school is smaller than a penthouse and you're clearly a long term resident of this education system if the teacher knew your name."

The boy's hazel eyes fluttered and looked unfocused as he stared up at Lucy. He would still be a head shorter than her even if she wasn't wearing her boots.

"Um yeah, I guess you could say we're small," The boy said, a Midwestern lilt touching his words. "Of course, it ain't too bad. It's nice to know everyone."

"It's nice to know the *idea* of people," Lucy remarked. "No one ever reveals their true self unless they get caught either in death or in love."

"Oh." The boy fluttered his eyes again. "Alright."

He led her down the hallway in silence. It wasn't long until they were sitting in two plastic chairs in a dimly-lit office. The walls were a faded, dusty-sort of sky blue and it was a tight enough space that Lucy's knees threatened to knock into the secretary's desk. To the side of the secretary was a freshly painted blue door with an iron horseshoe fixated to the center of it. The secretary, a frail woman thin enough to practically be a skeleton and visibly old enough to reflect the sentiment, tapped very slowly at the ancient computer with her two index fingers.

Tap.

A pause, to look over her oval glasses at the pink paper sitting on her desk. Her dull blue eyes etched across the pink paper just as slowly as she typed out each letter. Finally she turned back to the computer.

Tap.

When the secretary turned back to the paper, Lucy brought her camera to her face and snapped a picture. Unlike the elderly teacher, the secretary's lack of reaction to the loud shutter clap and the blinding flash of light seemed to indicate a lack of awareness of the situation rather than stubborn resistance. After a moment, the secretary turned back to her computer.

Tap.

The wooden door stationed aside the plastic chairs burst open, a loud explosion of old wood and rusted metal scraping across a floor desperate for a new waxing. The little Hunter boy let out a shout of surprise as a large man lumbered through. With broad shoulders and a fresh blue flannel shirt, the man immediately caught the secretary's attention. As she thoroughly examined the visitor's dark hair mand dark eyes, she adjusted her glasses.

"You must be the little Hunter boy's father," She cooed. "I must say, sir, it's an honor to *finally* have you here and we deeply thank-"

"Lucy, what the hell did you do?" Mike Vitalis said, his voice booming loud and clear in the office.

"I just took some pictures, Dad," Lucy said. "It distressed Hunter so a bitter teacher who cares about justice as much as she cares about her appearance sent us both here."

"My first name isn't Hunter," The boy squeaked. "That's my last name. Everyone just calls-"

"I'm sorry sir, but you're *this* girl's father?" The secretary said, nodding her head towards Lucy and completely ignoring the little Hunter boy.

"The one and only," Mike Vitalis grunted.

"Despite my mother's frequent infidelity, the paternity test he took for sole custody during the divorce proceedings proves against other implications," Lucy stated.

The secretary looked between the dark haired father and his acutely blonde daughter.

"Well then." She cleared her throat. "Since you're the first here, go right in and see Principal Hansen."

With a soft nod, Lucy pulled herself up from the chair and led her father into the blue door that led into the principal's office. At the large desk centered in the middle of the broom closet of an office, Principal Hansen was tending to an electric waffle iron. The sweet smell of fresh waffles hung in the tiny space, lingering with each sizzling sound discharged from the waffle iron. Around him, the walls were decorated with various forms of religious artifacts with a collection of wind chimes dangling from the ceiling. When the shutter from Lucy's camera as she took a picture of the odd interior design clicked, the man centered in the middle of the chaotic room looked up and promptly tossed the waffle iron onto the floor, uncaring whether it was still hot or not.

Sterben High's principal was a scrawny man with large dusty brown hair that puffed out everywhere in bushy curls. Stubble graced his jawline and a cheap thrift store suit sat loosely on his bony frame. Folding his thin fingers on his desk, he nodded to the two folding chairs stationed in front of the metal desk.

"Please take a seat!" Principal Hansen said. "My name is Mr. er, *Principal* Hansen, and I am the principal of this high school. Yes. I am the principal. What can I help with you today?"

Lucy ignored the principal's lapse in grammar and sat down in the folding chair, crossing her ankles. Quietly aiming her camera at the principal, she tried to frame his untamed hair in the cork board that sat behind him. Her father stepped forward and pushed her camera down to her lap, never breaking eye contact with the school official.

"You called me," Mike said. "My daughter Lucy is in trouble."

"Ah yes! Sweet Lucille." Principal Hansen smiled widely. "Yes. Such a bright student. Frankly when Mrs. Bobby called me to tell me she got in trouble, I was frankly very disappointed and frankly very angered that one of Sterben High's brightest students could possibly-"

"Lucy just started school here today," Mike said. "We're new in town...I'm sorry, but are you the real principal?"

"The real principal? Ha!" Hitting his fist against his desk, Principal Hansen stood up to reveal a towering height. "Good sir, I don't know who you are, but I have a Master's in Education from Kansas State University and a true passion to guide these students to success! That may not mean much from where you're from, but here that may mean just about the same thing from where you are from." The principal looked confused, yet proud for a moment as he sat back down in his chair and looked thoughtfully to a portrait of a white Jesus on the wall. "Dear, sweet Luanne will serve a lunch detention for her misdeeds. Make sure it doesn't happen again. My secretary, Teri, will write up your referral. Please send me the little Hunter boy after your departure."

"Fascinating," Lucy said, her eyes growing wide. "Dad, this school has an *actual* incompetent-"

"I don't need the reminder," Mike grunted. "Now c'mon. I've got to get back home so I can start looking into some good online schools for you."

"I think I like it here." Lucy picked up her bag and followed her father out of the principal's office. "It's an interesting contrast to our previous setting. Everyone and everything is just so...rustic. It should provide some fascinating pieces for my portfolio."

"No, I think you like it here because you don't get in trouble for assaulting other students," Mike said.

"The only assault my photography commits is the truth."

"Yeah well as your father I say you were assaulting another student and you're grounded." With a deep breath, Mike stopped by Teri the secretary's desk and looked around wildly. "No..." His eyes settled on Lucy's camera. "No more pictures!" Lucy frowned and Mike's face relaxed. "...for the rest of the day."

Tap.

"I concede." Not breaking eye contact, Lucy handed her camera over and only felt a twinge of hesitation as he grabbed the lens with his calloused hands. "However I do continue to vouch for my innocence with injustice of pre-bias as the only crime."

"Yeah well you're still going to apologize to the poor boy." Mike nodded to the little Hunter boy still sitting on the plastic chair. "In your terms, consider it an empathetic amendment."

"And in your terms?" Lucy asked.

"Being a nice person," Mike said. "Which includes *not* shoving your camera in random people's faces without their permission."

"Photography is not always a kind mistress."

"Make it one," Mike warned. "Make some friends too while you're at it. We'll be here a while until I can finish the job."

"Good! I could use the portfolio boost," Lucy said.

Tap.

"Yeah well same here." Mike sighed as he looked at his daughter, shaking his head ever so softly as he turned to the door. "Don't get into any more trouble, kiddo."

Lucy watched her father storm out of the tiny office, holding her camera protectively against his chest. Teri, the secretary, made another singular tap on the keyboard as the door swung close. The little Hunter boy stared at Lucy.

"You don't have to apologize if you don't want to," The boy said. "I'm used to people making fun of me. At least you didn't mean it."

"If it is of any consolation, I did not intend harm with my actions," Lucy said. "In fact, quite the opposite. My intentions were so that you would forever be immortalized in the art of the still image."

"Uh...okay?" The boy looked confused. "Thanks?"

The door burst open again. This time a young man with the same golden hair and hazel eyes as the boy in the plastic chair walked through. However, unlike the boy in the plastic chair, this young man was tall with lean muscles and a chiseled jaw. If she had her camera, Lucy would've taken a picture of the man's golden skin tanned from long days working outside as it contrasted against the sky blue walls and dusty lighting. None of the male models in New York could compete with this farm boy's roughened beauty.

Tap.

Teri looked up from her work.

"Chase!" The secretary smiled at the newcomer. "I thought we called your parents for your little brother?"

"My name's Chevy," The boy on the plastic chair said. "Everyone in this room can call me that. It's okay."

"They couldn't make it," Chase answered, ignoring his brother. "Work on the farm."

With a grumble, Teri shook her head. "It's *always* work on the farm."

As the aged secretary returned to her own work, Chase nodded at Lucy. "You must be that new girl everyone's talking about. Lucy, right? Did you really talk back to old Mrs. Bobby like that?"

"You bet she did!" The boy piped up. "She even said Mrs. Bobby was bitter and-"

"Chevy, I know what she said." Chase sighed before turning back to Lucy. "I can't say I admire the disrespect, but I can admire the gumption. I heard the last kid that spoke back to her got transferred to Lebenville."

"She made the same threat against me," Lucy said. "However, I found no real offense to it."

"Are you kidding?" Chevy spoke up. "Nobody good ever comes from Lebenville!"

"Perhaps your perception of Lebenville is stemmed from the bias that, as the closest city to you, they're your economic and social competitor that pose a threat to your city's well-being," Lucy said. "I'm sure local athletics are a factor as well, but I doubt your unfavorable opinion of Lebenville is broiled in too much fact and, as I have had no experience with Lebenville, I cannot say I take offense to it."

The room went silent. For the tenth time that day, all eyes were on Lucy. Even the aged secretary had abandoned her work to stare at the new girl in disdain. Slowly, Principal Hansen's door opened and the incompetent school official popped his head out.

"Did I just hear someone defend Lebenville?" Principal Hansen said in a grave voice. "No one defends Lebenville in *my* school."

"It's okay, sir!" Chase said, looking nervous. "She's from out of town. She doesn't know!"

"Unacceptable!" Principal Hansen shouted. "Lulu! Go to detention *right now!*"

"But sir I have yet to go to class and-"

"*Right now!*"

Principal Hansen slammed the door behind him, causing a slight tremor that shook the walls. Teri shook her head disapprovingly at Lucy before returning to her slow typing. Shaking his head softly as well, Chase let out a deep sigh.

"You've got a lot to learn about Sterben, new kid." He tapped his brother's shoulder. "Alright c'mon Chevy. Let's go talk to Principal Hansen."

"I can talk to him by myself!" Chevy jumped to his feet. "I ain't in middle school anymore! I don't need you looking after me like I'm some baby."

"Yeah well maybe you shouldn't have worn pull-ups till you were twelve," Chase said.

Glancing at Lucy, Chevy's face went beet red. "They're more environmentally friendly than regular underwear!"

"Oh what do you know about the environment?" Chase asked. "We grow corn for a living."

"I know plenty!" Chevy was quick on Chase's heel. "Like did you know that most underwears are created with oil-based synthetics that contribute to the overall declining-"

"Remember how hard you cried when Chadron replaced your Elmo pull-ups with boxers?" Chase asked as the principal's door closed behind them. "Cause I do."

The Hunter boys were gone and Lucy continued to stand in the office, awkwardly trying to figure out how to bide her time without her camera. The secretary made another lone tap on her keyboard before looking up at Lucy with a glare over her oval glasses.

"Don't you have a detention to serve, Lebenville-supporter?" Teri snarled.

"You never told me where and how," Lucy said.

There was a certain viciousness carved into the secretary's dull blue eyes now that reminded Lucy of her mother.

"I don't know! Just wander around until you find an empty classroom and sit in there for a while," Teri said. "Once I get this referral written up, I'm sure Principal Hansen will think of a more severe punishment for you."

Adjusting her messenger bag's strap, Lucy turned to walk to the door.

"Oh and Ms. Vitalis?" Teri held up a thin finger. When Lucy looked over at the frail secretary, Teri puckered her lips. "Is there any way, you know…I could see your father again?"

Lucy blinked slowly a few times.

"While I do understand your desire for romantic relations, I'm afraid you won't find that with my father," Lucy stated. "My mother's severe infidelity has discouraged my father from further romantic pursuits."

"We will see, dear." Teri's mouth twisted into a sly smile, her cheap lipstick cracked against her gray teeth. "We will see." Turning back to her computer, she looked down at her paper and then back at the screen.

Tap.

It took some time for Lucy to find an empty classroom. The high school was a small building with just enough classrooms for its 157 students so each room was filled. When Lucy peered into the window of Mrs. Bobby's class, the elderly teacher responded by locking eyes with Lucy and sharply smacking her yardstick on her desk. Without a second to waste, Lucy moved on from Mrs. Bobby's classroom. The only room Lucy could find remotely empty was a science lab in the deepest corner of the school.

Science lab was a loose term for the room. There were tables instead of desks with beakers gracing the counters and a skeleton dutifully stood next to the chalkboard, but it looked like it was mostly used for storage. Old posters were flat on the floor with cardboard boxes filled with outdated textbooks stacked up along the walls. An orange bicycle had even found its way into the room. The room's only occupant, an African-American girl with curly natural black hair held up in two pigtail buns and purple framed glasses, didn't seem to mind. She just kept working on her refreshingly high-tech laptop, constantly referencing her notebook with an orange mechanical pencil as she sped her fingers across the keyboard.

"Hello," Lucy stated, her soft voice echoing in the room. The girl turned around, her brown eyes searching for the new voice. When she finally found the voice's origin, Lucy gave a short wave before continuing. "I was told to serve detention in an empty classroom?"

"This is probably your best bet then." Hopping off her stool, the girl offered her hand and a wide smile as she approached Lucy. "I'm Natalie. You must be Lucy. I heard you stood up to Mrs. Bobby!"

"So word does travel fast in small schools." Lucy firmly shook Natalie's hand. "Fascinating."

"Well you're the first new kid since, well, me and I came here in Kindergarten." Natalie skipped back to her table and hopped onto her stool. "Plus I've been hoping that someone would stand up to Mrs. Bobby for a while. She's a terrible teacher, but she's probably going to be here until she's dead. Things don't change much in Sterben." She looked back over to Lucy. "You can sit at my table if you want. I don't have anywhere to be until fifth period history. How long is your detention?"

"They never said," Lucy said, sitting on the stool next to Natalie. "Are you in detention too?"

Natalie laughed. "Nah. I just take AP and honors courses online. If I want to make it into Brown, I've gotta be the best of the best."

"Brown University?"

"Yeah." Natalie assured. "Their neuroscience program is one of the best in the country, but nobody from this school has made it farther than K-State. If I can get into Brown, I'll be the first person in the school's history to make it into an out-of-state let alone an Ivy."

"That's fascinating," Lucy beamed. "What class are you?"

"Junior," Natalie said. "I should be a sophomore, but I was moved up a grade. I should be moved up another grade, but the school didn't let me. What class are you?"

"I'm a junior too!" Lucy exclaimed. "My last school was nontraditional so I'm fairly fascinated with the idea of a GPA. Is your entire future really dependent on a simple number?"

"Unfortunately," Natalie said. "But if I'm going to get into Brown, I've gotta have good ACT and SAT scores as well. I've already taken the practice tests eight times each. My last ACT score was 35 so I think when I take the real thing, I'll be able to pull off a 36. How have you been doing with your ACT and SAT prep?"

"I've never heard of the two," Lucy said. "I've just been building my photography portfolio so I can get into NYU."

"Don't you need an ACT or SAT score to get into *any* college?"

"Perhaps," Lucy said. "I guess if I don't get into NYU, I can just always do photography full-time."

With a soft shake of her head, Natalie let out a low whistle. "I wish I could be as relaxed as you when it comes to this college stuff. But you have the benefit of a higher education from wherever you came from-"

"New York City," Lucy stated.

"See? Even better!" Natalie said. "I've been stuck in this town's stupid school system since I was five. None of the teachers have had an education better than Kansas State and all of them are only here because they can't go anywhere else." She returned her attention to her computer. "Not to mention, Principal Hansen is only principal because his mom was a big deal in Sterben way back when. This whole system is a mess, but I'm not going to let it ruin my dream to become the best biomedical engineer in the country."

She returned to her work with more ferocity and determination. As Natalie worked, Lucy watched. Analyzing her every move, memorizing how effortlessly she would move the pencil from her ear to her notebook and then back to her ear, Lucy was already planning how she would photograph this girl once she got her hands on her camera again. But, in the meantime, Lucy pulled out her tablet and went through her portfolio, organizing and reorganizing the endless amounts of photos.

When lunchtime rolled around, nobody came to retrieve Lucy from detention yet so the girls split their meals and shared their lunch in the science lab. Natalie exchanged half of her egg salad sandwich for half of Lucy's cold cheese pizza and they combined their shares of pretzels and pistachios. With

Natalie's laptop, they traded cat video recommendations and giggled when one of them would start laughing with a mouth full of food. It was one of the most enjoyable meals either of the girls could remember having.

Eventually Natalie left for her fifth period history class and still nobody had returned to retrieve Lucy yet. She took her free time to read through the outdated textbooks. When Natalie returned, she let Lucy borrow one of her SAT prep books. While Lucy did not agree with the principle of standardized testing or defining one's education on a single number, she was grateful for her new friend's generosity and skimmed the book until the school day ended.

The final bell rang and the girls traded phone numbers before heading off in separate directions; Natalie on her orange bike and Lucy in her father's truck. Natalie let Lucy take the SAT prep book home with her ("I've already gone through it twice," She assured), so Lucy was holding it as she stepped into her father's truck. He looked at it with wide eyes.

"One day at a normal high school and you're already concerned with standardized testing," He said. "We should've moved *years* ago."

"It's a gift from a friend," Lucy said.

"A friend?" Mike said. "Dang. I thought you'd hate it here. I was even considering calling your mother to see if she would take you if you got too miserable."

Lucy pursed her lips.

"I'd rather not be with her." She looked out of the window. "Even if Sterben, Kansas was plunged into hell, I would rather be here than with her."

"Tone it down, Luce," Mike grunted as he pushed the truck into drive. "Sterben isn't at that critical of a situation...yet."

They drove out of the school parking lot. Two minutes later, Mike was pulling the truck into the brick driveway of their old one floor house. It was originally painted a bright yellow that had faded with the passage of time. Weeds had taken over the front yard and cracked pavements. For Mike, it was a cheap enough place for them to live until he got this job done. For Lucy, it was portfolio boosting heaven. She took enough pictures to fill up her first memory card and would've filled up another one if her father didn't require her to unpack before she went off to school the next morning.

Mike unlocked the front door and they walked into the house. Despite managing to unpack every box the night before, Mike and Lucy's home was still relatively empty. Their apartment in New York was smaller than the house so there was a lot of empty space between the limited furniture. However, Lucy ensured that the walls didn't have the same problem and had covered them with her own photography along with some of her favorite pieces from other photographers. The only walls she left clear was her father's bedroom. She knew they would be covered soon with evidence from his investigation. Their last apartment didn't have enough walls for his work.

"Can I have my camera back?" She asked as soon as they were in the house. "I want to print my pictures from today."

"Well you did make a friend today," Mike said as he closed the door behind them. "I guess it wouldn't hurt to give your camera back a little early."

Someone knocked on the door. Lucy raised an eyebrow. With a sigh, Mike opened the door he just closed. A young couple stood in the doorway with wide smiles and plastic containers in their arms. The man with broad shoulders and kind eyes as gray and deep as the ocean stood tall while the blonde woman held a glowing smile, her bright blue eyes twinkling as she looked over Mike and Lucy.

"Hi!" The young couple chimed in unison. "We're Chris and Kierra! We're your new neighbors!"

Before Mike and Lucy could respond, the woman gasped and looked at the man. "Babe, that was so good!"

"I know!" The man exclaimed. "We worked so hard on it!"

The couple shifted their respective plastic containers to their hips so that they could high-five each other. After the high-five ended, they turned back to Mike and Lucy with giggly smiles.

"Sorry, we're a little excited," Kierra said. "You guys are our first new neighbors!"

"We just got married a month ago," Chris explained. "Oh, babe, we should put this on our Facebook page!"

"Oh right!" Kierra shoved the plastic container of cookies into Mike's arms. Pulling a small black tube out of her jeans pocket, she attached her phone to it and extended it out. As she adjusted the selfie stick, Chris posed next to Mike. "Okay everyone, 3...2...1...welcome to the neighborhood!"

Right before Kierra could take the picture, Lucy moved her hat from the top of her head and covered her face in time for the picture. As Kierra pulled the selfie stick back and dismounted the phone, Lucy quietly moved her hat back to the top of her head and smoothed out her hair. Chris peeked around Kierra's shoulder to look at the picture.

"Ah man you gotta love these selfie sticks. They're really the best." With a laugh, he looked down at the picture. Suddenly Chris's smile fell and he looked up at Lucy with a frown. "Aw your hat must have fell while the picture was being taken."

"Every photo is a narrative," Lucy stated. "and I have chosen the path of the narrator."

Both Chris and Kierra gave her a look.

"My daughter, Lucy, is a photographer," Mike explained. "She can be a little pretentious about it sometimes." Before Lucy could protest, Mike extended his hand to the couple. "I'm Mike. Thank you so much for your warm welcome."

"Oh anything to make you feel comfortable!" Kierra said as she enthusiastically shook his hand. Chris repeated her action with the same enthusiasm. "So where's the Missus? We thought we would catch her during the day, but no one was around!"

"Location varies as she is draining some testosterone challenged man's retirement fund," Lucy said. "We can send an email and get a response within two to three years to answer your query."

"Lucy's mother and I are divorced," Mike translated. "We don't hear much from her these days."

Both Chris and Kierra gasped.

"How *tragic*," Chris said.

"I...I couldn't even *imagine*..." Kierra said.

"45 to 50% of all first marriages end in divorce," Lucy stated. "Not to mention, couples married in their early 20's only have a 64% chance of remaining married within the next ten years."

There was a moment of silence before Kierra let out a horrified whine.

"Why don't you guys come in for dinner?" Mike said. "We only have frozen pizzas for now, but-"

Mike's change of topic worked and the couple reverted back to their original enthusiastic mood without skipping a beat.

"Oh that sounds terrific! We wish we could," Chris smiled. "But we can't stay for long. Kierra has the night shift tonight."

"I'm a nurse over at the hospital!" Kierra said, the horror of Lucy's statistics passed. "The only acceptable reason to be near Lebenville, am I right?"

Chris and Kierra both laughed loudly as Mike managed a polite smile. Lucy remained stone-faced, wishing she had her camera to capture the jovial yet awkward exchange.

"Isn't she a superstar?" Chris said with a loving sigh. "Oh and she makes the *best* cookies ever. They're the bomb!"

"Oh stop it, babe." Kierra playfully elbowed his side. "Chris made a pretty good Jello for you guys too."

"I put little bits of fruit in it!" Chris placed the plastic container on top of the cookie container in Mike's arms. "Just to add that little pinch of flavor, you know?"

"Delightful," Mike stated.

"We can come over with a casserole tomorrow if you want," Kierra said. "Like my mom always said, everyone loves a good casserole."

"Oh wait not tomorrow, babe," Chris said. "I've got auditions tomorrow."

"Auditions?" Mike said.

"Chris is an *actor*," Kierra cooed. "One of the best I've seen! He's like a superhero when it comes to it."

"Is that your primary profession?" Lucy asked. "I wouldn't imagine being an actor in the middle of Kansas to be an easy career."

"Hey now! Community theatre is *very* important," Chris said. "We're actually performing Shakespeare's *All's Well That Ends Well* this time if you guys are considering auditioning. Lucy, I know you would make a terrific Violenta!"

Mike tossed a hopeful glance to Lucy. She ignored it.

"I'm sorry, but I've already dedicated myself to the art of photography," Lucy said. "I'll leave the art of the stage to professionals as yourself."

Chris blushed and shrugged as Kierra held his arm and proudly leaned her head against his shoulder. "I mean I wouldn't call myself too much of a professional but, you know...I *did* study it at Kansas State, so you know..." With another shrug, he cleared his voice and faced Mike. "So what do you do, Mike? What brings you to Sterben? Was it our community theatre?"

Kierra let out an endearing laugh and gave her husband's arm a pat.

"No, no," Mike said as he set the couple's goodies on the end table near the door. "I'm a paranormal private investigator."

The couple's smiles never faded, but both of them fluttered their eyes at his comment.

"Excuse me, did you say *paranormal*?" Kierra said.

"Yes," Mike stated. "Basically I investigate the paranormal and try to clear it from the area. Your mayor has hired me to deal with a recurring problem in your town so here we are."

"Wait..." Chris held up a finger. "So what you're saying...is that you're a ghostbuster?"

Mike sighed. "No. I'm not a ghostbuster."

"Oh my god I *love* those movies!" Kierra said. "Babe we should watch them when I get home from work tonight."

"But, babe, you know how I feel about ghosts," Chris said. "They give me the heebie-jeebies!"

"Oh alright. We'll watch *The Little Mermaid* again," Kierra said. Chris made a fist pump. "Well it was lovely meeting you guys! Good luck on your ghost-busting, Mike. If you need any help at all, just let us know."

"Yeah Kierra is a *great* hunter," Chris said. "She once shot a buck from fifty feet away."

"Oh babe, stop!" Kierra said. "You're so embarrassing."

"No you're so embarrassing!" Chris teased.

"Am I still your date to the Oscars?"

"Forever and always, babe!"

"Aw, babe."

"Dad I don't think they'll mind us closing the door on them," Lucy whispered. "They seem to be preoccupied in the euphoria of their honeymoon period."

"Agreed," Mike said. "Alright we'll see you two later!"

Mike shut the door as the young couple continued to canoodle. He let out a loud sigh before picking up the containers of food.

"So how do you feel about cookies and jello for supper tonight, kiddo?"

It was a supper Lucy hardly touched. She made her plate of Jello and cookies and then disappeared into the laundry room where she had made her makeshift darkroom. Even though Lucy worked primarily with digital, she still enjoyed having her own space to print photos. To add to the authenticity of her photography space, she even had the dying fluorescent bulbs in the room replaced with red ones and draped black sheets over the room's single window. Her Macbook laptop positioned on a rickety end table that came with the house offered the only glow of normal light. Pictures from last night's shoot of the house were already hanging on a clothesline that swung over the laundry machines.

As Lucy waited for the picture to finish printing, she set her hat on the hanger fixated on the back of the door before examining last night's prints. They were...moderately decent. Not her best work, but she had struggled to find the feel for the place in the beginning. She had inaccurately assumed there had to be more to the small town in the middle of nowhere than the stereotypes given to her through the books and movies. But, as one day in the town proved, small towns were rarely more than what they appeared.

Beep.

She rushed over to the enlarger positioned on the aged dryer and pulled out the print she was most excited to develop. Normally Lucy would save her best work for last after she had ensured the ink would print correctly, but she couldn't wait any longer to see how this piece would turn out. She carefully pulled it from the printer tray, careful not to let the glow of the laptop light touch it before the ink settled. This eye was going to be glorious, the shining achievement in her portfolio. Her ticket into Soho, her pass into recognition as a professional-

That wasn't normal.

A spot had appeared in the center of the iris. It was misshapen, an anomaly for a misprint. Putting caution to the wind, Lucy moved the print to the light of her laptop to get a better look at the spot. Despite the bright fluorescence of the laptop threatening to ruin the color of her print, Lucy could see she made no mistake in her rush to print the photograph. The spot wasn't her doing. It was part of the image. But Lucy still hoped beyond hope that it was something fixable.

As the photo hung with the other images, the spot mocked the expert photographer. She couldn't even move onto the other images of the day. What could she have possibly done wrong? The lighting was perfect, the subject was perfect, and Lucy was better than both of them. There was no error. Perhaps it was her rush to develop the image that ruined it. But as she continued to stare at the stain, she recognized the shape.

At this revelation, Lucy snapped the photo off the line and bolted out of the room. The sudden shift in lighting threw her off and she ran into the wall. Protecting the picture, she ran down the small hallway and into her father's room. He was sitting at his modest desk, his plate of cookies and jello also ignored as he worked diligently on his computer with old newspapers spread across the floor.

"Hey Luce." Mike didn't even look up. "Got anything good today? Anything worth getting in trouble over?"

"Absolutely." Lucy shoved the picture in front of her father's face. With a trained delicateness, he softly pinched the picture between his index finger and thumb to further examine the image. "Do you see it?"

"See what?" Mike squinted at the picture.

"The boy," Lucy pointed to the spot. "That's imprinted in the eye."

"It's not a stain?"

"No." Lucy said almost a little too proudly. "The little Hunter boy...he must have seen something that left an impression. Something not of this world."

After a moment, Mike cracked a wide smile.

"Luce," He said. "The Sterben case is officially open."

Tip #2:

Leave haunted houses alone.

MIKE AND LUCY SAT IN the ancient town hall lobby. While it wasn't as dilapidated as the principal's office, it was definitely aged. The couch they shared looked, and felt, like it was from the early 1900's. Oil paintings of old men, and eventually women, that all vaguely looked the same surrounded the room. A bookcase with large volumes dating back to the 1800's stood tall behind the secretary's desk.

The secretary tapped slowly at her computer. She was a plump woman with rosy cheeks and bobbed brown hair that came out of a 1950's catalogue. Lucy picked up her camera and focused in on the woman. She adored how the secretary's 1950's appearance contrasted against the decor of the 1900's. It was eerie. As soon as the shutter snapped, Mike gave Lucy a warning glance. She ignored him.

Two obnoxiously large walnut doors located in the center of the room slowly opened. In the center of the doors making his dramatic entrance was a short young man with a top hat and fake gray moustache pasted onto his upper lip. It was obvious it was fake because the taped on moustache refused to move with the rest of his face and the hair on top of his head was a dirty blonde color. As soon as he had managed to push the heavy doors open, the man beamed at Mike and Lucy.

"Ah! Mr. Vitalis!" He strode to Mike in wide steps. "New York City's second best paranormal private investigator according to GhostHunters.com. Such a pleasure to finally meet you. I am Mayor Hansen."

"Do you happen be related to Principal Hansen down at the high school?" Mike asked as he firmly shook Mayor Hansen's hand.

"Ah yes!" Mayor Hansen said, stroking his fake moustache. "Principal Hansen is my brother and another similarly great man! Now come; we have much to discuss."

Mayor Hansen turned on his heel and strode to the magnificent doors. Mike turned to Lucy.

"Listen this guy signs my paychecks so don't treat him like the idiot you know he is," He whispered. "If you do that for me, I'll buy the next set of inks for your printer."

"Bribery to assure submission," Lucy cooed. "Once again, your parenting methods prove competence in practicality but not in morality."

"You're not dead or in jail yet," Mike said.

With a shrug, Lucy followed her father with a skip in her step. When they walked past the massive doors, Mayor Hansen shoved them closed with a mixture of grunts, groans, and good ole shoulder shoves. In his office, a beautifully crafted desk made of the same wood as the doors sat in the back of the room with a shiny Mac computer positioned on top of it. The walls of the office were lined with shelves of thick, leather bound books similar to the bookcase positioned behind the secretary in the lobby. Behind the desk was a massive oil portrait of Mayor Hansen, the fake gray moustache still pasted on his baby face. When the doors clicked shut, Mayor Hansen turned to the Vitalises and tried to hide his short breath.

"Don't...don't be shy," He said in between massive gulps of breath. "Please...sit...catch your breath."

The mayor hobbled to his desk, still catching his breath. Mike shot Lucy another warning look to keep her mouth shut before they followed him to the desk. They sat down in the black Edwardian armchairs as Mayor Hansen fell into his wooden chair, coughing and hacking up a lung until he took a puff of an inhaler. With a deep breath, he composed himself and faced Mike and Lucy.

"With all respect, sir." Mike jabbed a thumb at the massive doors. "Have you ever considered replacing those with smaller doors?"

"I mean, yeah," Mayor Hansen said. "But then what will the city do when the zombie apocalypse happens? Zombies can't penetrate those doors. People can't even penetrate those doors. We're safe from the zombie apocalypse in here."

"Don't forget the liberals." Lucy piped up. "You're safe from them here too."

Mayor Hansen pointed at Lucy excitedly.

"*Yes!*" He exclaimed. "That's exactly right. The last thing we need in Sterben are...*Democrats.*"

Mayor Hansen let out a dramatic shudder. Lucy only nodded in mocking agreement as Mike let out an exasperated sigh. The mayor composed himself and looked back to his guests.

"Uh so?" Mayor Hansen drummed his hands on his desk. "You got something for me? A ghost? A demon? Maybe a giant marshmallow man?"

"A picture." Mike nodded at Lucy. She opened up her folder and neatly pulled out the picture of the eye. When she presented it to Mayor Hansen, the man gave the picture one look and let out a high pitched shrill, falling backwards out of his seat in fright. Lucy looked at her father and then back to the image. Suddenly the walnut doors behind them opened.

"Mayor Hansen?" The portly secretary cooed. "Is everything alright?"

"Fine!" The mayor squeaked, struggling to get to his feet. "Keep sending your emails, Jeri."

Puckering her lips into a small smile, Jeri nodded and closed the door almost as effortlessly as she opened it. Straightening his top hat, Mayor Hansen sat back down in his chair and cleared his throat.

"Interesting picture you have there. Definitely not...a giant marshmallow man," Mayor Hansen said. "Is that a, uh, ghost, in that black void of nothingness?"

"We're not sure," Mike said. "Ghosts have been known to leave impressions in photographs, but this impression is ingrained in the boy's eye. That means this boy has seen the spirit haunting your town. "

"The flash of my camera captured whatever he had seen," Lucy added. "If I had not used flash, it would've remained a shadow in his iris."

"I'm sorry are you a ghostbuster as well or...?" Mayor Hansen asked.

"Neither of us are ghostbusters, sir." Mike furrowed his eyebrows in annoyance. "My daughter Lucy is well versed in the paranormal from helping me on my investigations."

"Ah, okay." Mayor Hansen stared at the photo once more. "And who's the boy who's seen the thing?"

"Chevy Hunter." Lucy answered. "He's-"

"The youngest Hunter boy." Mayor Hansen handed the photo back to Lucy. "Well this was a neat picture, super cool ghost you got there, but unfortunately you guys are going to have to start your investigation elsewhere. The Hunters are untouchable. They've got the biggest plot of land in Sterben and I'm not pulling them off of it to tell them their youngest son has seen a ghost."

"Why not?" Mike snapped. "We just wanna talk to the kid."

"Yeah, okay, but *no one* talks to the Hunters," Mayor Hansen said. "Their two youngest go to the high school and that's it. They don't even go to church for crying out loud. If anyone managed to convince them to leave that farm-" He shook his head. "It's never happened and we don't want it to happen."

"Well we'll go there then," Mike said. "Look you hired me for this job and I intend to-" Mike stopped talking as Mayor Hansen fumbled with something under his desk. "What are you doing?"

"Nothing," Mayor Hansen said. "Please continue your argument. Very debative. Reminds me of when I got my master's in political science at Kansas State."

"I think he's looking for a panic button," Lucy stated.

"I'm not *looking* for a *panic* button," Mayor Hansen grunted as he continued to fumble under the desk. "That would be ridiculous. I would have to be *panicking* to use a panic button-" A click occurred. "Aha! Got it!"

"Got what?" Mike said.

"Uh, nothing."

"He pushed the panic button," Lucy said.

"Uh no." Mayor Hansen furrowed his eyebrows in fake confusion. "There's no *panic* button back here that gets me out of uncomfortable situations. That would be dumb. I'm a leader this community looks up to. I can't just push a button to get out of situations I don't want to be in."

Something slammed against the large doors. Mike and Lucy turned to see a police officer shove his way into the room through the giant wooden doors, struggling just as the mayor did a few minutes earlier. However, unlike the mayor, the officer in his faded blue Sterben police uniform had an actual moustache that matched the chestnut color of his hair. He was a thicker man, tall and bulky, that crumpled into himself to heave in a heavy breath as soon as he made it past the office doors. Once the officer caught his breath, he looked up at the mayor.

"I got here as soon as I could, Mayor," The officer said. "What did you press the panic button for?"

Both Mike and Lucy looked at Mayor Hansen who looked pale, but remained composed as he addressed the officer.

"Officer Hansen, please escort these two out of my office," He ordered. "They were, uh, just...just get them out of here."

"Let me guess: another brother of yours." Mike let out a loud sigh. "Is *your* secretary named Sheri, Officer?"

"I don't have a secretary," Officer Hansen said. "But my wife's name is Susie! Now c'mon. You've wasted enough of the mayor's time."

The police officer grabbed Mike roughly by his bicep and dragged him out of the office. Lucy happily followed along, snapping pictures of her father's struggle as he was continually dragged with force despite his protest that he would leave quietly. Finally, they all reached the outside of the magnificent brick building. The officer threw Mike towards the sidewalk.

"It's nothing personal, man," Officer Hansen said. "I just gotta do what the mayor says. It's my job as the only police officer of this town. You understand, right?"

"I guess." Mike straightened out his flannel shirt. "But you don't have to roughhouse me next time."

With an almost giddy smile, Officer Hansen beamed. "Are you giving me critique?"

Mike shot a wary glance at his daughter before addressing the officer again.

"Um...I guess?"

"Oh boy!" Officer Hansen whipped out a notepad and jotted something down in it. "Don't...roughhouse...the criminals." He looked back up at Mike with eager eyes. "What else can I do better?"

"Run a town based on merit rather than family ties?" Lucy offered.

"Luce, what did I tell you about treating idiots like idiots?" Mike said.

"Only when they sign your paychecks." Lucy picked up her camera and took a picture. "I'm not sure this man knows his own name let alone how to sign a paycheck."

"Lucy Vitalis, I swear-"

"Excuse me, how do you spell merit?" Officer Hansen interrupted, looking eagerly between Lucy and Mike.

All Mike Vitalis could do is roll his eyes and pace in a circle as his daughter helped the police officer with his spelling. Once the officer finished his note, he gave the both of them a big smile and folded the notepad back into his shirt.

"You guys are so nice!" Officer Hansen said. "No one ever wants to help me on my policeman duties. They think my brothers will yell at them, but I just want to do the best job possible, you know? Honestly if there's anything you guys want me to do, let me know and I'll get it done so fast you won't know what hit ya!"

"Can you grant me a warrant to search the Hunter family's property?" Mike asked.

"Okay maybe not that," Officer Hansen said, still keeping his wide smile. "But I can, you know, give you free rides in my cop car. If I turn the siren on, oh man is it a fun time! You can go anywhere in town in like a minute with that siren on."

"Can you take my daughter Lucy back to school?" Mike said, annoyance glazing over his eyes. "If no one here will allow me to investigate the Hunter family, then I need to get started on a new lead as soon as possible."

"Absolutely!" Officer Hansen saluted Mike. "You can trust me, sir! I will get your daughter to school as quickly and as safely as possible."

Mike immediately turned to Lucy.

"Wear your seatbelt and put me on speed dial," He stated. "It might be a late one tonight for me, but call if something happens."

"As always," Lucy said.

With a serious nod, Mike stormed off to his own vehicle. Officer Hansen tipped his hat at Lucy.

"Alright, you ready to go to school, little girl?"

"I'm sixteen," Lucy stated.

Before the police officer could react, she snapped a picture of him in his dull blue uniform contrasting against the dull gray sky. It was a fascinating portrait of the witless officer looking towards her as if she were a child. Her only wish was that she would've framed the gun holstered to his side. That would've really added a political aspect to her portfolio.

But her disappointment was appeased with the more artistic pieces she caught as the officer sped through the streets of Sterben, Kansas, his sirens blaring the entire time. He ended up getting lost a handful of times which gave her more opportunities to capture the moment of elderly people diving out of the way of the police car. She got a great one of one particular woman who snatched up her tiny dog just in time and looked awfully frightened as they zoomed past. The expression was flawless and, with enough blur in the background, became the focus point of the piece.

By the time Lucy arrived at school for the day, it was already lunch period. Everyone was mulling on the front lawn or near their massive trucks in the parking lot, enjoying the cool fall day. Lucy ignored all of the stares and muttered jokes at her expense as she made her way to the hidden science lab. Natalie was sitting at her table, legs propped up on another stool as she ate her sandwich.

She turned to Lucy when the door closed behind her and smiled.

"Oh good! You're back! I thought Mrs. Bobby actually transferred you." Natalie took her legs off of the neighboring stool and shuffled through her Star Wars lunch box. "My mom packed some extra pretzels and I downloaded a Ted Talk about the education system for us to watch while we eat. It's fascinating stuff!"

"Maybe in a little bit," Lucy said. "Do you know where I can find Chase Hunter?"

"Uh yeah. He's usually out by his truck with some of the other seniors for lunch," Natalie bit into her sandwich. "Why?"

"His little brother has seen a spirit and my father needs to investigate the matter," Lucy stated. "We need access to the Hunter farm."

Natalie stared at Lucy in horror before carefully swallowing the bite of egg salad sandwich in her mouth.

"I'm sorry, could you repeat that?" She asked. "So little Chevy Hunter saw what now?"

"A spirit," Lucy said. "Not a ghost, but certainly not a demon. It's somewhere in between and my father needs to find it before it takes over the town."

Turning on the heel of her black boot, Lucy made her way back to the parking lot. Natalie caught up to her side in no time.

"Lucy, there's no such thing as ghosts, right?" She adjusted her glasses. "I mean, everything we have studied on death has been purely philosophical so there's no saying on which is right, but current studies of the brain point to a lack of ability to function after death and therefore-"

"Is science not hindered by philosophical bias as well?" Lucy interrupted. "You can prove anything with science with the right mindset."

Natalie was quiet for a moment and, for once, Lucy was worried that she offended her new friend.

"You pose a fair argument about confirmation bias," Natalie said. "Okay. Well there's no better way to test a hypothesis than with a field study. Let's find Chase. "

With a smile, Natalie took the lead in their search. The light from the front entrance was a backlight against her frame, muting the brightness of Natalie's yellow cardigan. Noting how her curls bounced ever so slightly, Lucy lifted her camera to her eye and stopped to snap a picture. After taking a few shots playing with thirds, Lucy caught up to her friend. When they made it to the parking lot, the seniors mulling around their trucks gave the incoming girls distrustful looks. Natalie happily twiddled her fingers at a few of them, calling people out by name and asking about their test grades. Lucy captured more pictures. With each new picture she took, she received more glares from Sterben High's senior class. Frowning, she wished they would just ignore her like everyone did in New York so she could accurately capture the scene as it was.

Finally they arrived at an old blue Chevy truck where the familiar farmer boy with golden hair sat on the tailgate, eating a sandwich. A horde of girls, varying only in age, gathered around him. He seemed to not realize their motivation for being there. Natalie fought her way to Chase's attention, bringing Lucy with her. Chase's hazel eyes lit up at the sight of the girls.

"Hey Natalie! Hey new kid!" He smiled. "Glad to see y'all outside. Wanna sit up on my truck? It's a lovely day."

"Lucy wants to talk to you about Chevy," Natalie said.

"The little Hunter boy?" One of the nearby girls asked.

"Why don't you go talk to him then?" Chase said. "He's in the cafeteria with the rest of the freshmen."

Natalie looked at Lucy, who kept her lips pressed together in disapproval as she looked at Chase.

"This is a matter best kept to ourselves than with your brother," Lucy said.

Taking a bite of his sandwich, Chase chewed on his food a little bit as he thought.

"Well shoot." He swallowed. "Let's talk inside my truck. It's a bit more private."

Hopping off the tailgate, he continued to eat his sandwich as he walked to the driver's side. Natalie walked first to the passenger side, sliding into the middle seat as Lucy took the passenger seat. Chase's fangirls dispersed when their entertainment had left, leaving the trio safe from anyone listening in. He bit into his sandwich again before addressing the girls.

"So what's the situation?" Chase asked. "Is this about his crush on Lucy? Honestly, he just would *not* shut up about you last night."

"No. Something, surprisingly, more horrifying than that notion," Lucy said. Opening her black messenger bag, she retrieved the folder holding the picture. She pulled the glossy image out and presented it to Chase. He grabbed it with his grubby sandwich hands and she cringed, silently begging to be reunited with her precious art.

"What's this?" Chase asked as he bit into his sandwich, letting crumbs nearly fall onto the photograph.

"*That-*" Lucy snatched the picture from his hands before he could ruin it further. "-is the picture of your little brother's eye."

Natalie stole it from Lucy's hand and looked over it, taking care not to nearly ruin it like Chase almost did.

"This is his eye?" She asked. "Why is there a person in it? Did you Photoshop this?"

"No." Lucy almost felt offended by the notion. "Photoshop is for amateurs with no eye for art. That is a spirit that Chevy Hunter has apparently witnessed. We need to investigate your home and stop this spirit before it worsens."

Raising an eyebrow, Chase looked at Natalie. "Is she talking 'bout ghosts?"

"Yes," Natalie said.

"Ghosts ain't real though," Chase said. "We just say that they are to freak out our little brothers and sisters."

"Ghosts and spirits are very real and I am very disappointed in both of your skepticisms when neither of you have considered the alternative," Lucy stated. "I can prove to you that ghosts exist and they are in Sterben, Kansas, just as they are in every place death has touched."

"Well you ain't gonna prove it on my parents' farm," Chase said. "We're private people. We don't need the town believing that we might be hiding something on our land that we ain't."

"Any abandoned building should do just fine for a test study. Are there any nearby?" Lucy asked. "The older and more rundown, but still with a solid structure, are preferable."

After a moment, Natalie laughed.

"Oh my god!" She exclaimed. "Are you serious?!"

Lucy furrowed her eyebrows.

"I thought you were interested in a field study," Lucy stated. "If you wish to just laugh at-"

"No, no not that!" Natalie shot a look at Chase before giving an amused smile to her new friend. "Lucy, we're in the middle of Kansas."

"There's more abandoned buildings around here than working ones!" Chase started his truck. "Barns, sheds, houses...it's just a matter of what you want. But fortunately for you, my friends, I know a place."

No one said a word as Chase drove them out of the school parking lot with half of the school day still incomplete. Lucy grew nervous as they exited the small town's borders. Her father had instilled in her that she was not supposed to interact with spirits unless she had the proper equipment to ensure they would not act malicious. Now she was travelling with two non-believers to empty farmland where the nearest help would be thirty minutes away.

At least her camera would record their final moments. That might offer some consolation to their families or, at the very least, make their way onto some clickbait article about the top ten most mysterious and possibly supernatural disappearances. The final photos of the great Lucy Vitalis, locked up in a clickbait article. The thought horrified Lucy more than the prospects of their unlikely demise at the hands of some unkindly spirit in the middle of nowhere.

Chase pulled up on a long dirt driveway overran with yellowing grass. Corn surrounded the lot of land and the bright mid-fall sky seemed to grow darker as they approached the gray husk of a house. Hardly any glass remained in any of the windows while a porch swing remained dangling precariously on rusted chains. Chase parked his old truck near the steps leading up to the towering farmhouse. Turning the truck off, he turned to the girls with a menacing smile.

"Spooky, innit?" He said. "It's old Harry Wilson's place. Old man wasn't too hard to be around, but his kids still took off for other parts of the state after school. After his death, he left the place to them and they just haven't come back for it. They rent the farmland out to my family though so we hopefully won't have an issue with trespassing."

"And if we do?" Natalie asked.

Chase thought about it for a moment.

"Well if they decide to press charges, we could argue that we were exercising our First Amendment rights in an effort to promote a bake sale at school," Chase said. "It's a tricky argument though, so instead if conflict arises I would recommend feigning ignorance that we're not allowed on the property and leaving after the first verbal warning. Choosing to stay after the first verbal warning would result in a serious penalty. Probably not jail though, which is comforting, but our parents will definitely be notified which is a penalty in its own right."

Natalie stared at Chase as Lucy slowly pulled up her camera and took a picture of the house.

"Are you studying to become a cop, Chase?" Natalie asked.

"Nah," He said. "I'm going to help my folks out on the farm when I graduate. I just like to read up on the subject."

"*How?!*" Natalie asked. "Our library has two and a half Harry Potter books and three copies of the Bible."

"Mayor Hansen's secretary lets me read those big books in his office whenever he's out," Chase said. "I just gotta give her a piece of my momma's pecan pie in return."

"As fascinating as the discourse on how a conventionally attractive son of a farmer could know so much about law is," Lucy stated. "I recommend that we investigate the house before night. The supernatural is most powerful, and thus most dangerous, when the world is in the universe's natural state."

Ignoring her friends' raised eyebrows, Lucy stepped out of the truck and approached the house with her camera. Taking off her hat, Lucy bowed her head towards the aged building.

"Spirits of this residence, allow us to enter and witness your afterlife in peace," She said softly. "We are just tourists wishing to pay respect, not discomfort. Also, if you are camera shy, please let me know peacefully and I will conclude the session."

After waiting another moment, Lucy stuck her hat back on her head and snapped some pictures of the house, focusing on the windows. She adored how they appeared to have the glass shattered by bored teenagers, a sight rarely seen in New York with the gleaming skyscrapers her father usually worked in. Usually, if the window was shattered, it was a supernatural matter, not a bored teenager in the middle of nowhere matter.

Natalie and Chase both exited the truck, slamming the doors behind them. Pulling her pencil from behind her ear, Natalie picked a small notebook out of the back pocket of her jeans. She pushed her purple framed glasses up her nose before jotting down some notes on it.

"So what was that prayer you just said, Lucy?" Natalie asked. "Is it a necessity to the ghost hunting profession?"

"It's more of a courtesy," Lucy stated, still snapping pictures. "Some spirits will be more inclined to not kill you if you show respect."

"And how likely are our chances of being killed by a spirit?" Natalie asked.

"It depends on the situation surrounding the spirits' death and the personality they held in life," Lucy asked. "Chase, why did you choose this place for us?"

The farm boy shrugged. "I dunno. My older brother told me it was haunted 'cause his friends told him it was haunted. So everyone's just been saying it's haunted. Probably because of the fact none of Old Man Harry Wilson's kids came back for the land."

"15% chance," Lucy said.

With a final shutter snap of the camera lens, Lucy strode up to the front door with massively confident steps. Natalie looked nervously up at the building as she jotted down some notes. Biting her lower lip, she shook the eraser part of her pencil at the building.

"Look — I don't know *what* kind of redneck you might've been," She said. "But I'm not here to steal from you or hurt you in any way, alright? I'm just here for the science. Okay? Are we clear? Science! Not spooky stuff! Okay?!"

Sticking her pencil behind her ear again, Natalie followed Lucy on her tiptoes, not wanting to make a sound that would set off the supposed spirits that lived there. With a deep breath, Chase stuck his hands into the pockets of his Wrangler jeans and looked up at the building.

"Uh, Lord Jesus?" He tried. "Please protect us as we go into Old Man Harry Wilson's place and please allow our not-guilty plea to trespassing hold up in the Klein County Municipal Court System. Amen."

After his prayer, he ran in after the girls who were already well into the building. Lucy was taking pictures intermittently, mostly when she saw something interesting. A picture of a cobwebbed covered rocking chair here, a focused-in shot of a crack in the floorboard there...usual old house stuff. Natalie was gingerly touching the walls and railing alongside the stairs, examining the dust residue on her fingers after she did so. Chase mulled behind them, hands continued to be balled deep into the pockets of his jeans.

"Alright Lucy," He said. "You said you could prove ghosts exist. Where are they?"

"They'll show themselves if they wish," Lucy said. "You don't drag an introvert to a house party, after all."

"So they might never show?" Natalie asked.

"Possibly." Lucy snapped a picture of the fireplace. "The only reason you should willingly summon a spirit is if you're planning on getting rid of it and that's rather rude, don't you think? Especially if you wish to summon a ghost. Ghosts are simple. They're nice and hardly cause any harm. To summon one and to leave it in a summoned state without purpose would inconvenience it terribly."

"But you said the ghost wouldn't harm us?" Chase asked.

"A ghost might not," Lucy said. "But if my picture is correct, which it is, then Sterben, Kansas is dealing with something stronger than just a regular ghost."

An old grandfather clock stationed in the living room clattered to life, shaking its massive chimes in a dying song that echoed through the empty house. Natalie and Chase both jumped as Lucy snapped a picture of their shocked reactions.

"That shouldn't be working, right?" Natalie said. "Old Man Harry Wilson died nearly fifteen years ago."

"Grandfather clocks were built to last," Chase said. He checked his phone for the time before furrowing his eyebrows at the device. "Huh. I don't have any service out here."

"Paranormal zones usually don't allow cell or internet service," Lucy said. "Too much electromagnetic energy."

"With that logic, all of rural Kansas is a paranormal zone," Natalie said. "That doesn't prove anything."

Lucy's face remained serious as she considered Natalie's statement. "Then why is the grandfather clock ringing?"

"It's 2 o'clock," Natalie responded. "It's supposed to be chiming now."

"It has chimed eight times," Lucy stated.

Dong.

"Nine."

Dong.

The rocking chair creaked as it rocked back and forth slowly.

"Ten."

Dong.

A loud crack echoed from the second floor.

"Eleven."

Dong.

Wind pushed through the broken windows, whipping Natalie and Chase's clothes.

"Twelve."

Dong.

Silence.

Lucy turned to her friends as the eerie silence continued to settle amongst the teenagers.

"Thirteen," She whispered, her eyes growing wide.

"What does that mean?!" Natalie exclaimed.

Before Lucy could answer, an invisible force grabbed Natalie by a fistful of her hair and yanked her to the side. With a yell, Natalie fell face first against the wall pasted in cheap green wallpaper. Chase moved to help her and his entire body jerked backwards as the invisible force shoved him away from Natalie. Lucy set to work taking as many pictures as she could as her friends freaked out.

"Lucy!" Natalie shouted as she got pulled to her feet by her hair once again. "What's going on?! What should we do?!"

"Do you have any holy water on you?" Lucy shot another picture of her troubled friend.

"Do I *look* like I've got holy water on me?!" Natalie screamed as she was pulled around the room. "Get it off me!"

"I got it, Natalie!" Chase shouted. He jumped with his arms outstretched to where the invisible force would be. His attempt to tackle whatever was messing with them ended as he landed face first into the hardwood floor. A sharp cackle of laughter later, Chase was suddenly floating towards the ceiling. He flailed his arms and legs, looking like he was trying to swim through whatever was pulling him up.

"Chase!" Natalie screamed.

Lucy joined her friend's side and took pictures of the floating boy, her camera shutter snapping open and close faster than one could blink.

"This is incredible!" Lucy exclaimed. "Whomever possesses this residence holds tremendous power."

"Would you quit taking pictures and help him?!" Natalie shouted. "You got us in this mess!"

"It's an ambivalent spirit," Lucy stated. "Trust me, if it was malevolent, you would be much more concerned."

"I *am* concerned!" Natalie asserted. "Now, for real, how do you get this thing to quit bothering us?!"

With a sigh, Lucy put her camera down from her eye. "Chase? Do you have any religious artifacts on you?"

"Got my cross!" He managed to reach to his t-shirt neckline and pulled out a metal cross fixated on a thick thread around his neck. "What do I do with it?"

Lucy was silent.

"*Lucy!*" Natalie exclaimed.

"Well I don't know then." Lucy looked up at Chase as he floated near the ceiling and shrugged. "Clearly the spirit does not answer to that religion."

"*I do not.*"

Within the blink of an eye, Chase was slammed against the wall with his back to it. He screamed as he was dragged down it at a quick speed. When his feet touched the floor, he stayed pressed against the wall and looked around wildly. His chest heaved with every heavy breath he took before he looked at the two girls.

"Did y'all say that?" He asked.

The girls shook their heads.

"*I did.*"

As the teenagers turned back to the fireplace, it lit itself with a green flame. Stepping out from the fire was a Japanese woman, her black hair flecked with streaks of grey and looking uncombed as it hung loose off of her shoulders. She wore a pure white kimono folded right over left that was dirtied at the bottom and she held an ashened walking cane. Her dark eyes glared at the trio, as if her spectacle didn't make it clear enough that they were unwelcome in the house.

"Fascinating!" Lucy snapped a picture. "I would not expect a yurei to be the spirit haunting Sterben, Kansas."

"I am neither of those things," The spirit hissed. "I am Murasaki Hashihime, the jibakurei who has claimed this land of Sterben, Kansas as under my protection and I intend to follow my purpose, including eradicating the spirit that does haunt this land." The green flames of the fireplace behind the spirit grew massively as she held up her cane, making green smoke crawl out from underneath her kimono in ominous tendrils. Chase and Natalie latched onto Lucy who barely regarded them as she took pictures of the scene. "You have interfered with my purpose, a divine purpose given to me by the gods upon my untimely death, and now you mere mortals will face the same untimely demise. A torturous, hellfire of-"

A soft mew echoed through the room. The trio looked down at their feet as a gray cat with bright green eyes sauntered at their feet, staring at the spirit with its tail tucked between its legs. All of a sudden, the tendrils of smoke retreated and the flames died to smoldering ashes. Murasaki's cane disappeared in a puff of green smoke and she looked at the cat with a saddened expression.

"Okiku, did I scare you?" Murasaki asked in a softened voice.

The cat mewed again before moving away from the spirit, darting between the trio's legs in its escape.

"Oh Okiku, you know I didn't mean it!" Pulling up her kimono, Murasaki chased after the cat. "Okiku, come back! Come back! Mommy loves you! Mommy didn't want to scare *you*! Come back."

"Okay, what is going on?!" Chase exclaimed. "Lucy, was this some sort of trick? Did you set this up because *wow* that trick on the ceiling..." He waved towards the sky. "That was super cool. You gotta do that for Chris's theatre show. Have you met Chris and Kierra yet, Lucy? Good people. Just got married last month. Nice wedding."

"So I've heard," Lucy stated.

"Yeah, my science on this is calling bologna sandwich," Natalie said, her eyes following the ancient spirit chase the cat around the house. "I mean, why else would a Japanese spirit be found in the middle of Kansas, America?"

"Because, as she stated, she is jibakurei," Lucy stated. "Jibakurei are spirits that protect a specific location...although it is typically limited to a location sentimental to the spirit. Not an insignificant town in the middle of a foreign continent."

She took a picture of the cat as it bolted across the wooden floors. The creature then climbed to the top of some ragged curtains and Murasaki set to work on talking it down with various coos and gentle promises.

Natalie let out a hum. "Either way, Chris would love to borrow this actress for some of his shows."

"Do not speak to me of the actors of your era." Murasaki whipped around and folded her arms across her chest. "Vapid creatures. In my age, they were *artists*. They trained for decades before seeing a minute of stage time. Now? Any fool with a terrible accent could pretend to be one."

"Then what about you, fancy shmancy spirit?" Chase said. "Are you done trying to kill us?"

"If my job were to kill innocent mortal children, it would be done." Murasaki rolled her eyes before returning her attention to the cat attached to the curtain. "I just wished to scare you off before you got too far deep into things you shouldn't be delving into. However, you-" She turned briefly to point a finger at Lucy. "-do not fear what you are dressed as and that is concerning behavior to influence friends with."

Chase and Natalie looked at Lucy and her all-black outfit perfect for a funeral. She ignored them to focus on the spirit.

"My father is the paranormal private investigator assigned to get rid of, assumedly, the same spirit you wish to protect this town from," Lucy said. "He could use your help."

"Mortals have no place in the spirit world." With some green smoke emanating from her fingertips, Murasaki was able to coax the cat down into her arms. Turning to the teenagers, she stroked the cat's fur and it purred softly in her arms. "Keep that in mind before you choose to become soldiers."

The clock chimed again and the jibakurei vanished with her cat in a wisp of a green flame. The teenagers stood there as the dust settled, staying huddled together. Finally, Chase let out a low whistle.

"You really went all out on making a believer out of us, Lucy," Chase said. "Seriously you've *gotta* get that actress to audition for Chris's shows. She was phenomenal. I nearly wet my pants with that damnation talk."

"Humans' ability to stay in their own reality despite the counter-evidence is astounding," Lucy said, snapping a picture of the empty space the spirit had left. "For the record, a jibakurei *is* a type of yurei so I was not wrong in my original assumption."

"Lucy, I'm sorry but you can't deny the scientific evidence." Natalie stepped out and faced her friend. "Boric acid, which made the green flames, is found in common cockroach sprays that was probably used on this house at one point. If Murasaki coated her hands in the stuff, she could easily pull off a magic trick not uncommon among-"

"Chadron?" The trio turned around and met eyes with an elderly man, white and vaguely transparent, hovering ever so slightly just a few inches away from Chase. "Chadron Hunter! Why I haven't seen ya in a hot minute! How's the team this year? Got that scholarship yet?"

At the sight of the ghost, Chase gave Lucy and Natalie a questioning look. Natalie looked just as shocked as Chase and Lucy captured a photo of the event. Swallowing his fear, Chase turned back to the Ghost of Old Man Wilson.

"Mr. Wilson, I'm Chadron's younger brother Chase," Chase offered quietly.

"That ain't right," The Ghost of Old Man Harry Wilson frowned. "Little Chase Hunter's just a baby. Quit trying to fool an old man. You know my heart's about to give out any day now." He looked over to Natalie and whistled. "Pretty lady friend you got there, Chadron. You know, you're lucky my wife's been gone for ten years now. Sweet woman, made a mean potato casserole, but the pig never had the open mind I do."

"Harry Wilson, what did you just call me?!" An elderly woman came hobble-hovering out of the kitchen, holding a dusty rolling pin that looked aged from abandonment. Lucy took a picture, hoping that the rolling pin would appear floating in the image. "No right man in his right mind would call his wife that word!"

"Jesus, Bernice!" The Ghost of Old Man Harry Wilson grabbed at his chest. "You're supposed to be dead! Quit trying to kill me, old woman."

"You're already *dead*, you dense moron," The Ghost of Bernice Wilson shook her rolling pin at her undead husband. "I've been gone for twenty-five years and the only time I was happy was when I was free of this fool for the first ten." She hover-hobbled back to the kitchen. "You're not getting any pot pie tonight, Harry!"

"Bernice, you're being unreasonable!" The Ghost of Old Man Harry Wilson shook his head. "I'm sorry, Chadron, I've gotta deal with my woman or I ain't getting any supper tonight." Chuckling, he tried to pat Chase on the shoulder and his hand flew through him instead. Chase shuddered. The Ghost of Old Man Harry Wilson didn't notice. "Always liked your family. I should give my farm to you happy lot rather than my ungrateful brats. Meh. I'll call my lawyer later." He hover-hobbled after his ghostly wife and vanished as he crossed the threshold into the kitchen.

After a moment of silence, Lucy snapped a picture of the doorway.

"Keep note." Lucy turned to Natalie. "Threshold from their world to ours is in the kitchen doorway and fireplace. However, the fireplace might just be something dramatic Murasaki invented herself to try and impress us. Feel free to investigate either in your field study. Neither will harm you unless you linger."

There were no protests from ether Chase or Natalie. Natalie simply pulled her notebook out and starting jotting notes down like crazy. Lucy tasked Chase to investigate the rest of the house, advising him to bring any personal objects to her for inspection. They all ended up exploring the haunted house for the rest of the afternoon. Lucy took picture after picture as Natalie carefully took samples of the wooden door frame entering the kitchen and some pieces of brick from the fireplace.

As the smell of chicken pot pie wafted through the air, the trio headed out of the house at Lucy's urging just as the sun was setting. They had gotten lucky that this haunted residence only held ambivalent spirits and she refused to risk it any further.

Regardless of the danger, Lucy found herself smiling as she and her friends piled back into Chase's truck. Natalie fawned over her samples, exclaiming that she couldn't wait to check them out with her personal lab equipment, and Chase kept re-accounting the story of their encounters with Murasaki and the Old Wilson couple, fighting that he didn't scream *that* much when Murasaki flung him to the ceiling. The two girls disagreed.

However, their lightened mood came to a sobering halt as they approached Sterben's city limits. It was dark now, which made the single Sterben police car's lights shine that much brighter as it barricaded the road into town. Chase slowed his truck to a stop and Officer Hansen approached the truck with his flashlight.

"Chase." The bumbling officer did not offer a warm smile as he did for Lucy earlier in the day. Just a courteous nod as he shone the flashlight into the bed of Chase's truck. "Where have you guys been tonight?"

"Out for a drive," Chase stated effortlessly. "Why? Are we in trouble?"

"All of you should call your parents," The police officer stated sternly. "They'll all be mighty relieved it wasn't none of you."

"None of us?" Natalie asked. "What is this about?"

Officer Hansen looked around before leaning into the truck.

"I shouldn't be telling you kids this, *but...*" Officer Hansen looked proud of his secret. "There's been a murder in Sterben."

Tip #3:
Cemeteries are not for romance.

LIKE MOST SMALL TOWNS, a murder had never happened in Sterben, Kansas before and so, like most small towns, everyone had to get involved with it. The murder had taken place in the town graveyard, a measly eight acre plot of land that nearly every family in Sterben owned a corner of. Officer Hansen, the brilliant police officer of the law, deduced the murder's location based on the fact the body remained stapled to the fence on the land, a trail of blood leading up to it. There were small, bloody footprints leading away from it, but they had vanished mid-step.

Clearly, that meant everyone in town had to go look for the murderer.

Every in-town Sterben resident had taken to the streets, holding some sort of weapon and lighting device, as they called out for the murderer. While Chase returned to his family's farm to see if they had seen anything, Natalie and Lucy stayed with Officer Hansen until their parents arrived. The Hendrixes were surprisingly forgiving given the circumstances. They greeted Lucy with warm hugs and thanked her for being such a good friend to Natalie before taking their daughter back home. Mike Vitalis did not share the same warmth when he arrived.

"Lucy, you *know* how dangerous my job is," Mike lectured as they drove away from the cop car. "When a never-happened-before murder has occurred and you never came back from school-"

"You should've assumed I was, at the very least, taking photos for my portfolio," Lucy stated. "It's what I did when we were in New York. Why would my habits change here?"

"Because it's more dangerous here," Mike said. "In New York, you knew to just stay away from an affected building or place. There's no escape here. There is *only* Sterben and Sterben is not safe."

Pursing her lips, Lucy decided not to tell her father about what she had found, about Murasaki and Old Man Harry Wilson and his spectral spouse. He didn't need to know about her willingness to seek out spirits recklessly without the proper safety procedures. But she also knew that the afternoon's divergence was not the last. Natalie and Chase were believers now. They were small town residents that had gotten a taste of a bigger world. Lucy just hoped whatever was haunting this town was not as dangerous as Murasaki and her father said it was.

As the Vitalises arrived at their house, Chris and Kierra were just leaving their place. Each of them had a matching headlamp on with Chris holding a foam prop sword and Kierra brandishing a hunting rifle. Kierra continued to load her gun as Lucy and Mike exited their truck. Chris waved at them with a jovial smile.

"Howdy neighbors!" He shouted. "Are you going out to search for the murderer? The whole town's in on it!"

Mike raised a hand. "Not for me, thanks! I've got some work to do." He dropped his hand onto his daughter's shoulder. "Why don't you take Lucy with you instead?"

In a rare show of shock, Lucy turned on the heel of her boot to face her father.

"Have you lost your mind?" Lucy whispered. "You *just* expressed your over-invested concern for my well-being and now you want to send me to search for a person who has physically killed someone with two people we barely know?"

"If you think I'm going to leave you home alone with a murderer running around, then *you* have lost your mind," Mike said. "Besides, you know they probably won't find the murderer. These are the safest people you can be with right now."

Lifting the gun, Kierra took a peek through her scope. "Don't worry, Lucy! We'll watch out for you!"

"Kierra's the best shot in Sterben!" Chris swung his plastic sword around. "And, I don't mean to toot my own horn here, but I've been praised for my swordsmanship on the stage in the Sterben Herald."

Lucy gave her father a worrying look. He shrugged.

"It'll be fun," He assured. "Think of it as an opportunity to practice taking pictures at night."

"I had plenty of practice in New York," Lucy said. "But, to appease your worries as a single parent and your effort to connect despite the disparity in the our shared interests, I will go with them."

Mike ran inside the house to grab Lucy a flashlight and her pepper spray for humans. There was equipment more appropriate against ghosts in her messenger bag, but Lucy was more than happy to accept something that would work against a murderer too. She clipped the pepper spray to her camera strap before turning the flashlight on and walking out with Chris and Kierra.

As they roamed the streets, they met with other residents of Sterben who cheerily greeted the couple before either commenting on Kierra's gun or the couple's recent wedding and subsequent honeymoon. With each person they met, Chris and Kierra were kind enough to include Lucy in their conversations as much as possible and introduce her to much of the town.

By the time they reached the graveyard, Lucy felt worn out from all of the half-hearted conversations about how excellent the night scope on Kierra's Mossberg was or what Chinese buffets were the best in Manhattan, Kansas. She was actually thrilled to finally see the first trace of blood on the grave plot. It started out thin, but soon carved a thick path of blood to the dead body still pinned to the pointed black fence lining the back of the graveyard.

Chris let out a gasp as his headlamp shined on the body.

"Oh no, isn't that one of the Morrison boys?!" He swallowed hard. "I mean, I know they're not the best family, but this is horrible."

"It's so disrespectful to leave the poor guy up there," Kierra said, shaking her head. "Why hasn't Officer Hansen taken him down yet?"

"Because this is a crime scene," Lucy stated. She snapped a picture of the body. "If there was a real police force in this town, we wouldn't even think to be here. We're interfering with evidence."

"Terrible." Kierra turned to her husband. "Chris, when I die, make sure my body isn't left up like that for hours."

"Babe, if you die, *I'll* die." Chris took his wife's hand. "Promise me you won't die."

"That's not a reasonable-"

"Promise me."

She sighed. "Of course, honey. I won't die if you won't die."

"You can't be my date to the Academy Awards if you're dead," Chris said.

"And you can't take me if you're dead."

"Then let's not die."

"Aw babe!"

As the newlyweds spoke, Lucy focused her attention on taking pictures of the crime scene. It was already littered with various footsteps from the visiting residents, but most of the evidence still remained. She captured several angles of the dead body before focusing on the path, snapping pictures of the blood trail leading back to the grave that it started at. Through her camera lens, she noticed the dates on the gravestone. Peeking out from behind her camera, she did the math in her head as she read the marker.

"What happened to Jonathan Gilbert?" Lucy asked. "He died when he was only eighteen. If the dates on here are correct, he would've been just a few grades older than you guys."

Chris and Kierra walked over to the grave hand-in-hand and stared at it for a moment.

"I've never heard of a Jonathan Gilbert in Sterben before…" Kierra said.

After another minute, Chris snapped his finger and looked at his wife. "Gilly! Remember Gilly? Used to hang out with Chevron Hunter all the time? His real name was Jonathan!"

"Oh Gilly!" Kierra exclaimed. "Of course I remember Gilly. He was always so funny."

"Poor guy died in a car crash the night after graduation," Chris sighed. "He had a theatre scholarship to DePaul University up in Chicago. Not going to lie, a lot of us were jealous he got it. But he worked hard for it, so I guess no complaints."

Lucy nodded towards the dead body still hanging out on the fence. "Did he have any connections to the Morrison boy?"

"The Morrison boy would've only been a kid when Gilly died," Chris explained. "I mean, he still is-*was* a kid, but Gilly would've never known him. Like I said, Gilly was a theatre kid through and through. The Morrisons have been the stars of the football team since their great-great-grandpa....or was it great-great-great grandpa?"

Lifting her camera to her eye again, Lucy focused her camera on the gravestone. When her finger flicked the shutter button, her viewfinder went black. She pulled away from her camera and looked at it. Dead battery. It made sense. She had forgotten to charge it the night before and after the afternoon's unexpected extensive photoshoot, she was surprised it didn't shut off after the first attempt to take a picture in the dark.

Mew.

Lucy, Chris, and Kierra all looked up. Sitting calmly and staring at them with its bright green eyes, a gray cat let its tail wave back and forth as it stared at the amateur investigators. After assessing the newlyweds, Okiku looked at Lucy and mewed before standing to its paws. It trampled off, allowing Lucy to watch where it went.

"What a pretty kitty!" Kierra said. "Poor thing. I hope it didn't see what happened here. It would be so traumatizing!"

"Let's follow it," Lucy said. "It might take us to someone who might know something."

Chris and Kierra followed almost reluctantly, keeping pace with Lucy only to fulfill her father's wish that they would keep an eye on her during their adventure. The trio followed the cat deeper and deeper into the dark, non-populated region of town, where tree branches turned into arms that snatched children in their nightmares and gave adults reason to trim their own hedges. Lucy continued to follow the cat, taking each stride with confidence.

The same could not be said for the huddled, shaking mass of Chris and Kierra.

With a leap, the cat flew into the arms of Murasaki who stood hidden behind a tree.

"Oh you are such a good kitty!" Murasaki said as she walked out from her hiding spot. "You make Mommy *so proud*!"

When she emerged, both Chris and Kierra gave a shout. Quickly composing herself, Kierra aimed her rifle at the ancient Japanese spirit.

"Are you the person who killed the Morrison boy?" She asked.

"I am neither of those things," Murasaki said, petting her cat. "I am the being whom arrived too late and was only able to save one life rather than the two."

"What are you talking about?" Chris asked.

With a sigh, she turned to Lucy. "Despite my previous assertion, I'm considering you my partner in this matter. I've never interacted so directly in the mortal world that I've sworn to protect and thus have no idea how to proceed."

"It's okay," Lucy whispered. "They're good people despite their naivety."

"Your trust better not be misplaced," Murasaki said. "I know how rash mortals act."

Turning her back to Lucy, Murasaki walked forward and snapped her fingers. A large green flame shone in the darkness, illuminating the empty space. Lucy aimed her flashlight towards the same space as Chris and Kierra joined her, their headlamps illuminating the area as well. Murasaki stepped to a tree and spoke behind it softly.

After a moment, Murasaki led a teenage girl out from behind it. With long blonde hair and bright blue eyes, the girl's beauty was nearly enough to distract from the dried blood splattered on one side of her body, completely ruining her pink blouse and white jeans. But the girl didn't seem to notice her distressing appearance. With a glowing smile, the girl wiggled her fingers at the newcomers.

"Hi everybody!" She exclaimed. "It's, like, *so* nice to meet you. Mara has told me that you guys are, like, really nice and stuff and, like, won't think I'm the murderer or anything which is *super* cool because I am definitely *not* the murderer, you know?" Her eyes landed on Lucy and the girl smiled widely again. "Ooo! Your outfit's cute! I like your hat! It kind of looks like a Frisbee!"

Awkwardly pinching the brim of her black hat, Lucy nodded politely. "Thank you."

"All of this sounds like something a murderer would say!" Chris said, lifting his foam sword towards the girl.

Stepping forward, Murasaki let her hand glow a threatening green as she confronted the actor. "I will attest for this girl myself that she is innocent of every crime except being in the wrong place at the wrong time. Do you understand?"

Staring at the mysteriously glowing hand, Chris nodded. Murasaki stepped back.

"Now. Back to the situation at hand." Murasaki took a deep breath. "The murder was taken place by-"

The spirit was interrupted by a flood of light originating from at least one car and fifteen people with various flashlights. When Murasaki and Okiku disappeared in a burst of a green flame, the bloodied girl ran and hid behind Chris and Kierra. Following the flood of light was a small mob, led by Mike Vitalis with Mayor Hansen and Officer Hansen closely behind him. Behind them was the majority of the town that was previously out searching for the murderer.

"Just a few more steps..." Mike didn't look up from the device beeping wildly in his hands. He stopped in the place that Murasaki stood in just a few moments before and the device shut down. With a happy sigh, he looked up. As soon as he made eye contact with his daughter, he frowned. "Lucy? What are you doing here?"

"You told me to try and find a murderer," Lucy stated. "So that's what I was doing. What are *you* doing here?"

"I had a lead on a potential spirit and everyone started following me," Mike said. "Have you seen anything?"

"Just a jibakurei and her cat," Lucy said.

"This isn't the time to joke, Luce," Mike said. "There's no way a Japanese spirit would be in the middle of Kansas."

Adjusting his top hat, Mayor Hansen stepped forward away from the crowd.

"Uh, so Mike?" Mayor Hansen said. "Where's the ghost? Where's the murderer?"

"Yeah who do I have to cuff?" Officer Hansen whipped out his handcuffs. "They are going *down!*"

The crowd cheered at Officer Hansen's declaration. He held his arms up in triumph and the crowd cheered louder. Mayor Hansen twiddled with his fake moustache proudly. Mike sighed and turned the device in his hands off.

"There's no murderer here," He announced. "Just a false lead on a potential spirit."

"What about her?" A woman shouted from the crowd, pointing a finger towards Lucy, Chris, and Kierra and the bloodied girl. "She looks like she's from Lebenville!"

The mob shouted in agreement. Mike held his arms out.

"That's my daughter!" He shouted. "She's innocent and I'm sure she has the photos to prove it!"

"Not that girl!" The woman shouted again. "*That* girl!"

"Carol, you were at our wedding!" Chris said. "You see Kierra at the grocery store every Tuesday on taco nights!"

"No, no!" The woman, Carol, sounded frustrated. "The girl behind all of you! Honestly, am I the only one who sees her or am I going crazy?!"

The reviews were mixed from the crowd. Finally, the bloodied girl emerged from her hiding place. The entire crowd gasped before immediately yelling for her arrest. Officer Hansen held his hands up.

"Good people of Sterben, do not fear!" He shouted. "I will arrest the dangerous murderer myself." Officer Hansen turned to his brother. "Mayor, would you do me the honors?"

With a nod, Mayor Hansen accepted a small stereo from a member of the crowd and plugged his phone into it. There was a long pause as Mayor Hansen fumbled with his phone, struggling to find what he was searching for. The crowd waited patiently in relative silence. Officer Hansen waited another beat until finally the Cops theme song blared from the stereo. As the crowd cheered at the song's beginning, Officer Hansen took confident strides towards the girl, flipping his handcuffs between his hands as if they were toy nunchucks. Lucy stepped in between the police officer and the girl.

"Hey, little girl, could you move?" Officer Hansen asked quietly. "The song is only so long and it takes a long time to arrest someone-"

"She's not the murderer," Lucy said. "Let her explain."

"She's going to lie just like every criminal I saw on Cops!" Officer Hansen insisted.

Mike stepped forward and placed a hand on the police officer's shoulder. "Just some more critique for you, but you generally don't arrest someone until you know for sure they're guilty. You'll get in trouble if you're wrong, es-pecially since she's probably innocent, right?"

Suddenly looking nervous, Officer Hansen turned to the crowd. "Al-right! Hold on everyone!"

With a huff of annoyance, Mayor Hansen paused the music as Officer Hansen looked increasingly nervous at the amount of eager eyes watching him. "Uh as part of my duty as your police officer of the peace, uh, I've gotta interrogate her real fast so just, like, chill, okay?"

The crowd groaned. Officer Hansen turned to the girl.

"Alright, make it quick," The police officer said. "I've gotta arrest some-one for this murder before it gets to morning when the old people wake up and start yelling at me."

"Well I don't know how you're going to arrest a ghost, Officer," The girl said.

Everyone went quiet. Mike Vitalis pushed the incompetent police officer out of the way and approached the girl.

"Ghost?" Mike said. "What makes you think it was a ghost?"

All eyes were on the very pretty blonde girl. She twiddled with her fin-gers nervously as she looked at everyone.

"Well okay first off, I'm not a slut okay? I, like, didn't even like John in that way," The girl explained. "When he said he wanted to play Ghost in the Graveyard with me, I, like, actually thought we were going to play that game because I *loved* that game when we were kids, you know? So he drove all the way to Lebenville to pick me up-"

"She *is* from Lebenville!" Carol shouted. "She's gotta be guilty! Arrest her, Officer!"

The crowd cheered again and Mike held up a hand to silence them. Once they fell silent, he turned to the girl and nodded, silently urging her to con-tinue. The girl took a deep breath.

"Well okay so he picks me up and he brings me to the graveyard and tells me to start counting mand, like, so I close my eyes and all of a sudden he starts kissing me and I was like well okay I guess I'll kiss you back?" The girl shrugged. "But, like, I'm not a slut, okay? I didn't even really want to kiss him, okay?"

"While his sexual assault is an issue, it's not the crime we're investigating at this time," Mike said. "How did John get murdered?"

"Oh it was the ghost! Mara told me!" The girl nodded excitedly. "Well, like, all I saw was him getting pulled off of me and then he started screaming and bleeding and I just thought maybe he started his period or whatever boys have instead of a period?" She ignored all of the incredulous stares from the people around her. "Anyway, like, and then the same thing was about to happen to *me* but then Mara saved me and Mara told me John was dead and that he was killed by a ghost or something and that it was very dangerous and she was just, like, so *brave* about it all."

"And what is your name?" Mike said.

"Georgia!" She smiled proudly. "Georgia Peaches."

"Well, uh, Miss Peaches?" Mike offered. "Where is this Mara now?"

"Her full name is Murasaki," Lucy said. "She was the jibakurei I was telling you about before you disregarded me."

After registering just what they were talking about, Officer Hansen's eyes grew wide as he looked between Mike and Georgia. Finally he turned to his brother and indicated for him to join their meeting. Mayor Hansen joined them with a skip in his step, pressing his fake moustache against his upper lip.

"Yo what's up?" The esteemed mayor of Sterben asked the group. "Is she the murderer? Can we blame her?"

"Uh, no." Officer Hansen said quietly. He leaned in closer to his brother. "The murderer was, uh, a ghost."

"A GHOST?!" Mayor Hansen exclaimed loudly. "YOU MEAN A GHOST KILLED THE MORRISON BOY?!"

The crowd muttered nervously between themselves. Risking a glance at the now nervous crowd, Mike shushed the mayor. "Could you keep it down? I feel like this is a strictly need-to-know basis."

"WHAT'S NEED TO KNOW?" Mayor Hansen continued to shout. "THAT A GHOST MURDERED THE MORRISON BOY IN COLD BLOOD AND THAT NO ONE IS SAFE FROM IT'S UNBRIDLED RAGE BUT WE CAN'T STOP IT BECAUSE IT'S A GHOST?!"

As Officer Hansen put his smaller brother into a headlock and smothered the mayor's mouth in his hand, the crowd screamed and shouted their concerns. Carol called to sacrifice Georgia Peaches to appease the spirit, while the rest of the group either agreed or argued to cast out the Vitalises instead, claiming that nothing bad happened before their arrival.

Chris and Kierra shared a glance before Kierra brought her index and middle fingers to her mouth. With an ear-piercing whistle, she single-handedly silenced the crowd, an act Lucy found remotely impressive. Kierra stepped to the side, adjusting her rifle and looking nonchalant at her ability to calm an angry mob with one whistle.

Georgia Peaches let out her own soft whistle. "What a badass."

"Hey now!" Not hearing Georgia, Chris stepped forward with his hands outdrawn. "Listen, I understand everyone's fear about this murderous ghost, but we can't kick out Mike and Lucy! They're part of the town now. Besides, Mike's an *actual* ghostbuster. He can save us all!"

The crowd muttered and nodded in agreement while Mike let out an exasperated sigh at the mention of him being a ghostbuster.

"What about the Lebenville slut?" Carol shouted. "Can we sacrifice her instead? There was no murderous ghosts before *she* stepped into this town."

The crowd muttered and nodded in agreement again. Georgia Peaches folded her arms across her heavy chest and frowned.

"I told you guys I'm not a slut!" Georgia whined.

Officer Hansen shouted out in surprise as Mayor Hansen licked his brother's hand to free himself from the headlock. Standing up straight and ensuring his moustache was still stuck to his upper lip, Mayor Hansen indicated for Mike and Officer Hansen to come in closer to him. To close the huddle, Lucy stepped forward as well.

"Alright listen...." Mayor Hansen said quietly. "It might not be....a *bad* idea to sacrifice the girl-"

"Are you crazy?" Mike asked. "What is this, Salem?"

"Nah Salina is farther east from us," Officer Hansen explained. "Just a few miles south of Manhattan."

"We could get Father O'Shannon to approve it!" Mayor Hansen said excitedly. "The burn pit is already prepped from homecoming weekend a few weeks ago. Would burning her at the stake work, Mike?"

"No it wouldn't," Mike said. "Sacrificing this girl would do nothing but lose an innocent life."

"I've gotta settle these people down somehow, Mike!" Mayor Hansen hissed. "If they want a sacrifice, then gosh darn it I'm going to give them a-"

"Why not just put her under custody?" Lucy offered. "Keep her in town until there's more evidence that it's her fault. It should appease your blood-hungry mob of probable devout Christians. Keep their hands washed of the crime until the crime is convicted."

The Hansens looked at each other.

"Works for me," Mayor Hansen said with a shrug.

With a sigh, Officer Hansen turned to the crowd. "Alright y'all! Change of plans. First off, there will be *no* sacrifice tonight."

The crowd shouted in protest and disappointment.

"Lebenville lover!" Carol spat.

"But..." Officer Hansen looked jovial as the crowd hushed in anticipation for what he could potentially offer them instead. "We *are* going to arrest Ms. Peaches and keep her in our custody until we get to the bottom of this ghost business."

"And then we'll sacrifice her?" Carol asked.

Officer Hansen looked towards his brother. The mayor shrugged.

"Sure!" Mayor Hansen said. "That sounds cool."

The crowd, and even Chris and Kierra, cheered. Georgia Peaches clapped and bounced ever so slightly. With a triumphant push of a button, Mayor Hansen let the *Cops* theme song play right where it left off. The cheers grew louder as Officer Hansen walked over to Georgia Peaches with his handcuffs in hand. Mike shook his head and turned to Lucy.

"Luce, could you keep an eye on Georgia while she's in Sterben?" Mike asked. "Just to make sure she isn't killed by this group of trigger-happy rednecks?"

"I don't know if my reasoning will be able to subdue them when the time comes," Lucy said. "But I will make a triumphant attempt."

"Hold on, Officer Hansen!" Carol came running up with her phone in hand. "Let me get a picture of you arresting the Lebenville delinquent for the Sterben Herald!"

Lucy cringed as the woman attempted to take a picture worthy of publication with her phone. Pausing the arrest, both Officer Hansen and Georgia Peaches smiled widely as Carol tapped her screen. The picture was taken and

Officer Hansen resumed putting the handcuffs on Georgia Peaches. Carol turned to Lucy and her father and pointed her phone at them.

"And now some pictures of Sterben's newest residents and heroes!" She exclaimed. Lucy turned away from the phone as the woman took the picture, blissfully unaware that Lucy's face would be obscured by a blur of blonde hair and her half of the picture would be completely unusable in any serious paper. With a happy sigh, Carol put her phone down.

"I can see the headline now!" Carol said. "Lebenville Punk Brings Murderous Ghost to Sterben; Only Mike Can Stop It!"

"I think there's been worse headlines in the world," Lucy said, fixing her hair. "Dewey defeats Truman comes to mind."

"Stop!" Mike shouted. "All of you! Listen to me!"

The crowd stopped happily talking amongst themselves and looked at Mike Vitalis. Mayor Hansen paused the music, causing Officer Hansen looked up from his pleasant conversation with Georgia Peaches. Mike stared at the group with a solemn expression.

"Do *not* tell anyone about this," Mike ordered. "Ghosts and spirits are quiet creatures who crave privacy. A media circus would only agitate them and worsen the situation. This was just one murder. This could happen ten times over if you do not allow me to finish my work in peace. Do you understand?"

Looking between each other, the crowd nodded numbly. Georgia Peaches attempted to raise her handcuffed hands. She stayed in that awkward position until Mike raised an eyebrow.

"Uh...Georgia?" He asked. "Do you have a question?"

"Yes!" She sang. "Is there a way I can see Mara again?"

"I don't know a Mara," Mike said.

"Murasaki," Lucy stated. "The jibakurei I keep trying to tell you about."

Mike sighed. "No. Don't seek out any ghosts or spirits and *don't* alert the media. Is everyone clear on that?!"

Carol raised a hand. "What defines a spirit? Because Mr. Carroll definitely has some spirits in our alcohol cabinet."

"Who's Mr. Carroll?" Mike asked.

"My husband, of course."

"Your name is Carol Carroll?" Lucy asked.

"Maiden name was Bells," Carol said sweetly.

"Well I think those spirits are okay in quantity," Mike explained. "Any other questions?"

Everyone in the crowd raised their hand. Chris and Kierra raised their hands. Even Georgia did her weird handcuffed elbow-hand raise again. Mike sighed.

"All people who somehow don't understand the whole 'don't tell anyone' thing, put your hand down," Mike said. "I mean it when I say it: don't tell anyone. You might die."

Half the crowd dropped their hands.

"If you have a question about finding ghosts," Mike said. "Put your hand down because I already told you to not find them. You might die."

Everyone else's hand went down. Only Mayor Hansen's hand remained. Mike nodded at him.

"Mayor?" He asked.

"So like when you say 'don't tell anyone', does that include my secretary?" Mayor Hansen asked.

"Yes," Mike answered begrudgingly. "Anyone means everyone."

"I can't keep this from Mr. Carroll," Carol said. "I've been married to him for fifteen years. He's the father of both of my kids. I've never kept a secret from him before!"

"Don't. Tell. Anyone." Mike repeated through gritted teeth.

For the next hour, Mike reiterated his statement over and over as the citizens of Sterben refused to believe their kids, grandmothers, brother, the mayor (someone was confused (it was Officer Hansen)), the principal (that was asked by the same man who asked about their brother (it was Mayor Hansen)), and whoever else they could think of would be excluded from knowing what had happened that night. Even though Mike had good intentions in his heart and was only following the protocol that he learned after his years of seeing what happened when he failed protocol, he had forgotten one thing and one thing only:

There are no secrets in small towns.

Tip #4:

Don't profit off the dead.

"$15 FOR A 'I SURVIVED Sterben' sweater," One vendor shouted from her table, competing with the busy Sterben street filled with tourists. "$10 for the 'Sterben Spooked Me' t-shirt!"

"Next ghost tour in twenty minutes!" Another man shouted into a megaphone. "See Sterben's finest dead people! Guided by Sterben's oldest living resident, Betty Bells!"

An elderly woman dressed in a pink, fuzzy bathrobe waved from her position on a large trailer with some metal folding chairs situated on it. Lucy lifted the thin black veil that fell from her black, flat-brimmed hat. Taking the picture, she prided herself on being able to capture the senile expression on the woman's face. She was almost tempted to take the tour, just to marvel in the ignorance of it all, but Natalie had already expressed her disgust at the idea.

"Oh look." Natalie sighed and pointed to the newest pop-up stand. "The Morrisons are trying to bastardize their son's death again."

Lucy snapped a picture. This was the family's third attempt. The funeral took place a week after the murder and the Morrisons were charging $5 admission to all wannabe ghost hunters. After the old ladies who enjoyed a good funeral and the goodies that came with it complained, they dropped the admission. The day after the funeral, they tried to resurrect their son through a seance that also had a $5 admission, but no one showed after Mike denounced it. So now they were finishing setting up a stand promoting their new DVDs of the documentary about how their son had died at the hand of a ghost. Natalie let out an audible sound of disgust.

"All of this is so terrible," Natalie said. "Does anyone even care that it's a school day?! Wait. Don't answer that. We both know the answer. One, two, three-"

"No," The girls said in unison.

"Because if anyone cared about education in Sterben-" Natalie started.

"-they wouldn't be in Sterben." Lucy finished.

Technically, the town of Sterben was celebrating the Harvest Festival which allowed the excused days off school. But also, technically, word of Sterben being haunted *somehow* spread past the town's borders which forced the Harvest Festival to extend into the school week. According to Mayor Hansen's official press release, the three days originally allotted weren't enough to fulfill the demands of the ghost seeking tourists that had overran Sterben and thus the Harvest Festival would continue until the tourists were gone.

Unrelated, this was the longest Harvest Festival to occur in Sterben's history to not include a single mention of any sort of harvest.

Smiling softly, Lucy adjusted the settings on her camera. "If you sold the samples you took from the Wilson house, I bet you could get a high enough bid to pay for your first textbooks at Brown."

"I'm in the middle of a study!" Natalie exclaimed. "You don't just *sell* your samples in the middle of a study. It's like selling your photos before you print them."

"You hurt my soul with that suggestion," Lucy said. "Where's the booth with my dad's action figures again? I promised I would get him something today."

"I think it's just past the 'Bust the Ghosts' carnival game stand," Natalie said. "You know? Right next to the face-painting station."

"Across from the inflatables?" Lucy asked.

"Yes!"

"Oh my gosh!" A woman wearing a 'Sterben Spooks Me' shirt ran up to them. "Are you guys *actual* Sterben natives?!"

"Nope," The girls said in unison again.

The woman looked disappointed before running off to bother someone else. Lucy and Natalie looked at each other and shrugged.

"I'm from New York," Lucy said.

"Kansas City," Natalie said.

Sharing their proud moment, the girls linked arms and walked down the street to look for the elusive action figure. People pointed cameras at them and Lucy bowed her head, unconcerned because her veil concealed her face well enough. It had become common for the ghost tours to mistake Lucy as a spirit on first glance. Once, they even convinced a tourist that Lucy was possessing Natalie and they got the poor guy to buy them each a Spooky Sterben Snowcone from Charlie Carroll's stand or risk getting haunted for the rest of his days. It wasn't their proudest moment, but he also touched Natalie's hair without her permission so they agreed it had to be done.

"Lucy!"

The girls turned to the voice. Chris and Kierra were standing at the street corner, passing out flyers in varying shades of purple, pink, and blue. Adamant in his work, Chris didn't look away from his potential customers as Kierra waved the girls over with fistfuls of flyers in each hand. Lucy and Natalie strolled over to the newlyweds.

"Hi Lucy, Hi Natalie!" Kierra said as she offered them a flyer. "You guys are coming to Chris's play, right? With all of these tourists, it's sure to be a packed house but we'll make sure to reserve seats opening night for our favorite neighbors and their guests!"

"I'm sure my father will require my attendance and I will require Natalie's companionship to endure the performance," Lucy said as she accepted the flyer. "Natalie? Would you be free for the play?"

"I never miss Chris's plays!" Natalie turned to Lucy and beamed. "You would be surprised on how charming they are. Plus, Chris is a pretty good actor. Who does he got co-starring this time, Kierra?"

"Well, of course Teri and Jeri will be in it," Kierra said. "And then the second grade class from Sterben Elementary will be helping out as well. It should be a good show this year!"

"I can't wait!" Natalie said with a huge smile before walking away, Lucy in tow, to leave Kierra to continue her work. For once, Lucy waited a respectable distance before she unleashed her offenses.

"A second grade class?" She asked. "Does he truly expect his work to be taken seriously when he's working with seven year olds?"

"He loves it," Natalie said. "It's so cute to see him inspire those little guys. Besides, second grade is good for him. The last show was kindergarten. It made an interesting *Richard III* to say the least."

A horn blared behind the girls. They both flinched as a truck carrying a flatbed trailer filled with tourists sped up and stopped right next to the girls with a jolt. Old Betty Bells didn't seem to notice the excitement as tourists stood to aim their cameras at Lucy and mutter amongst themselves as they took pictures.

"Delilah, is that you?" Betty Bells croaked into her crackling megaphone, squinting at Lucy. "Delilah! It's me, Betty! Remember when we went to the prom and drank an entire bottle of whiskey behind the porta-potty? Oh those were good times. It's a shame Jimmy had to knock ya up. You woulda been a great nurse!"

"Hank!" Natalie shouted. "You *know* this is Lucy Vitalis, a living breathing human!"

"Wait—she's still alive?" One of the tourists exclaimed.

The driver squinted at the girls. "Oh. Yeah. I guess it is. False alarm, everyone!"

The flatbed trailer filled with tourists sighed sadly as the driver smiled ever so slightly before driving off. Betty Bells waved to the girls with a wide, senile smile.

"Ring me when the line is clear, Delilah!" She shouted. "I already got the bottle of whiskey ready!"

Lucy took a picture of the tourist attraction as it sped off. Glaring at the fleeing makeshift tour group, Natalie waited for Lucy to finish taking her photos before continuing their walk.

"Honestly, doesn't it bother you that they're treating you like this?" Natalie said.

"As long as they don't capture a clear image of me, I have no qualms," Lucy said. "Besides, it could be worse."

Halting in her tracks, Lucy looked across the street. Natalie followed her gaze and let her jaw drop at the spectacle.

"Meet the girl behind the Morrison boy's murder!" Carol Carroll shouted from the booth the girls stared at. "Georgia Peaches, right here in the flesh! Fresh from Sterben jail! $10 for an autograph, $5 for a photo!"

Decked out in a orange long-sleeve blouse and black sweatpants someone had attempted to spray paint orange, Georgia Peaches was smiling and signing autographs with a handful of tourists. Natalie and Lucy only shared one curious glance before striding over to the station. Carol Carroll regarded her visitors with a warm smile.

"Oh howdy girls!" Carol said. "Have you heard of our discount for Sterben residents? There's an even better discount for those who were in attendance of the murder!"

"Shouldn't Georgia be with Officer Hansen?" Lucy asked. "As I recall, no bail has been posted and it's unlawful to parade a suspect for financial purposes, not to mention the ethics of it all."

"Yeah well it was unethical for this Lebenville slut to kill the Morrison boy too, but you don't see Father O'Shannon condemning the girl to hell," Carol Carroll explained.

"That's because Father O'Shannon is too busy offering exorcism classes," Natalie said. She turned her head towards Lucy. "$20 donation to the church a pop. My parents are actually taking it just in case, you know, my studies go haywire or something. But at least it's supporting the church?"

Lucy rolled her eyes. "Regardless, Georgia Peaches should be with Officer Hansen. She definitely should not be with a woman who can keep her mouth shut as well as a thirteen year old near their crush."

With a frown, Carol Carroll furrowed her eyebrows at Lucy. "Didn't your father ever teach you to respect your elders? If he did, you would be more understanding of the fact Officer Hansen has his hands filled trying to keep the peace with all of these tourists and Mrs. Hansen has a crafts table to run. It's more productive for Georgia to be out here raising some money and settling her debt than watching TV at the Hansens' place."

The tour truck came to a screeching halt behind them. The girls turned to it and Betty Bells waved as more cameras flashed in Lucy's direction.

"Delilah, hello!" With another wide, nearly toothless smile, Betty Bells reached under her robe and pulled out a handle of whiskey nearly as big as the old woman's head and just about as empty as it too. "I told ya I'd bring the good stuff!"

"Hey, hey! Five bucks a photo!" Carol Carroll stormed over to the truck to discourage the tourists from their freebie Snapchat pictures.

Georgia's last batch of fans finished their photos and walked away. With her free moment, she smiled and waved at Lucy and Natalie.

"Hi guys!!" She sang. "Isn't this great? It's like a little party to celebrate ghosts!"

"A boy was murdered by a spirit we know nothing about and the town is profiting off of it," Lucy said, folding her arms across her chest. "I wouldn't call it an admirable party."

"Some might even call profiting off of others' suffering deplorable," Natalie mumbled.

"But Mara knows all about the spirit!" Georgia said. "She was telling me all about it when she saved me. By the way, um..." She looked around as her cheeks flushed slightly. "Have...have you guys seen her?"

"One should not actively seek out spirits, especially ones with power," Lucy said. "But no. We haven't."

Georgia frowned. "Do you think the festival is upsetting her?"

"I think it would upset anyone with half a brain in this town," Natalie said.

Shaking her head, Georgia sighed deeply. "Mara is so smart too. I hope she didn't leave forever."

"I also hope the same," Lucy said. "My father has made no progress on his investigation since the tourists began so she continues to be the one barrier standing between us and the spirit trying to kill us."

"Well, like, if you guys see her...can you tell her I said hi?" Georgia offered.

The girls agreed as another group of tourists approached Georgia with cameras in hand. Carol Carroll abandoned her cause with the ghost tour and rejoined her sideshow act, hastily punching in numbers to her tablet to accommodate the new guests. Lucy and Natalie continued their journey to the action figure table. After bartering for a hot minute, Lucy managed to get her hands on an action figure of her father for only $3. The action figure was just the body of a Ghostbuster toy mashed with the head of a Superman doll, but Lucy loved it and knew it would get a rise out of her father. If anything, it would be an excellent souvenir of their adventure in Sterben.

"Lucy! Natalie!"

The girls looked to see Chase with a wide smile, waving at them as his little brother Chevy trailed behind him, tugging at the back of his shirt while looking wide-eyed at Lucy. Lucy snapped a picture of the brothers as they made their ways to the girls.

"It's a nice surprise to see you guys out and about," Natalie said. "Your folks don't need help on the farm?"

"They do. I just told them Chevy and I would come to town for some parts real fast," Chase answered. "Chevy also wanted to tell y'all something. Go ahead." He smacked his younger brother's shoulder. "Tell them."

Chevy's already wide eyes got even wider as Lucy and Natalie looked down at the youngest Hunter boy expectedly. Chevy looked back up at his brother who nodded towards the girls. Swallowing hard, Chevy kicked his feet around.

"Ah well-" Chevy cleared his throat. "Lucy, I just think you're pretty and smart and-"

"No! Not that, you dingus." Chase rolled his eyes. "I'm talking about that ghost you were telling Chadron about."

"I told you about that five weeks ago!" Chevy whined. "Chadron was just askin' why we had so little chickens and so I was telling him about the fox-"

"Your stupid fox ain't important," Chase said. "Just tell the girls about the ghost."

"Well if my fox is so stupid, then I guess that's all to the story." Chevy folded his arms across his chest. "I saw a ghost. The end."

As Chase tried in vain to get his younger brother to explain what he saw, Lucy found her father. It was an easy accomplishment given the fact Mike Vitalis was a not-small man balancing several planks of wood on one shoulder while using his other arm to gesture wildly during his loud conversation with Mayor Hansen in the middle of the town square. Lucy approached her father and young mayor cautiously, joining the small crowd circling the grown men, as her friends remained behind to continue their own argument.

"You are dooming your town, sir!" Mike yelled. "You hired me to help you with your paranormal problem and this is me helping you. If you don't end this foolish-"

"My city is prospering!" Mayor Hansen stated proudly, twirling his fake moustache. "You have done excellent work, Mike. You've made the problem into a booming tourist industry! I couldn't have done better myself."

"Yeah, which is exactly why I'll be spending my weekend building a shelter for my daughter, myself, and anyone else who would rather live than die an unimaginable death at the hands of an unstoppable spirit," Mike said, glancing around the crowd. "From firsthand experience, I will tell you it's unpleasant enough to simply witness a death at the hands of a spirit. I couldn't imagine experiencing it."

The small crowd muttered in worry amongst themselves. Mayor Hansen smiled widely and clapped his hands together.

"That sounds *terrific*, Mike!" He exclaimed. "When do you think you'll have that little project done? I think that would be a *great* event for next weekend. You could do tours or maybe a "how-to" workshop-"

He didn't get to finish his thought before Mike shook his head and walked off. The mayor didn't seem to notice Mike's annoyance. Mayor Hansen just shrugged and moved to talk with a tourist holding a camera and wearing a "I See Dead People....in Sterben!" t-shirt. Lucy ran ahead to catch her father, clutching her $3 action figure.

"Dad!" She shouted ahead. Mike stopped and waited for his daughter. Lucy smiled softly as she approached him. "I have acquired a trinket for satirical amusement and symbolic remembrance of-"

The all too familiar sound of screeching truck brakes echoed through the air. Mike looked beyond Lucy's shoulder to watch as the flatbed trailer full of tourists took more pictures of his daughter.

"Oh it's Delilah!" Betty Bells sang. "Hello Delilah! Do you remember me? It's your old pal, Betty! From high school? Delil-"

"Lucille?!" A woman shouted from the trailer. "Michael?!"

While initially apathetic to the tour truck's return, Lucy's eyes widened at the sound of the voice, but she remained in place. Mike's shoulders stiffened, but he still lifted his free hand in a cold greeting.

"Hi Nora."

The ex-wife of Mike Vitalis and mother to Lucy Vitalis hobbled to the end of the trailer, precariously balanced on two sharp high heels with a tight black pencil skirt wrapped around her legs. Her platinum blonde hair that matched her daughter's was tied in a low ponytail that slicked down the back of her hot pink blouse. When she reached the ground, an old man stood and waved her down.

"Nora, lovely, wait for me-" He said, using his dark wooden cane as support. The elderly man clambering for Lucy's mother was dressed in a sharp suit, a custom made Armani, with a crisp purple shirt and bowler cap to accent it. Nora reached to help the old man off the trailer, keeping fragile balance on the toes of her heels as she did so.

Lucy looked at the back of her bare wrist. "Well unfortunately, I have a timetable to meet and my mother is not an option on it-"

As Lucy tried to walk past Mike, he grabbed her by the shoulder.

"Oh no. You're not flaking out on me again," Mike said. "Just suffer for three minutes, I'll do all the talking, and you can go on your way."

Pursing her lips, Lucy slowly turned around to face her mother, stuffing the action figure of her father into her messenger bag as she did so. Nora came hobbling over to them with a large smile, showing off her laser-whitened teeth and fresh Botox, as she held onto the old man's arm, both of them acting like he did not require her assistance off the trailer just moments ago.

"Oh my god!" Nora detached herself from the old man and approached her former family with wide arms. "What a small world to see you guys here of all places! Of course I should've known you would be behind this, Michael. You *are* the second best paranormal private investigator in the world, after all." She hugged Mike first and he half-heartedly hugged back with one arm, grimacing when she kissed his cheek as she pulled away. Nora turned to Lucy, the twinkle in her eyes diminishing ever so slightly at the sight of her daughter. "And Lucille! You've gotten so *gorgeous*, sweetie, but there's always room for improvement."

Nora hugged her daughter, but Lucy didn't bother to fake any affection for her mother. Pulling away after a long, awkward moment, Nora cleared her throat before returning to the old man's side.

"You guys already know Diesel Edmund." Nora took the old man's arm again. "Diesel, do you remember my ex-husband and daughter?"

The old man smiled graciously and extended a hand. "Diesel Edmund, at your service. It's an honor to finally meet the man my wife calls 'the best-" He stopped himself when he noticed Lucy and then promptly cleared his throat. "-uh, *tango dancer* of her life.'"

Mike gave a terse smile. "Funny how there were still about twenty nine other men between us who danced with her, Mr. Edmund."

"Twenty seven according to the court documents and *dancing* isn't everything, Michael," Nora cooed. "A woman has to be satisfied in other ways as well."

"When other woman say that, they usually mean something along the lines of emotional intimacy or intellectual conversation," Lucy stated. "They're usually not talking about financial security."

Pursing her lips, Nora shot a cold glare towards her daughter. Meanwhile, Diesel Edmund chuckled.

"Oh man if I had a penny every time someone called one of my wives a gold digger," Diesel said. "Well...I'd make my fortune twice over."

Putting on her biggest, brightest smile again, Nora held onto Diesel's arm tighter. "So...what are you guys doing here? Michael, don't tell me you're here to ruin the fun!"

"I am here for business, yes," Mike stated.

"You came here all the way from New York to settle some silly small town hocus pocus?" Nora laughed. "Oh my! Business *must* be as bad as they say it is in our old hometown. Diesel and I haven't been there in *ages* because of the supernatural shortage."

"Our tour of the paranormal *has* been lacking in the Big Apple," Diesel said. "Of course, once you've toured the Roman catacombs to the fullest and discovered the first knife that stabbed Caesar, it's sort of hard to settle for the usual urban haunts, eh?"

Mike remained silent on the matter.

"How on earth were you able to afford this trip then, Michael?" Nora asked. "*And* you brought Lucille along? My child support doesn't pay for vacations, you know."

"We are aware," Lucy said. "If you cared, you would notice I address my annual 'thank you' card to Diesel."

Nora glared at her daughter as Mike bounced on the heels of his feet.

"We're, uh, actually living here," Mike said. "Temporarily. Until the business is finished. Then we'll be back in New York."

"Well I would hope so!" Nora snorted. "Lucy doesn't belong here. She belongs in New York, where we can dock Diesel's yacht and see her every so often. Not to mention, this place can't support her...picture taking or whatever. It's so...ugly. That's probably why she looks so miserable! You're abusing our child, Michael!"

Lucy pursed her lips and kept her face blank.

"Your tour stopped two times before you recognized your own daughter," Lucy said. "I don't think you get a say in what is good and what isn't good for me."

"You can't blame me, sweetheart," Nora stated. "That hideous veil would make it hard for *anyone* to recognize you, let alone someone you've been avoiding for six years."

Checking the back of her bare wrist again, Lucy looked up at her father.

"My three minutes are up," She said. "Diesel, thank you for the financial support. Nora, thank you for inconveniencing yourself for nine months to birth me. Now, if you'll excuse me."

Turning on her heel, Lucy stormed back to her friends. Natalie smiled as Lucy approached, unaware of her friend's rage.

"Lucy! This is great!" Natalie said. "Your picture was right. Chevy *has* seen a ghost."

"It wasn't a ghost!" Chevy whined again. "I keep trying to tell y'all that it wasn't!"

"I know I was a non-believer at one point too, Chevy," Chase said. "But from what you said, you definitely saw one and I'm surprised you didn't wet your diaper."

Looking wide-eyed between Lucy and his brother, Chevy shook a wavering finger at Chase. "You *know* I quit wearing pull-ups years ago! And I know what a ghost is. I've visited the Wilsons plenty of times."

"Wait, you knew about the Wilsons?!" Chase asked. "Why didn't you tell me?"

"I *did* try to tell you!" Chevy exclaimed. "Remember when I was asking you about where Mom got her sweet potato recipe from and you told me she got it from the Rowlands and then I asked where the Rowlands got it from and you told me to mind my business?"

"...yeah?"

"Well Mrs. Wilson was the one that asked me for it!" Chevy said. "She was mighty disappointed when I didn't bring it to her."

"Why didn't you just come out and say you'd seen a ghost?" Chase asked.

Chevy shrugged. "I dunno. You never asked."

The girls shared a look as Chase groaned and facepalmed.

"A'ight, Chevy..." Chase said with a resigned sigh. "Now why didn't you tell me about the second ghost you saw? The one in Lucy's picture?"

"First off, it wasn't a ghost," Chevy said. "Second, you said my fox wasn't important!"

Chase looked like he was three seconds away from an aneurysm.

"How is the fox important?" He asked with forced patience.

"Because that's how I found the not-ghost-ghost," Chevy explained. "The dead guy!"

Lucy squinted her eyes. "Define dead guy."

A blush washed over Chevy's face. "Well I tried to look him up in the school computers and all that came up was some funny word from that demon book Father O'Shannon warned us not to read."

"Harry Potter?" Natalie offered.

"Yeah!" Chevy said. "I don't remember how to spell it, but I think it was called-"

Before Chevy could finish his thought, the world tried to do a backflip. At least, that's what it felt like as the ground shook tremendously with the loud roar of the earth shifting against itself echoing from the depths of the underground. The town's festivities came to a stop as everyone struggled to catch their balance, and their displays, as the earthquake threatened to undo the morning's work.

There was a deep, resonating snap that crept up from the core of the earth. Everyone turned to the noise. Old Betty Bells's ghost tour was sinking quickly, and deeply, into the ground. Most of the tourists had jumped off the trailer in time and was running away from the sinkhole. But Betty Bells remained, clutching onto the gooseneck of the trailer with one hand and her whiskey with the other as the driver tried to reach down into the hole to grab the old woman, risking his own life in the process.

"C'mon, Betty!" He shouted. "Grab my hand!"

"Hold my whiskey, Hank!" Betty Bells swung the bottle towards him and he grabbed it before it could be smashed against the dirt wall. "I'm finally gonna get my dance with the devil!"

Despite the driver's protests, Betty Bells went cheering into the underground to her long awaited death. A handful of men ran forward and pulled the driver to safety. The town of Sterben, Kansas and its newfound tourists could only watch in disconnected horror as the sinkhole consumed the senile old woman. Once she was well deep into the ground, the earth trembled and the ground rose to fill its own sinkhole. Even as the earth stopped trembling, Betty Bells's audience stood frozen in their place.

"That was..." Mayor Hansen said. "...a *spectacular* show! Good work, Hank!"

Many of the town's residents and tourists clapped and cheered. However, a large portion was silenced in horror. Lucy and her friends, Mike, Nora and Diesel, Hank the driver, and, most notably, Carol Carroll and her family all remained quiet as they knew this was far from an elaborate spectacle to entertain tourists. Their knowledge was confirmed as suddenly a high-pitched shriek ruptured the air, transforming every window of the modest town center into a shower of shattered glass. A large gust of wind came from every direction and overturned every display the townspeople tried to protect from the earthquake. Lucy even had to hold onto her hat to prevent it from flying off in the wind.

And as suddenly as the commotion began, it had stopped. Cheap trinkets and signs were scattered around the ground along with the beads of broken glass, the festival decidedly concluded due to the sheer mess of the town center. Once everyone took note of what had happened, they all turned to Mayor Hansen who was frozen in place with wide eyes that at first stared in horror at nothing, but then darted around to the people staring at him. His terrified vision rested on Mike, who was doing his best to look neutral rather than smug at the confirmation of his prediction.

When it became apparent Mike wouldn't save him, Mayor Hansen instead cleared his throat and twirled his moustache in a false appearance of confidence.

"Good people and visitors of Sterben!" He said. "There's a good reason for this odd coincidence of activity and that is...."

Holding up a finger, the inept mayor of Sterben's mouth fell open as he prepared to address the crowd with inspiring words of wisdom. But instead of a bumbling soliloquy filled with false metaphors, a low voice echoed from the mayor's throat.

"*You all will payyyyyy.*"

Slapping his hands over his mouth, Mayor Hansen's eyes were filled with panic at his stolen voice. The town of Sterben, Kansas remained frozen with their fearless leader for just a moment. Finally, Diesel Edmund thumped his cane against the ground and sighed.

"Welp. It was fun while it lasted." Diesel patted Mike's shoulder. "Good luck with your demon-possessed town, Mike."

Diesel's encouragement broke the frozen spell holding the town hostage and a woman let out a scream. All of the tourists immediately bolted towards their respective vehicles and even the local residents' vehicles when they determined their car was too far away. Sterben residents either joined the tourists' escape, continued to stand around trying to figure out what to do next, or desperately tried to save their displays from the cruel ground. Mayor Hansen continued to have his hands smothering his mouth, but tried to bark orders or convince people to stick around while doing so. Diesel Edmund was on his cell phone, speaking merrily to someone as his wife glared at her ex-husband. Mike just looked resigned at the ensuing chaos. Lucy whipped around to Chevy.

"*What* did you see?" She asked sternly. "No games."

With Chase and Natalie staring him down too, Chevy fell into himself.

"A-a..." He swallowed hard. "...poltergeist."

Something heavy settled into Lucy's heart and she glanced at her friends to see they felt the same weight of their situation. The fact she didn't even need to inform them that a poltergeist was the worst thing this town could face was enough confirmation that they were in some serious trouble. And if this poltergeist could do this much damage with such little effort....

Then this was knees deep into a New York sewage line and Lucy knew they could still get deeper.

Tip #5:
Don't mess with curses.

ON ANY OTHER DAY, IN any other city, Lucy would be thrilled to go to a show. Mike had been taking her monthly to Broadway and Off-Broadway shows alike since she was six years old. It had only been in recent months when Mike's work had been low-paying that Lucy had willingly skipped them, telling her father she felt ill or had photos to print. But she had been hopeful to break that habit tonight. In fact, ever since the incident at the festival, she actually kept a note of Chris's play in hopes that it would be able to distract her father for just an evening.

But now, as she adjusted her black hat in her bedroom mirror, she risked a glance outside of her window and found her father hard at work on his half-finished bunker. With a sigh, she watched him work for another minute before heading out there to confirm what she already knew. When she approached him, he barely acknowledged her with a glance before climbing onto his ladder with a plank of wood balanced on his shoulder.

"Hey," Mike said. "What's going on? Where's your camera?"

"Chris's play is tonight," Lucy stated. "I'm sure it'll be a dismal interpretation of Shakespeare due to the inexperience and inadequate education of both the producer and his audience, but Kierra said she saved us some seats. As an additional bonus, I don't believe the reservations correspond with your newfound popularity but rather true charity."

"Uh-huh." Sticking some nails in his lips, Mike shifted the board over and placed it on the roof of the bunker. Removing the nails from his mouth, he examined his work. "Why don't you go on without me, Luce? If the entire town's at this play, I might actually get to finish our bunker tonight rather than answer false alarm calls."

Mike hammered the plank of wood onto the bunker's framework, answering his own question with each thundering pound into the cheap wood.

Even though her heart was heavy with the notion of leaving her father behind for him to do work when he should be taking a well-needed break, Lucy knew she would've sounded like a spoiled child if she tried to change his mind otherwise. On the other side, if she refused his request and stayed at home with him, he would insist they go and she would feel guilty for pulling him away from his intended task.

But, for a rare moment in her life, she wasn't going to disclose this predicament to her father.

"Well as there is little entertainment in this area aside from the community theatre, I'm sure you'll receive minimal additional ways to dispose of your time tonight," Lucy said. "How is your investigation going? Any clues on the identity of the poltergeist?"

"Not one bit," Mike stated. "I've been too busy checking Mayor Hansen's various body parts for demonic possession to look into it further."

"What about the boy, Jonathan Gilbert?" Lucy asked. "His death was early in his life, right when he had the most potential. Surely his spirit might be restless enough to-"

"Lucy." Mike stopped working to turn to his daughter. "I know I let you help me on cases in New York, but this is different. I don't want you going anywhere *near* anything paranormal in this town, okay? It's too dangerous." He returned his attention to the bunker. "Just...pretend to be a normal kid for once, okay? Go to the play. Hang out with Natalie. Read your SAT prep book. Forget about Jonathan Gilbert and whatever else weird things go on in this insane town, alright? We'll be home before you know it."

Almost unwillingly, Lucy took a step back and reached for the absent camera that usually held loyally around her neck for comfort. Never in her sixteen years of life had her father directly stated that she wasn't a normal kid. She knew she wasn't and she knew her father believed that she wasn't, but it still hurt to hear her father directly say it.

"Okay," She said. "I'm going to the play now. Don't forget to eat something."

Turning on her heel, she went to walk towards the street so she could walk to the high school where the play was being held. Behind her, Lucy could hear her father sigh deeply, a sign that he knew of his failures as a parent but was unresolved on his ability to fix these errors.

"Luce!" He called out. She turned around. Mike raised his hand, then promptly dropped it when he gave up on his idea. "Just...call me if you need anything."

Lifting her phone, Lucy waved it in the air. "As always!"

With a slight nod, Mike returned to building the bunker and Lucy walked to the high school in silence, wishing she had her camera on her to not only entertain her lonely walk, but to offer her security as well. But she knew proper theatre etiquette and she wouldn't dare disrupt that etiquette with the implication that she didn't respect it. However, Lucy's insecurities faded away as she approached the high school and Natalie came running over from her parents' side with a welcoming smile only fitting for a close friend or food at a restaurant after a long wait. Natalie took Lucy's wrist.

"I'm so excited you made it!" Natalie said. "Seriously, you're going to *love* this! It's everything we love about Sterben and so much more. Even Mrs. Bobby comes out to the show and she hates everyone."

"Well I'm sure the fact that most other forms of entertainment are forty minutes away or in your rival town contribute to the popularity of an otherwise mediocre experience," Lucy said. "However, of the things we supposedly *love* about Sterben, I do hope we don't encounter any malevolent spirits this evening. That would assuredly dampen the otherwise jovial mood."

"Speaking of that, I think I have a theory on why Chase won't take us to his farm to investigate..." Natalie looked around before leaning into her friend to ensure nobody overheard their conversation. "I think his family is hiding something."

"I would only assume as much given their unusual stringency for privacy even for a region that seemingly promotes reclusion," Lucy said. "But what could they have hiding on their farm that would relate to the poltergeist?"

"I don't know," Natalie confessed. "But given Chase's hyper-interest in law, his resistance to allow us to investigate his family, even though his brother is the only known person in town to see the spirit, and their lack of interaction with the rest of town is very suspicious. Something is definitely up with them."

Before Lucy could offer her own thoughts, a soft mew purred from their feet. Both girls looked down to see a familiar gray cat with bright green eyes looking up at them. As they gazed down upon the feline, he rolled over on his back and kicked his paws in the air. His bright green eyes still looked at the girls with happiness as he purred at them again.

Lucy looked up at Natalie. "It appears I was wrong about the appearance of a malevolent spirit."

"I have told you before, girl dressed of death, I am not your enemy."

The girls turned to the voice to see Murasaki approach them, wearing the same clothes they first witnessed her in. However, on her side was Georgia Peaches in a tulle pink dress and her long blond hair done up in curls. Her cheeks were flushed pink as well, but not of a result of the excessive make-up Georgia had done herself up with.

Georgia beamed and waved. "Hiya guys! I hope we're not too late. Okie had ran off and Mara had to find him before we could go."

"Wow," Natalie said. "I thought I was exaggerating when I said everyone would be here tonight, but it really looks like everyone *is* here."

Murasaki sighed. "As the appointed protector of Sterben, my presence is required at functions with majority of the town's population in attendance."

"Where were you at during the festival then?" Lucy asked.

"A ghost-seeking tourist attraction is not an attractive place for a jibakurei as myself to be," Murasaki said. "I did not expect the spirit to be powerful enough to attack so publicly and violently and therefore I did not expect my presence to be necessary."

"Mara ain't much of a people person," Georgia translated. "It took me *forever* to convince her to come out with me."

"Yes. I am here now, as I will be at all future Sterben events to ensure no one other than Betty Bells has to die a tragic death at the hands of this awful spirit," Murasaki said, her dark eyes burning into Lucy and Natalie. "Any other doubts?"

With more pink returning to her cheeks, Georgia took Murasaki's arm and giggled. "Ain't she the bravest! She's gonna save us all from that mean ghost that killed John!" Pulling on Murasaki's arm, Georgia tugged her date towards the school. "Now c'mon! I wanna get some good seats for the show!"

Surrendering to Georgia's insistence, Murasaki turned to the cat as she got pulled past the girls. "Okiku! Stand guard."

The gray cat mewed again before rolling back onto its paws and scampering off. When Murasaki and Georgia were out of earshot, Natalie turned to

Lucy. "We better find our seats too. They won't start the play until everyone's there."

So the girls followed Georgia and Murasaki at a respectable distance through the school until they arrived at a very overcrowded gymnasium. Temporary black platforms had been placed underneath the far basketball hoop with red fabric strung up on a wire to portray the illusion of a stage. Lucy noted that, if he were there, her father would've either tried to convince her to not make fun of the small town's pathetic excuse of a theatre or commented on the fire hazards of the crowding situation. If he were there, of course.

"Aw, we're too late," Natalie said with a pout. "C'mon. Let's find my parents. Maybe they were able to save us some-"

"Miss Vitalis!"

Lucy's face remained neutral as she turned to the Mayor, twirling his fake moustache proudly as his brother, Officer Hansen, stayed at his side. They both wore a clip-on bowtie with their usual outfits. However, Mayor Hansen went the extra distance and put a clip-on bowtie on his top hat as well.

"Come to enjoy the show, I see? Aha! I knew Sterben's culture would entice you eventually," Mayor Hansen said, his eyes wandering the crowds around them. "By the way, where is your dear papa?"

"My father is using the distraction of the community event to complete his work on our paranormal bunker," Lucy said. "I believe he fears for the safety of this provincial residence which remains at the whim of an incompetent, self-serving schlemiel and thus is willing to sacrifice a night of leisure to ensure survival."

"Wait...so your dad isn't here?! Who's gonna protect us from the poltergeist?!" Mayor Hansen's proud demeanor vanished and was swiftly replaced by the all too familiar look of panic in his eyes. He immediately grabbed onto the front of Officer Hansen's collared shirt and pulled the officer into himself, even though the mayor was much smaller. "*Officer!* You can *not* leave my side at all tonight! Do you understand me?!"

"I wasn't planning on it!" Officer Hansen said. "We've got seats next to each other."

"*Promise me, darn it!*" Mayor Hansen shook Officer Hansen vigorously. "You watched all of those training videos I sent you, right?!"

"Ah gee whiz," Officer Hansen said. "You know Ghostbusters scares me."

"Gosh *dang it*, Officer Hansen!" Mayor Hansen slapped his brother across the face before letting go, allowing the police officer to stumble to the floor. The mayor immediately petted his fake moustache nervously as he paced in a tiny circle. "Okay, don't panic. You're the mayor. You just have to get the police to *demand* the professional ghostbuster to be here!" He looked down at his brother who was crying and holding onto his struck cheek. "Okay not the police...uhh...."

"Lucy! I've been looking for you!" Kierra, dressed to the nines in a shimmering blue dress and pearls, approached the group with a wide smile. "Oh hi Natalie! It's nice to see you again as well." Her smiled dropped as she looked at the Hansen brothers in their varying states of distress. "Mayor and Officer? Are you guys okay?"

"No!" Officer Hansen wailed, tears still streaming down his face. "This ghost has got everyone all stressed out and angry and I *told* the mayor that we never should've-"

"If you shut up right now, I'll let you watch Pokemon on my Crunchy-Roll account!" Mayor Hansen said, sticking his finger into his brother's face.

Officer Hansen quit crying and looked up at his brother. "Really? Even the new season?"

"Okay no, but like the old seasons. The good stuff." Mayor Hansen's voice grew gentle as he rubbed his brother's back. "Does that sound good to you, buddy?"

Officer Hansen nodded and Mayor Hansen helped his brother up. With Officer Hansen sniffling under his arm, Mayor Hansen smiled at the girls. "We'll be getting to our seats now! Have a good one."

The Hansen brothers walked off and Kierra turned to the girls with her hands on her hips. "Well as long as the Hansens are alright, Lucy, I've got some seats up front for you and your dad! But if your dad isn't going to be here, then Natalie can claim it."

"Wow!" Natalie said. "Thanks Kierra! That's really generous of you."

"Ah it's nothing for my favorite neighbors and my future boss at Lebenville Medical!" Kierra said. "Now c'mon! Chris is *so* excited to have some new eyes on his performance. You'll have to tell him all of your thoughts of the show at the after party."

As soon as the girls sat down in the only three seats left open in the front row, Kierra gave a wide smile and two big thumbs up to someone peeking around the red fabric. The person, assumedly Chris, dashed away from view. After a moment, the lights dimmed and the gymnasium quieted. From the cheap speakers of the gymnasium cackled a slow funeral tune, a soundtrack to the slow rise of dusty curtains that revealed Chris, Jeri, Teri, and a small second grade boy wearing a comically large fake beard for his face. All of them were dressed in various shades of black as they walked out on stage. Chris strode with confidence, at ease with his acting abilities as he looked dramatically downtrodden towards off-stage. Teri toddled after him, holding a handkerchief to her crooked nose and acting just as dramatic but without the ease of talent. Jeri and the second grade boy mostly stood off to the side, as if they forgot the entire town was watching them.

"In DELIVERING a sON from MEEE-" Teri wailed. "I hast bury thy second husband! Ohhhhh!" She blew dramatically into her handkerchief.

A flash of annoyance crossed Chris's face, but true to the testament of his acting ability, he remained downtrodden for the scene. With a deep sigh, he looked down at his feet before gazing off-scene again as if he were in deep thought.

"And I in going, madam, weep o'er my father's death anew." He took a moment to look sad again, before striding towards Teri who was still wailing dramatically with regained confidence. "But I must attend his majesty's command, to whom I am now in ward, evermore in subjection."

The second grader stepped forward and heaved in a heavy breath from his chest.

"You shall find the king a...husband, ma'am!" He shouted towards the audience. Panic hit his little face and he looked over to Chris. Two parents deep within the audience holding a camcorder made the indication for their precious angel to keep going. Chris nodded as well at the child. The second grader nodded back and swallowed back his stage fright. "He that is so good, generally must have...nec-necess-neccessessity to hold virtue. Whose worthiness stirs and not lack a-bun-dance."

The second grader smiled widely at his parents and they waved at him, beaming with pride. The rest of play continued in a similar fashion. Second graders took the roles meant for serious, classically trained adult-aged actors and Teri and Jeri delivered their lines either with too much convection in an effort to impress an unaware Chris or as a second grader would if they were asked to read aloud to the class. Chris was the only redeeming factor to the mess. His performance was stunning given his working conditions and, during his soliloquies, Lucy actually believed she was witnessing a production worthy of Shakespeare's approval. Then Jeri or Teri would interrupt and she would be dutifully reminded of her current location.

Unfortunately the tire of theatre had hit the cast hard during Act III. Most of the second graders had given up and were now playing a game of tag off-stage. Only Chris, Teri, and Jeri remained, skipping through the missing second graders' roles as if they were used to the inconvenience. Chris had retained his energy, somehow giving off enough of it to continue the audience's engagement with the performance. Unfortunately, Teri and Jeri had taken the way of their younger co-stars and they had fizzled out as well, only remaining on stage as evidence of their devotion to Chris or because they were sleepwalking. The difference was lost on Lucy since Act II.

"You came, I think, from....uh...." Jeri closed her eyes a little bit, nearly falling asleep on stage, before jolting up. "FRANCE! You came from France"

Lucy could swear she could see Chris behind the curtain, nervously twisting his own script as he kept glancing between the train wreck on stage and the rest of his cast playing tag off of it.

"I did," Teri said. Her eyes went wide. "So! I did so!"

"Here you shall see a country...country...*man* of yours," Jeri said. "That has done worthy service."

"His name?" Teri asked. When Jeri remained quiet, her eyes pleading for her co-star to continue, Teri snapped her fingers. "His name, I pray? I pray *you.*"

But the damage from Teri's stumble and the sheer magnitude of the script they had to memorize had already done its toll. Jeri looked lost trying to remember the name of the valiant countryman.

"The Count....The Count, uh-" Jeri shrugged. "Ma-Macbeth?"

Lucy, Natalie, and Kierra all sucked in a collective gasp. Even Chris broke his personal rules of theatre to peek out from behind the curtain in horror at his cast member's unredeemable error. As expected, Jeri and Teri didn't realize the severity of their blunder and kept going.

"There is a gentleman that serves the count," Teri said. "Reports but badly of her."

"And what was his name?" Jeri asked.

"Mister, uh...." Now Teri looked lost. "Hamlet? No! *He* was Macbeth. You got your name wrong, Widow!"

"I am not Widow, I am Helena!" Jeri shouted.

"No I'm Helena!" Teri said. "Not that you would know! You don't even know the difference between The Count Rousillon and Macbe-"

"STOP!" Chris shouted. The crowd gasped. Kierra was clutching her chest looking worried towards her husband. He ignored the audience's reaction and kept focused on the two amateur actors. "Ladies, skips ahead to scene six and don't say the M-word again!"

"What M-word?" Jeri asked.

"Macbeth?" Teri asked.

"Why can't we say Macbeth?" Jeri asked. "He was Shakespeare right?"

"*She* was Shakespeare," Teri corrected. "Macbeth was a lady."

"No that was Lady Macbeth!" Jeri said. "And neither are in this Shakespeare-"

A low, but loud, roar from a wild animal reverberated through the gymnasium. The second graders stopped their game and the entire audience looked around to try and locate the source. From the very back row, Murasaki stood to her feet.

"False actresses, leave the stage now!" The spirit shouted. "You've done over enough to awaken-"

"Who are you?!" Teri shouted, squinting into the crowd. "Seriously, has anyone seen this lady before?"

An invisible force slammed Teri and Jeri into the curtains behind the stage, tangling them into the fabrics. The children screamed and ran back to their parents as Chris escaped the chaos, making a magnificent leap away from the self-destructing stage. As the women struggled to escape their confines, a gray fog lifted from the stage in eerie tendrils that etched down towards the thin aisles.

"Hung be the heavens," An omnipresent voice cooed out. "Yield day to *night*."

At the last word, the studio lights dimmed before fixating themselves to the center of the stage where the fog was curling in a neat spiral. Everyone was standing to their feet, eager to see the new event far more captivating than the previous play.

"In fair Sterben, where we lay our scene," The omnipresent voice reported. "From ancient grudge break to new mutiny, where civil blood makes civil hands unclean."

From the spiral in the fog, a semi-transparent man rose with a dramatic twirl. Half of the crowd gasped or awed at the spectacle. He wore an old fashioned 1600's outfit with a frilly neck thing tied around his neck and poofy sleeves, but his face was young and he had a full head of luscious hair in addition to a fine goatee on his chin.

"'Tis I, the Ghost of William Shakespeare!" The ghost echoed, proving ownership to the previous omnipresent voice. "Summoned by great disrespect, a cunning foe. To thee offenders, fixed over there." He pointed to Teri and Jeri. The action caused the curtains to unfurl themselves to release the women. They both looked at the Ghost of Shakespeare in horror. He held up a single finger.

"Time shall unfold what plighted cunning hides," The Ghost of William Shakespeare said. "Who cover faults, at last shame them derides."

Their faces immediately fell and the two women held their hands up.

"Are you talking about the boy?" Teri shouted. "We were just doing our jobs!"

"We didn't know the truth until later!" Jeri argued. "Please sir-"

"Oftentimes excusing of a fault, doth make the fault the worse by the excuse," The Ghost of William Shakespeare shouted, floating above the stage. "Live in thy shame, but die not shame with thee!"

The women and audience were quiet. After a long moment, The Ghost of William Shakespeare turned around to face the audience.

"Doth thou all speak English?" He asked. "I believe to speak as fair as I allow."

"He, like, wants y'all to confess to something!" Georgia Peaches's voice shouted from the back of the crowded gymnasium. "You know? Like clear your conscious or something?"

Teri and Jeri offered a nervous glance to the other.

"We-we can't!" Jeri said.

"We swore we wouldn't!" Teri said. "We'd lose our jobs and be forced to work in...Lebenville."

Both women shuddered as The Ghost of William Shakespeare straightened his stance, hovering above the women.

"Loyalty is held well to the fools," He said. "You will follow your master to the last gasp, but see if he will do the same!" The famous playwright moved his hand to the sky. "Tis by my word that until thy master come forward, to speak with truth and fair, the offended shall exit...pursued by *bear*."

The animal's roar materialized again, this time accompanying a ferocious bear that appeared with a burst of fog in the far corner of the gym. Standing on its hind legs, the beast let out another mighty roar as the audience cleared out in a panic, sprinting to every nearby exit. The mighty grizzly bear fell forward onto four legs and took off in a dead sprint towards the women. Teri and Jeri let out a shriek and bolted in the opposite direction. The bear continued its pursuit, never letting its eyes off of the actresses.

"Child of death!" Murasaki pushed against the retreating crowd to reach Lucy and Natalie in the front row. Georgia Peaches was towed behind the spirit, happily holding onto her hand as if the entire room hadn't been descended into madness by the Ghost of William Shakespeare and his spectral bear. Murasaki handed Georgia over to Lucy and Natalie. "Seek out a solution to this spirit's wrath while I calm the beast. Care for Georgia as well as I do so."

Before Lucy and Natalie could protest, Murasaki ran off in the direction of the bear that had chased Teri and Jeri to the remainder of the school. Holding her hands close to her heart, Georgia let out a deep sigh.

"She is just, like, so brave, right?" Georgia said.

The other two girls ignored Georgia as they mutually turned to each other at the same time.

"Alright, Lucy, what do we have to do?" Natalie asked. "Should we call your dad?"

"I can assure you Mayor Hansen has handled that chore," Lucy said. She stared up at the Ghost of William Shakespeare who continued to float above the stage, taunting Chris and Kierra who were threatening him with the prop swords the second graders had left behind. "This summoning began with the utterance of the Scottish Play's true name. Despite the unusual severity of the consequences, a common curse has common solutions. We just need to look up the proper cleansing rituals and-"

Lucy was distracted by Georgia as the Lebenville native promptly spun around three times. At the end of the third spin, she spat over her left shoulder before she noticed and acknowledged Natalie and Lucy's incredulous stare. Georgia shrugged.

"What? That's like how you cleanse yourself of the curse, right?" Georgia said. "I mean, like, if we wanted to get *real* about it we could go outside and do it before entering, but like we didn't do anything. Those secretaries said it."

Still holding her incredulous stare, Natalie could only point at Georgia. "How did you know that?"

"Um...doesn't *every*body?" Georgia rolled her eyes. "Whatever. I'm going to go talk to Mr. Shakespeare and see if we can't get all of this cleared up."

As Georgia strode confidently over to the Ghost of William Shakespeare, Lucy and Natalie shared a somewhat worried glance before repeating Georgia's previous actions of spinning and spitting. They finished their cleanse before hustling over to Georgia who had just captured the Ghost of William Shakespeare's attention.

"Fair thoughts and happy hours attend on you," Georgia said with a curtsy towards the ghostly playwright. "If we shadows have offended, angels and ministers of grace defend us."

With a sly smile on his face, the Ghost of William Shakespeare spread his arms apart and the chaos in the room ceased. When Chris and Kierra ran forward, intending to attack, he swept them to the side with a flourish of his hand and floated down to face Georgia Peaches.

"These violent delights have violent ends," The Ghost of William Shakespeare said. "And in their triumph die, like fire and powder"

"O father, what a hell of witchcraft lies," Georgia stated eloquently. "In the small orb of one particular tear."

"Tis not a small tear to qualm," The Ghost of William Shakespeare said with a raised finger. "A man can die but once. He wears the rose of youth upon him. Nothing in his life became him like the leaving it, and yet no deep repentance has been issued."

With a clap, Natalie turned to Lucy with wide, incredulous eyes.

"Shakespeare is literally quoting himself," Natalie said. "How is this happening?"

Before Lucy could respond, Georgia held up a finger to quiet Natalie, never looking away from her conversation partner.

"Time doth transfix the flourish set on youth," Georgia said. "But screw your courage to the sticking place! Thou know'st 'tis common; all that lives must die, passing through nature to eternity."

The Ghost of William Shakespeare shook his head.

"So wise so young, they say do never live long," He said. "When beggars die, there are no comets seen; the heavens themselves blaze forth the death of princes. Woe, destruction, ruin, and decay; the worst is death, and death will have his day."

"We have some salt of our youth in us!" Georgia said, placing her hands on her hips. "You speak an infinite deal of nothing. Murder's out of tune, and sweet revenge grows harsh."

A mighty bear roar echoed throughout the building, haunting the remaining audience members still dazed from the panic. Even Lucy and Natalie stepped towards each other, their eyes darting around the room to follow the ominous echo. The only dramatic movement was Chris and Kierra who made another valiant rush towards the spectral Bard with their foam swords. As he pushed them away with another invisible force, the Ghost of William Shakespeare remained stoic without looking away from Georgia.

"For he being dead, with him is beauty slain, and, beauty dead, black chaos comes again." The Ghost of William Shakespeare looked sad as he looked upon his new friend. "Doomsday is near; die all, die merrily."

With that, he disappeared into a fold of reality no mortal eyes could witness. Murasaki burst back into the gymnasium, blood splattered over her white kimono. All eyes turned to the spirit and she stopped in her face, clenching her fists to her side as she realized the amount of people staring.

"The beast is slain," Murasaki announced. "However, I had failed to calm it before the women fell to its rage. Teri and Jeri are no more."

The Sterben residents whispered worryingly amongst themselves. Not so subtly putting her hand up to cover her face, Murasaki quietly walked towards the trio of girls. Lucy and Natalie turned to Georgia.

"Okay, what did you say to Shakespeare?" Natalie asked, pulling out her notebook and pencil. "What did he say back?"

Georgia gave the girls an incredulous look. "Weren't you listening? He was, like, talking about the poltergeist or whatever. He was just trying to help it avenge its wrongful death or, like, whatever." She gave a wide smile as she clapped her hands together. "But I think I convinced him we were innocent so we should be safe from his unbinding wrath next time!"

"Why would the Ghost of William Shakespeare be so keen to assist a vengeful spirit such as our poltergeist?" Lucy asked. "Surely the curse of the Scottish Play wouldn't be enough to invoke such destruction."

"Theatre is a powerful ally," Murasaki spoke as she approached the group. "The bond between those that invoke its power cannot be breached. Perhaps our poltergeist was a fan of theatre in a previous life? One with enough devotion to be able to call upon those with similar passion?"

Slamming her pencil into her notebook, Natalie gave the jibakurei a hard look. "Do you guys know how hard it is to take notes when you only speak in riddles?"

"I think she talks really pretty," Georgia said, a blush forming on her cheeks.

"Jonathan Gilbert," Lucy said. "He died young and was devoted enough to the stage to acquire a scholarship far exceeding this town's academic expectations. If the Bard didn't mislead us, he is definitely our poltergeist. But the question is, how did he die?"

"A car accident," Natalie said. "Nobody in town talks about it, but it happened right near the edge of town off of the...." She paused as realization crossed her eyes. "Hunter property."

"The Hunters?" Lucy asked. "As in Chase and Chevy?"

"And their older brothers Chadron and Chevron, yeah," Natalie said. "Chadron's quite a bit older than all of them, but Chevron was the same grade as Gilly. He disappeared onto the Hunter property around the same time Gilly died. Do you think-"

"Absolutely," Lucy said. "The Hunters are involved somehow. How else would Chevy be able to see the spirit and no one else?"

"But, like, Shakespeare said Teri and Jeri were involved which is why he unleashed the bear on them!" Georgia said. "Honestly, did, like, anyone listen?"

Lucy and Natalie shared another look.

"Two leads," Lucy said, unable to hold back a soft smile. "Both alike in dignity."

Placing her pencil behind her ear, Natalie smirked. "Something wicked this way comes."

"Excuse me, everyone!"

Everyone turned to the voice. Kierra was standing center stage, still looking stunning in her Oscar worthy dress, and waved cheerily at the remaining audience members. It was almost like the fact she just lost a fight to the ghost of a famous playwright didn't phase her in the slightest.

"If y'all don't mind, my husband Chris and I believe we could all use the distraction from what just happened," Kierra said. "So without further ado, I present One Man Shakespeare: *All's Well That Ends Well* featuring my own husband, Chris!"

As a splattering of applause overtook the survivors, Kierra hurried back to her destroyed folding chair as Chris took the stage with a plastic crown on his head. He held up a plastic sword as he looked valiantly off stage.

"Let us from point to point this story know," He shouted. "To make the even truth in pleasure flow."

Picking up one of the remaining folding chairs, Lucy watched the remainder of the performance with her friends and could only hope the truth would free them from the hell of the past's mistakes.

Tip #6:

Don't insult the dead.

FOLLOWING THE VERY public appearance of the Ghost of William Shakespeare and the following destruction that came from it, the town of Sterben was under an unofficial lockdown. However, the man who should've called the lockdown, Mayor Hansen, and the man who would've enforced it, Officer Hansen, had disappeared during the chaos of the destroyed gymnasium. As school was cancelled for the time being until someone figured out how to remove the dead bear carcass from the building and Mike Vitalis was ignoring the investigation in favor of spirit-proofing his own property, Lucy and Natalie were free to explore the town as they pleased for their own investigation.

Their first stop was the Gilbert residence.

"Jonathan?" Mrs. Gilbert asked. "No, no Jonathan ever lived here."

Natalie furrowed her eyebrows at the old woman.

"What are you talking about?" She asked. "He was your son! Of course he lived here."

Mrs. Gilbert's eyes went wide as she shook her head.

"No, please, leave us alone," Mrs. Gilbert said. "We don't have a son. We've never had one."

Remembering her night in the cemetery, Lucy lifted her camera and took a picture of the woman. When she checked her camera, the screen reflected back a portrait of a sad woman in dull blouse and faded high-waisted jeans.

"This selective amnesia is not of the poltergeist's doing," Lucy stated. "If it were, he would've shut off my camera as he did in the cemetery when I attempted a photo of his grave."

Licking her lips, Natalie looked at the woman with curious eyes.

"So either Mr. Gilbert has some severe amnesia caused by extended grief from losing her only child," Natalie said. "Or she's willingly hiding something from us."

Mrs. Gilbert raised her hands. "Ladies, if I knew anything about the ghost terrorizing our town, I'd tell ya. But for now-"

"We never said we were here to ask about the ghost," Lucy said. "Also it's a poltergeist, not a ghost. If you're not going to honor your dead son by giving us more information about his death so we may properly put him to rest, the least you could do is use the proper nouns for him. It might convince him to spare you when he finally decides to kill us all."

With tears in her eyes, Mrs. Gilbert pointed a shaky finger at Lucy.

"We were fine until you and your deadbeat of a father came along!" She shouted. "Everything was *fine!* But now look! You've ruined everything!" With a shaky inhale of breath, Mrs. Gilbert glared at Lucy. "Now go before I call Officer Hansen to take you away."

The grieving mother slammed the door in Lucy and Natalie's face. Natalie turned to Lucy.

"She didn't mean that," Natalie said.

"She did or else she wouldn't have said it." Lucy snapped a picture of the front door, appreciating its alignment with the windows Mrs. Gilbert was hastily closing the curtains over. "However, the outburst is easy to forgive as it is a result of small town narrow-mindedness. Some people just don't like when things change."

"Or...perhaps she was hiding something and used the outburst as an excuse to exit the conversation," Natalie said as they stepped off the front porch. "The Hunters have money. They've got to since they're the second largest landowners in Sterben. Maybe they're paying her off?"

Lucy considered it as she took a few more pictures of the general scenery of Sterben.

"Perhaps," Lucy said. "We should take a closer look at the police report of the accident. One would've had to been filed for the fatality that occurred. If it were the case that the Hunters are the ones paying her off, they would've had a narrow window to bribe her between when the body was discovered and when she was notified."

"All of the police reports would be filed at town hall," Natalie said. "And, you know, with Jeri's death and Mayor Hansen on his little vacation, I'm sure all of those police reports just became public domain."

With a brisk walk through the empty streets of Sterben, the girls arrived at town hall with no further problems. The small town hall was as abandoned as the rest of the town, with whatever remained of the staff on leave for Teri and Jeri's funeral. However, when they arrived in Mayor Hansen's office, the girls encountered the only living soul left in the building.

"Chase?!" Natalie exclaimed. "What are you doing here?"

The young farmer boy perked up from his spot on the vintage couch where he was previously laid out in a comfortable position, reading from one of the thick books that graced the story-level bookcases in the office. Sitting up straight, he nervously ran his fingers through his hair as he looked over at the girls.

"Oh! Hiya ladies!" Chase said. "Uh...I feel mighty bad about it, but I came into town for some more parts and saw that everyone was hiding away because of the ghost and realized that Jeri was gone too so I figured that I could come here to read for a bit, um...." He blushed. "Don't tell anyone, okay? I recognize it's an invasion of privacy during a time of mourning and-" His hazel eyes went hard as he looked at Natalie and Lucy. "Wait...what are *you* guys doing here?"

"Attempting to solve the mystery of Jonathan Gilbert's untimely death in an effort to put the poltergeist to rest," Lucy stated. "May I ask what you're reading?"

Chase looked at cover of the book in his hand. "*Attacking and Defending Drunk Driving Tests*? I dunno. It was a fresh copy I found in Mayor Hansen's collection, but it mostly seems to be about the effects of alcohol on the body rather than the laws around it which is disappointing-"

"Are you sure you're not reading it to defend your own family?" Natalie said.

Chase raised an eyebrow.

"I hate to break it to ya, friend, but I'm the only one who has driven off our property since my brother Chevron graduated school nearly ten years ago," Chase said. "And you ain't going to catch me drinking at this age. That's an offense of K.S.A. 41-727 and under Kansas Law, that's a minimum of a citation and maximum of incarceration. So no. I'm not reading this to somehow defend my family."

Natalie and Lucy shared a glance, trying to decipher their friend's innocence. It took a moment for Chase to realize the situation.

"Y'all think my family's involved in Gilly's death, don't you?" Chase said. When the girls remained quiet, he sighed and threw the book onto the open space next to him on the couch. "I mean, I don't blame ya. He did technically die on our property and given my brother's involvement with him and our private nature as a family, you did have enough circumstantial evidence to suspect us."

"We're sorry, Chase," Natalie said. "But your family is our top lead."

Chase shrugged.

"It's fine," He said. "But only because we're completely innocent. You can check the police report if you want for Chevron's statement. They're over here in Miss Jeri's filing cabinet."

Lifting himself off the couch, Chase led them to the area behind Jeri's abandoned desk. He reached under the lamp on the desk and fished out a small key. As he moved to unlock the filing cabinet, he shrugged at the girls.

"Miss Jeri had me organize some things for her too when I didn't have any pie," Chase said. He dragged open the filing cabinet to reveal folders dated back to the 1930's. "I never really went through the police reports though. Most of them are a drag or complaints from the old ladies in town. They get really basic once Officer Hansen took over."

"And when was that?" Lucy asked.

"Nearly ten years ago," Chase said, going through the folders as he spoke. "Poor guy was held back enough in high school that they just graduated him with his brothers and he joined the force the day after graduation."

"His dad was the police officer at the time so it was just a matter of handing the uniform over," Natalie added. "Then, of course, their mom was the mayor so it's not like anyone had any right to complain about it."

"The audacity for such blatant nepotism in this town is admirable," Lucy said. "Do you not hold elections for these things?"

Continuing to sort through the files, Chase snorted. "It wouldn't be a Sterben election without a Hansen on the ballot is what my paw always said."

"It's not like people would vote for anyone else," Natalie said. "Like you said, people in small towns don't like change."

"And as the largest landowners in Sterben, the Hansens have always been in charge," Chase said. He furrowed his eyebrows as he flipped between two different folders. "Pardon my language, ladies, but goddamn I cannot find this report. I know I might have my years mixed up on when my brother graduated, but the report isn't in any of these files."

"Let us look," Natalie said, stepping forward.

All three of them grabbed a handful of folders to look into to see if the report had gotten misplaced. When that handful didn't have anything useful, they would grab another stack from the cabinet. By the end of the hour, the entire office was covered in old police reports and empty folders. Chase ran his fingers into his hair, looking around wildly at the mess around them.

"This doesn't make sense," He said. "Where's the report?! It's required to be taken for any sort of fatal car accident, regardless of whether or not it happened on private property."

"We have reports of all of the old ladies' complaints about loud dogs, every single speeding ticket ever issued, and even a report of when Officer Hansen kicked Lucy and her dad out of the building," Natalie said, throwing the report she was reading on top of her pile. "But not a single one about the only fatal car accident to ever occur in Sterben, Kansas."

Lucy took a couple pictures of her distressed friends amongst the pile of papers before she set her camera to the side. Unleashing her long blond hair from the ponytail holder, she smoothed it with her hands before putting her black hat back on.

"I believe the report has been willingly removed from the record," Lucy said. "If the Ghost of William Shakespeare is to be correct, then the secretaries were involved with this as well. There might be a solution to this conundrum in their personal files."

Frustrated by the situation, Chase and Natalie moved with aggressive swiftness to the secretary's computer. Lucy reached them as they booted it up using the password found on an old sticky note. Natalie took charge of the keyboard and searched the computer's files for "Jonathan Gilbert", "Gilly", and "Gilbert". The only thing the search brought up was invoices for Mrs. Gilbert's gardening services.

"These checks are regular, but cheap," Natalie said. "Only $50 for 12 hours of service?"

"I mean, after nearly a decade, it kind of all adds up," Chase said. "I gotta tell ya though, I've never seen Mrs. Gilbert outside of her house."

"Try the Google Calendar," Lucy stated. "Perhaps there's a schedule for Mrs. Gilbert's services that we can see if the invoices line up."

Natalie logged onto the Google account and opened up the Calendar application. As soon as the application finished loading, a notification appeared on screen. Natalie automatically moved to close out of it, but Lucy stopped her hand.

"147 days overdue," She read out loud. "Annual Hansen Brother Get Together?"

She clicked on the notification, letting it lead to a page that showed the event was shared with Officer and Principal Hansen. There was also an address in the location field on the form. Chase pointed at it.

"That's my address!" He exclaimed. "But the Hansen brothers have never visited my farm. They're not big on my family if y'all haven't noticed."

"They're not big on any family that could threaten their rule on the town," Natalie said. "If your family ever left that farm, Mayor Hansen might have some competition on his next ballot."

Chase shook his head. "Not possible. There's too much work to be done on the farm for one of us to be running the city along with all of it."

"Small town family rivalries aside, I suggest we keep focus on our mission to protect the town and find a way to contact the Hansen brothers to ask them of this event," Lucy said. "Georgia has already promised to alert us to Officer Hansen's whereabouts if he does happen to return home. That leaves Mayor Hansen and Principal Hansen."

"Mayor Hansen wouldn't tell us anything anyway," Natalie said. "But I know where we can find Principal Hansen!"

"Where?" Lucy asked.

"The same place he always is," Chase said. "C'mon, I'll take y'all there in my truck."

"Oh no, it's fine!" Natalie said. "If you still have to grab your parts, Lucy and I can walk. I know the way."

"I appreciate the thoughtfulness, but I need to prove my family's innocence," Chase said, bouncing up from his spot behind the desk. "Not to mention, there's a possible obstruction of justice with this missing police report. I ain't letting that slide."

In their hustle, the trio left the mayor's office in the same mess they caused. Lucy took a last, fleeting picture before following Chase and Natalie out to Chase's truck. As they raced out to the truck, Lucy noted how the previously bleak gray fall sky now had dark clouds swirling within it. Not unusual weather for a Midwest autumn, she assumed given Chase and Natalie's lack of reaction, but certainly an omen. It was compelling enough for Lucy to capture a photo of it before returning her attention to her friends and their mission.

The drive from the town hall was short, but solemn. Natalie spent her time sitting in between Lucy and Chase going over the notes in her notebook and jotting down questions to ask the esteemed principal. Chase was silent, thinking intently over something he refused to reveal to the girls. Lucy kept alternating between fidgeting with her camera strap, glancing up at the threatening sky, and considering texting her father. But she knew revealing her whereabouts would make him overprotective again and he would threaten to keep her in the house until the end of his investigation or...worse.

By the time the trio reached Sterben High School, they were all ready for answers. They wasted no time heading into the school, storming down the empty hallways, avoiding the dead bear carcass that *still* remained, and going straight to Principal Hansen's office. However, their momentum was tarnished when they entered the office to see a woman sitting at Teri's desk.

Tap.

While Chase and Natalie stood there in horrified shock, Lucy snapped a photo. The spectral secretary looked up from her work at the sound of the shutter.

"Oh! Miss Vitalis!" Teri smiled. "How's your father?"

"Mz. Teri, you're-" Chase stammered before turning to his friend. "Lucy, does she know she died?"

"Possibly," Lucy answered.

"How is this possible?" Natalie asked, pulling out her pencil and notebook again. "What would compel Teri to stay as a ghost, but not Jeri?"

"Unfinished business is always a compelling motive for any soul to stay alive beyond the body," Lucy said. "However, the unfinished business would have to be compelling enough for a soul to be willing to avoid eternal heavenly bliss in exchange to complete it. Or, perhaps, it's the other way around. Perhaps she is avoiding eternal damnation."

Tap.

Teri looked up from her work and glared at Lucy.

"Are you saying I should be in hell, young lady?" Teri said. She pointed her translucent bony finger at the girl. "You're lucky Principal Hansen ain't here or I'd have him serve you a detention!"

Chase and Natalie both gave the ghost a look.

"What do you mean he's not here?!" Chase exclaimed. "He's always here! He never leaves his office!"

"Yeah I walked in on him sleeping under his desk before," Natalie said. "There was another time where he tried to make me waffles in honor of an academic achievement. The guy definitely lives in there."

"Lives where?!" Teri exclaimed, looking around. "This is the only room here!"

As Chase and Natalie gaped at the secretary's ignorance, Lucy lifted her camera and took a picture of the door leading to the principal's office.

"It's the door," Lucy said. "Painted blue and fixated with a assumedly blessed horseshoe to ward off spirits. I had just attributed it to poor design choices common in the Midwest, but it appears to be purposeful in its intent."

"What is the intent?" Natalie asked.

"To keep that brat Gilly away from him of course."

The trio turned to the new voice in the doorway behind them. Mrs. Bobby was giving them all a cold glare icy enough to freeze all of their souls into place. In her hand was a particularly sharp looking yardstick that remained still in her iron grip. Lucy lifted her camera to take the picture of the woman's look, but a terrified Natalie brought her hand up to push the camera back down. Chase's Adam's Apple bobbed before he stepped forward.

"Ma'am, do you know anything about Gilly's death?" Chase asked. "My family is bein-"

"Be quiet, Mr. Hunter!" Mrs. Bobby pointed her yardstick at Chase. "I know plenty about who your family is! A bunch of heathens threatening to tarnish the good name of Sterben, that's for sure! If Gilly hadn't gotten to your brother-" She shook her head. "I knew he'd be trouble from the start. Starting that gay club-"

"Dr-drama club," Chase stammered to Natalie and Lucy. "She means drama club. Not-mhmm...." He shook his head and looked down at his feet. "So offensive."

"I know what I said!" Mrs. Bobby shouted. "And Gilly was the worst of them! Always whining and complaining and writing his papers about how stupid everyone in town was...he was disrespecting the whole town so I told him what I knew, I did. I told him he would die as he lived, stuck in Sterben, Kansas like the rest of us!"

There was a crack of lightning. Natalie unintentionally clutched Lucy's arm for safety. Noting her best friend's fear, Lucy looked the old teacher in the eye.

"Please, Mrs. Bobby, this is a sensitive time to be disgracing a spirit's death," Lucy said. "Especially if the area is vulnerable enough for Principal Hansen to warrant creating his own barrier between here and the spirit world-"

"I don't care!" Mrs. Bobby shouted. "Sterben is a nice place, a safe place! When the rest of the world goes to hell, you can always trust Sterben to be the same and that brat was trying to ruin it all!"

Thunder rumbled loud enough to shake the building, causing the cheap lockers to rattle in fear and a distant echo of Principal Hansen's wind chimes to sing. But Mrs. Bobby continued on with the perseverance of a seasoned lecturer. "And now *you* troublemakers are trying to ruin everything too! Why couldn't you just let the little jerk be dead? Well I'm going to finally do what I should've done a month ago! Teri!"

"Yes, Mrs. Bobby?" The spectral secretary asked, acting oblivious to the teacher's rage.

As Mrs. Bobby pointed her yardstick at Lucy, there was another low rumble of thunder reverberated through the school.

"Set up the paperwork to transfer Miss Lucy Vitalis to Lebenville High!" Mrs. Bobby ordered. "I've am *done* dealing with disrespectful troublemakers and this one!" Her yardstick shook as she pointed it at Lucy. "This one deserves a fate worse than Jonathan Gilbert's."

There was another crack of lightning and thunder. It was powerful enough to set off the fire alarm sprinklers in the hallway. Chase, Natalie, and Lucy all instinctively stepped back into the principal's office area to remain dry. Mrs. Bobby glared up at the fire sprinklers and shook her yardstick at it.

"You stupid system!" Mrs. Bobby shouted. "We should've replaced these years ago instead of waxing the dang floors-"

The sound of distant rushing water caused Mrs. Bobby to stop her rant and look to her right. The trio all popped their heads out of the doorway at the noise to see a wave of water at waist height flooding into the hallway. Mrs. Bobby's eyes went wide and she moved to run into the principal's office. But when she lifted her legs, her feet remained glued to the floor. When Mrs. Bobby looked up at the trio in a rare show of vulnerability, Chase stepped forward to help the elderly teacher. An invisible force knocked the trio backwards and onto the floor of the small space before the principal's office, slamming the office door behind them.

Chase was quick to get back onto his feet and ran back to the door just as the waist high water reached Mrs. Bobby. He twisted the doorknob restlessly and used all of his strength in his attempt to yank open the door. The door didn't even budge. The trio and Teri could only watch from the window in the door to see the water slowly rising around Mrs. Bobby. She kept her arms above the water and continued to shout at the students, her cries for help lost in the door separating them.

Lucy lifted her camera and took a picture. At the sound of the shutter, Natalie whipped around and glared at Lucy.

"This isn't the time!" She shouted. "Mrs. Bobby's about to die!"

"And we need to prove our innocence!" Lucy argued back. "I'm proving we could not have saved her life if we tried. Passivity when action could've been taken is as worse as the crime committed."

"I concur!"

The trio turned to the newest voice to see Principal Hansen poking his head out of his blue door office, his previously poofy hair tied back in a bun as he wore a green facial mask.

"Not from personal experience ah-" Principal Hansen said. "I certainly have not witnessed an unjust murder nor caused such an atrocity! That would be ridiculous! Why else would I hide in this ghost proof room for nearly a decade? I wouldn't! That's why!"

Natalie and Lucy shared a look.

"Oh! Principal Hansen, there you are!" Ghost Teri exclaimed. "Shall I continue Mrs. Bobby's request for an official student transfer-"

"No! Forget all of your paperwork! Just get out of here!" Principal Hansen shouted. "Children, please join me in my office before Gilly gets to you too!"

With a shrug, Ghost Teri disappeared into an invisible fold of reality. The water levels in the hallways were at Mrs. Bobby's neck level. Tears were streaming down her face as she moved her head up, desperate to get as much air as possible before she couldn't. Shivering, Natalie turned away from the scene.

"As long as I don't have to witness *that* any longer," Natalie said. "I'm good with hiding out in a teeny tiny room with a possible murderer if you guys are."

"I am!" Chase said, lifting his hand.

Chase and Natalie led the way into Principal Hansen's office while Lucy took the rear. She offered a fleeting glance to the aged teacher before ducking into Principal Hansen's office, being sure to lock the blue door behind herself. Chase and Natalie gave her a worried look as they all settled into the tiny room. Lucy knew her friends were valid in their fears.

In the middle of a ghost town, Lucy probably just locked them in with a murderer.

Tip #7:
Murder is bad.

PRINCIPAL HANSEN WAS never an intimidating sort of man. With his lanky build, fluffy hair, and bumbling personality, he looked innocent enough to get away with anything in the town of Sterben. When he continually ordered wind chimes after wind chimes, the mailman didn't judge him. When he requested Father O'Shannon to come by every Sunday to bless his office, even during the summer, the priest didn't question it. When he disappeared into his office after college graduation for nearly a decade, only leaving in the early mornings to use the bathroom and get fresh supplies, hardly anyone had noticed.

Now the esteemed educator was sitting behind his desk, calmly lighting candles as one of his most experienced teachers drowned in a supernatural flash flood right outside of his office. Natalie, Chase, and Lucy all stared at their principal, trying to believe that he would be the mastermind behind Jonathan Gilbert's death. As Lucy took a picture of the odd scene, being sure to include the way the candle light reflected against the many wind chimes above them, Chase half-lifted an index finger.

"Uh excuse me, Mr. Hansen?" Chase asked. "If you don't mind me asking, what *exactly* are ya doing?"

"An excellent question, Third Hunter Boy!" Principal Hansen said. He shook out the match he was using to light the candles as he looked up at the children. "I am cleaning my aura! It is one of the more enjoyable techniques of preventing Gil-I mean, ghosts into my life. It is a ghost prevention technique, yes."

"Is that why you're wearing a facial mask too?" Natalie asked. "The...green stuff?"

"Oh! Does this work too to prevent Gil-GHOSTS?" Principal Hansen gave his green cheeks a soft pat. "It came free with one of my candle orders and I just *love* how soft it makes my face. Tell me, Lupita, can my facial masks also prevent Gil-GHOSTS? SPIRITS? NOT SPECIFICALLY GILLY GILBERT?"

Lucy gave a glance to Natalie before looking back to the principal who was now tapping his finger incessantly against his desk, hoping Lucy couldn't see through his thin facade.

"I suppose mixing it with sage could provide some preventative measures, but coconut oil would be a more productive substance if you're going to add anything to your skincare routine," Lucy stated. "But I would argue this conversation is hardly a priority given the-"

"Hey!" Principal Hansen pointed a stern index finger at Lucy. "Self-care is always important. If you can't love yourself, no one else will, am I right? Up top, Third Hunter boy!"

The principal raised his hand towards Chase, inviting him for a high-five. Chase shook his head.

"Sorry sir," Chase said. "While I agree with your sentiments, my family's honor is on the line and your family has probable cause for obstruction of justice. I can't high-five to that."

Principal Hansen waited a long minute with his hand in the air before he decided Chase was serious in his refusal.

"Fine," Principal Hansen said. He slapped his own hand before leaning back in his chair. Putting his feet up on his desk, he revealed a pair of fuzzy pink slippers on his feet. "So what shall we discuss until the ghosties are gone? I have a waffle-maker!"

There was a heavy silence between the trio and the principal. Wiggling the toes of his fuzzy pink slippers, Principal Hansen waited another minute longer. When it became obvious that none of them would accept his offer for waffles, his nostrils flared as he continued to look at the teens, his brown eyes continually darting nervously between the three.

"Crazy weather we're having, right?" Principal Hansen said. "I tell you what, when I woke up this morning, I did *not* expect it to start flooding in my hallways here, let me tell you. Maybe a light drizzle-"

"Did you kill Jonathan Gilbert?" Natalie blurted out. "What about the police report of the homicide? Where is it? Did you hide it?"

Principal Hansen stared at Natalie with panicked eyes. Lucy lifted her camera to her eye.

"Subtle work, Detective Hendrix," Lucy said. She snapped a picture of the principal's horrified expression.

"Well what else do you want from me?!" Natalie exclaimed. "I'm a future scientist! Not a...detective or whatever we're doing."

"I don't...know....what you children are talking about," Principal Hansen said. He sat up straight in his chair, bringing his feet off of the desk, and fumbled under his desk for something. "There's...nothing....I know...about this-"

"Do you also have a panic button under your desk similar to that of Mayor Hansen's?" Lucy asked. "If so, I thought you'd like to know your brothers are-"

"Gone?" Principal Hansen said. "I know of my brothers' untimely disappearance. But that doesn't mean I can't panic!"

With a sigh, Lucy stepped forward and placed both hands on the principal's desk, leaning forward into him.

"Your incompetence has exceeded tolerance," Lucy stated. "The sooner we can determine Jonathan Gilbert's true cause of death, the sooner we can potentially put his spirit to rest, and the sooner Sterben will be safe."

"Potentially?" Natalie questioned.

Lucy looked over her shoulder. "I will have to consult with my father, but poltergeists are hard enough to appease when they're weak let alone strong enough to cause a flash flood in an indoor building or summon the ghost of a centuries dead playwright."

Natalie and Chase exchanged a nervous glance. Principal Hansen gave Lucy a hard stare before shaking a finger in her face.

"You...are a student and you do not...you do not scare me!" He stammered, his voice cracking on the last word. "You will *not* get me to say a word against my brotherly oath to not say a word about the thing we made a brotherly oath on!"

The flames on the candles wavered with the principal's stern warning. Lucy kept her face neutral, struggling to find the words to convince the principal otherwise. There were many things to criticize and demean the incompetent principal for, but his loyalty to his brothers was not one of them. Not to mention, Lucy knew all too well how powerful personal oaths could be and their potential to become curses if broken.

"Don't worry, Lucy," Chase said. "I can make him talk."

Blindly trusting her friend, Lucy stepped back to allow Chase to awkwardly shuffle past her in the broom closet-like space. After a moment to settle into Lucy's old spot with Lucy taking Chase's spot next to Natalie, Chase folded his arms in front of his chest and tried to look stern with Principal Hansen. Principal Hansen looked smug in his green facial mask, leaning back again in his chair with a proud smirk before copying Chase's stance.

"Ah, the Third Hunter Boy," Principal Hansen said. "The rivalry between our families is as well known as it is infamous. What could you possibly say to convince me to reveal my family's deepest darkest family secret to you?"

"On the contrary, Principal Hansen, our family holds no animosity against yours. It ain't our style," Chase said. "However, what is my style is ensuring the full extent of the law is fulfilled to the best of its ability. For example, the mission statement of the Kansas Board of Education is to prepare Kansas students for lifelong success through rigorous, quality academic instruction, career training and character development according to each student's gifts and talents." He indicated to Principal Hansen. "As you are the principal of this school, it is your job to fulfill this mission statement. Failing to educate your students may result in a loss of your school leadership license."

As Principal Hansen's smug expression fell, Chase merely shrugged. "We're your students, sir, and we're just askin' you to educate us on the death of Jonathan Gilbert to the best of your knowledge."

Pursing his lips, Principal Hansen nodded his head slowly as he considered Chase's words.

"If I lose my license..." Principal Hansen said. "I...can't stay in my office?"

"That's right, sir," Chase said.

After a long moment of consideration, Principal Hansen nodded.

"Well... I *do* have a true passion for leading my students to success," Principal Hansen said. "Alright! You got me, Third Hunter Boy! It must have been our connection as fellow third brothers, although technically I'm the oldest, but I am the third in power so..." Shaking his head, he moved himself off of his chair. "Anyways, I'll be right back, children! When I return, be ready to get educated!"

The principal ducked under his desk. With a small, proud smile, Chase leaned back to the girls.

"There really ain't any legal repercussions to be made if he doesn't do his job," Chase whispered. "Unless someone privately sues him, of course, but he doesn't have to know that."

Natalie let out a low whistle.

"You should really consider a career in law, Chase," Natalie said. "You've got a natural talent for it."

Chase's cheeks reddened. "Well, I-"

"I'm back!" Principal Hansen sprung up from his spot underneath the desk. His green facial mask was scrubbed off and he had freed his poofy hair from its bun. He had also somehow changed out of his robe and slippers into a thrifty tweed jacket and thin rimmed glasses that made him look distinguished.

Blinking rapidly, Natalie pointed at the principal.

"That...wow," Natalie said. She turned to Lucy. "I thought that only happened in movies."

Brushing the dust off of his jacket, Principal Hansen ignored Natalie's remark and nodded at the trio. "Are we ready to be educated?"

Even though the students made no effort to respond, Principal Hansen reached up to the ceiling and pulled down a blank screen. Whipping out a remote control from his coat pocket, he pushed a button on it with a flourish and the light of a projector above the trio's head lit the screen. As Principal Hansen worked to get his presentation on screen, Natalie shook her head.

"This is a waste of school money," She said.

"*This* is how I'm going to educate you so what's the waste of money now?" Principal Hansen pointed at Natalie. "You are!" When she gave him a hard glare, he stuttered on his confidence. "I...I didn't mean that, Natasha. You know you're our best student and your exemplary test scores are the only reason why this school hasn't been closed yet."

Folding her arms over her chest, Natalie smirked. "You got that right."

"Now onto the education!" Principal Hansen said.

Principal Hansen pushed a button and a school picture of Jonathan Gilbert appeared on the screen. Even though the image was in black and white, it was clear that Jonathan was, at one point, a handsome young man. Sharp cheekbones with tousled dark hair and piercing dark eyes that matched unsmiling thin lips, Lucy could now see why he would want a career where everyone could see his face. If only he had the opportunity to grow into his young face...Jonathan Gilbert would've made a very good model for her photographs.

Clearing his throat in anticipation for his lecture, Principal Hansen faced the projector screen. "This is and/or was-"

"Wait, hold on," Natalie said. "How do you already have a presentation prepared for this?"

"First off, dear Natsuki, try not to interrupt a teacher when they're educating, okay? Raise your hand if you have to," Principal Hansen said. "Second off, yes I do suffer from an extreme form of guilt that grips me in the middle of the lonely nights and sometimes that extreme guilt compels me to create an entire, very well-detailed PowerPoint presentation in the hopes that someone, someday, will call me out on my guilt and I can finally talk about it in a healthy environment in the only way I know how. Thank you for asking."

Doubling over, Principal Hansen took a deep breath and held up a finger to the students.

Lucy nodded. "No please. Take your time. That was quite the run-on sentence."

"Yeah I mean, there's only a bloodthirsty poltergeist waiting to kill us once we get out of this office," Natalie said. "So just catch your breath. We're good over here."

"You guys are the best," Principal Hansen choked out.

The principal sucked in a heavy breath before standing straight again. "Now back to the education! This is and/or was Jonathan Gilbert." Principal Hansen pointed to the school picture on screen. "He graduated in the same class as my two brothers. What is notable about him is that he had received a theatre scholarship to DePaul University in Chicago, Illinois. He was the first student in Sterben High history to receive admission to an out-of-state university, which was great for him because he would *not* shut up about leaving Sterben. In fact..."

Principal Hansen clicked a button and the slide changed to a picture of Jonathan Gilbert in his graduation gown flipping off the entire gymnasium with his diploma tucked under his arm.

"He vowed to leave Sterben that night after graduation and never return!" Principal Hansen said. "It was kind of sad. He skipped all of the good graduation parties just to leave sooner."

"Oh, yeah, I knew that," Chase said. "He came over to-uh....never mind."

Lucy and Natalie gave Chase a look while Principal Hansen continued his lecture.

"Anyways, my brothers and I did *not* know that!" Principal Hansen said. He flipped the slide and it showed a picture of all three brothers together with a fake moustache-less Mayor Hansen and a fully moustached Officer Hansen still in their graduation robes. "And we had decided to celebrate that night because Officer had finally graduated and Mayor was on his way to Kansas State!"

Lucy held up a finger. "Pardon the interruption...but your names are *actually* Mayor, Officer, and Principal? They're not just titles?"

Now Natalie and Chase turned to give her an incredulous look.

"Yeah?" Natalie said.

"What else would we call them by if those weren't their names?" Chase said.

"Really, Luna, you need to start paying attention," Principal Hansen scolded. "We've told you our names several times by now."

All the budding photographer could do was shake her head.

"I can't say I'm too terribly surprised," Lucy stated. "Continue your exposition, Principal. I apologize for the delay."

"Thank you," Principal Hansen said. "And so, on that night of graduation-" He switched the slide and the picture transitioned from a happy picture of three celebrating brothers to a slide of a demolished car on the side of a dirt road. "-we got into a devastating car accident with Gilly and accidentally murdered him because we were too scared to call an ambulance and get in trouble. The end!"

"Whoa, whoa!" Chase put his hand up. "That was quite the leap in narrative."

"Yeah!" Natalie said. "What gives?"

"I always got too sad whenever I got to this part," Principal Hansen admitted. "So I just skipped some details to get to the point."

"I will argue the details are the most essential part of the story, especially since we're attempting to determine how this poltergeist came to be," Lucy said. "For example, what was the blood alcohol content at the scene of the crime?"

"It was...um," Principal Hansen said. "...two?"

"He doesn't know what a BAC is," Natalie stated.

"It don't matter," Chase said. "If he were underage and had *any* alcohol in his system at the scene of a vehicular manslaughter, then he is subjected to a level four felony and he should've served jail time."

"Exactly!" Principal Hansen said. "That's why we used our family influence and considerable wealth to hide the crime and tried to blame your family instead! My mom said that kind of felony could ruin a life."

"Death can also ruin a life," Lucy stated. "So let me guess: once you successfully covered up a crime you *definitely* should've paid for in some capacity, unexplained phenomenons began to occur to you and your brothers?"

"Yes! Exactly!" Principal Hansen pointed at Lucy enthusiastically. "Well, first, our parents died in their own equally tragic accident, *that* was sad. Then you know, my walls started bleeding, Gilly's voice followed us around whispering "you did this..." and "Sterben will fall", Mayor couldn't grow a moustache, and it was just a real hinderance, you know. So, with my Master's in education, I did some expert Googling and found some solutions like locking myself in my office with some wind chimes."

"And the meeting once a year on the day of Gilly's death at his death site?" Lucy asked. "Is this related?"

"Yes!" Principal Hansen said. "We discovered that if we met once a year to pay our respects to Gilly, the weird stuff stopped happening! But then Mayor decided we couldn't keep doing that for the rest of our lives so we stopped going this year and the weird stuff started happening, but worse. So that's why we called your dad! To get rid of Gilly!"

"But you didn't tell him *why* he needed to get rid of Gilly," Lucy said.

"Of course not! Then we'd look like bad guys and he wouldn't help us," Principal Hansen said. "We couldn't have that. My brothers and I have a town to run and Gilly-"

"Gilly is trying to avenge his own death and your interference has prevented my father from doing his job," Lucy said, anger bubbling under her words. "Not only that, but your family's selfish pride has jeopardized the safety of the citizens of this town by allowing Gilly to continue to grow in power due to your blatant disregard for basic respect for human life."

Principal Hansen regarded Lucy's words with a contemplative nod.

"Maybe so," Principal Hansen said. "But at least we didn't intentionally kill Betty Bells, Teri, Jeri, and um...someone else." After a moment of thought, he snapped his fingers. "The Morrison Boy! That's right! He was a student here...in hindsight, I should've thought of him first. That's on me, y'all."

Before the teens could berate the principal further, the door behind them shook violently as something heavy crashed into it. They all turned to face it. Principal Hansen let out a high-pitched shriek and ducked behind his desk again.

"He found me! Gilly found me!" Principal Hansen shrieked. "I knew I shouldn't have saved the children! Teri! *Teri*! Escort them out! TERI!"

With the second crash, a thick crack appeared directly in the middle of the blue door. Lucy instinctively grabbed onto her friends' arms, a feeling of dread creeping up in the back of her spine. She had gone too far. She thought she was helping, but, in this moment, she could see she was just putting herself in the center of the danger. She would now face the repercussions meant for the Hansens, right here and right now.

Finally, on the third crash, the door splintered open. Lucy, Natalie, and Chase all flinched with Lucy tightening her grip on her friends. When the chaos settled, Lucy was surprised to see not the undead spirit of Jonathan Gilbert, but instead the most badass person in Sterben, Kansas appear in the destroyed doorway.

"If there's any ghosts in here, you better watch out!" Kierra shouted. "I just bashed this door in with a softball bat and I'm not afraid to do the same to your head!"

Principal Hansen popped his head up so his eyes were peeking over the desk. He looked directly at Kierra.

"Ohhhhhhh no," He whispered. "I'm going to die."

Once Kierra looked at the group before her, she relaxed considerably.

"Oh thank-" Kierra turned back to the room behind her. "Mike! She's in here."

As Kierra shuffled out of the way to allow Mike Vitalis into view, Lucy dropped her friends' arms and tried to keep her face neutral. Despite her heart had now sank into the deepest pit of her stomach, Lucy couldn't let her father know the relief she felt in that moment. She had to appear confident so he would never know the fear she felt. However, her heart took a sharper dive when Mike's concerned face appeared in the doorway, his eyes sad until they landed on Lucy. He let out his own sigh of relief.

"Luce!" Mike reached out for her. "What are you doing here?! The jibakurei who informed us about the paranormal activity warned that you'd might be here."

"Murasaki?" Lucy questioned as she accepted her father's help out of the office. "She revealed herself to you?"

"I did," Murasaki said. "The threat posed by the poltergeist at this location proved too much for me to handle alone. Even it risked my own life in the process, I needed help from a fellow enemy of this spirit. Georgia was able to convey my intentions to the spirit seeker."

"I just said she was real nice and stuff and that she saved my life!" Georgia exclaimed from behind the spirit. "I also pointed out the door when she couldn't see it."

"It had confounded me at first, but now I see it clear as day," Murasaki said. "It appears this brave warrior with the power to heal has brought it into my vision."

"That's my Kierra for ya!" Chris shouted from the hallway. "She's a badass, alright! By the way, Mrs. Bobby's dead and her body's kind of creeping me out here."

Natalie poked her head through the doorway. "Good Lord, how many people are even here?"

"Are any of y'all qualified to make an arrest?" Chase shouted. "We've got a man we need to charge with involuntary vehicular manslaughter and obstruction of justice!"

Mike turned to the rest of the group. Kierra gave Chris a glance. He shook his head at his wife before she turned and shrugged at Mike. Georgia tried raising her hand, but Murasaki immediately pushed it back down again. With a sigh, Mike turned back to Chase.

"I guess I have some authority to make an arrest if it's involved with my investigation," Mike said. "Why? What's this about?"

"Oh, uh-" Chase jabbed a thumb behind him. "Principal Hansen and his brothers killed Gilly in a possible underage drunk driving accident, then used their family influence to cover the crime, which made Gilly into the poltergeist that's been terrorizing the town."

"Tattletale!" Principal Hansen shouted from his hiding spot. "My momma was right about not trusting a Hunter!"

"You killed a guy, sir!" Chase said. "If I didn't admit the crime, we'd all be accessories to it."

"Alrighty, time to get you kiddos away from the murderer," Mike said as he offered his hand to Natalie to guide her over the destroyed doorway. Kierra stepped forward to help Chase out.

"Oh c'mon!" Principal Hansen groaned. "I didn't *mean* to murder him. Officer was at the wheel! I was just the passenger!"

Mike paused for a second. "Wait...your names are *actually*-"

"It's okay, Dad," Lucy said, patting her father on the shoulder. "I forgot where we were residing too."

"This is slander!" Principal Hansen shouted. "Heresy! Blasphemy! Mutiny!"

"Heresy can only apply to those with opinions in contrast to religious doctrine," Murasaki stated. "Just so you know, for future attempts of blame deflection."

"Holy-is that a ghost?!" Principal Hansen jumped back. "How-how can you see me?! How-" His eyes widened as he looked at the destroyed doorway. "The door! The door is broken! Gilly can see me now! He's going to come for me like he came for my brothers! Please! Put it back up, put it-"

The wind chimes sang softly, almost mocking the principal's cries for help. Mike stood at alert, his instincts as a seasoned ghost hunter kicking in. Noting Mike's heightened awareness, Kierra lifted her softball bat.

"There's a ghost here, isn't there?" Kierra said. "And it's Gil-"

"Shhh," Mike hushed. "Don't say it's name. It will increase its power."

"Oh! Like Harry Potter?" Georgia exclaimed.

"I understand that reference!" Chris shouted.

"I do not," Murasaki said.

"Ooo we can have a movie night!" Georgia said. "I'll ask Mrs. Hansen if we can-"

"Folks...not now!" Mike shouted.

The wind chimes were now rustling aggressively, taunting the poor man in his office. Lucy brought her camera to her eye and framed her shot. Before she could take the pictures, all of the various religious artifacts on the walls dropped to the floor in one go. Principal Hansen let out a yell and ducked further under his table, the wind chimes continuing to rattle violently above him. When Kierra raised her softball bat above her head, Mike snatched it out of her hands. Murasaki stepped forward, her hands dripping with green smoke as she worked to calm the aura around them. With Kierra's softball bat, Mike leaned forward and stretched it out to Principal Hansen.

"Principal! Grab onto the bat!" Mike said. "I'll drag you to safety!"

"No! The office is safe," Principal said, rocking back and forth on the floor in the fetal position. "The office is safe, the office is *safe*."

The office was, in fact, not safe. All of the wind chimes stopped mid-chime. The cacophony of silence was deafening, causing both Mike and Murasaki to break their concentration to stare up at the chimes in curiosity. Soon, Principal Hansen poked his head up to inspect the mystery as well. When he did, a ring of fire appeared on the projector screen above his head. Within the ring of fire was a pit of darkness, appearing never-ending to the human eye.

The principal turned to the projector screen. As he did so, something gripped two tufts of hair on the top of his head. He let out a scream as he was lifted up in the air, his lanky legs kicking the desk below him. Murasaki positioned herself towards the floating principal, the tendrils of green smoke growing thicker around her fingers. With the sign of the cross, Mike hurried into the office with Kierra's softball bat and swung at the space above Principal Hansen. The principal dropped onto the desk with a heavy slam.

An overwhelming wave of fear overtook Lucy as Mike lifted the bat in front of him in a defensive position. Running in front of everyone, she turned the flash on her camera and set it to continuous shooting. Clicking the button, she lifted it above her head and closed her eyes. Flashes of light overtook the room, reflecting off all of the shiny wind chimes and even causing her father to flinch away from the blinding light.

Lucy took a peek to see if her emergency plan was working. To her surprise, she could see the shadow of a boy among the flashes of light. His head was turned towards her but he looked back down to the principal who was covering his eyes from the camera flash. The shadow then bent down and lifted the principal by his ankles. Principal Hansen only let out a shout of surprise as he was once again lifted into the air.

Before Lucy could do anything, the shadow tossed Principal Hansen into the ring of fire in the screen. The principal's screams echoed as the shadow jumped towards the hole, offering Lucy one last head turn before he followed the principal into the void. The continuous shooting on her camera ran out shortly after and the room returned to its normal fluorescent lighting. Mike took a moment to let his eyes adjust to the new lighting before he noticed the missing principal. He then turned to Lucy with fire in his eyes.

"...why did you do that?" Mike's voice shimmered with a restrained frustration.

Lucy was at a loss for words. She could feel all of her friends' eyes burrowing into her, blaming her for the principal's disappearance. Swallowing, Lucy fiddled with her camera strap nervously.

"To be completely honest," Lucy said. "Perhaps taking the soul of an accused Hansen brother will appease the spirit rather than-"

"Lucille Lorraine Vitalis," Mike seethed. He lifted a shaking finger to his daughter. "You *know* sacrificing a human life to appease a spirit is the absolute *last* thing we do."

"But Dad-"

"I don't *care* how incompetent he was or how terrible he acted or whatever the hell he did!" Mike shouted. "The first order of this job is protecting life by respecting death and you've done none of those things today!" He took a deep breath. "As soon as I get your mess cleaned up, I'm calling your mother. Sterben is clearly too-"

"No, Dad!" Lucy shouted. All eyes were still on her and she was feeling the weight of their judgement. "Don't send me to live with Nora. I-I won't get involved again! I swear!"

Mike gave her a hard look. Never had his responsibilities as the second best paranormal investigator in the world been threatened by his responsibilities as a father. Not only as a father, but as the only true parent to Lucy Vitalis. Sighing, Mike straightened his shoulders as he faced his daughter.

"One more chance," Mike said. "But the next time I catch you sniffing around my investigation, you're on the first flight to New York. Understood?"

All Lucy could do was nod solemnly at her father's wishes. He barely regarded her reaction before turning to the rest of the group.

"Chris and Kierra? Can you make sure these girls get home safe?" He asked. "Murasaki, the same with Georgia. Chase, I need to talk to you about investigating your family's property if these accusations about Jonathan Gilbert's death are true."

Chase nodded. "I'll discuss it with my family."

With another nod, Mike returned his attention to the principal's office to investigate the scene fully. In a normal investigation, Mike wouldn't mind having Lucy around. In fact, sometimes he invited her so she could take pictures for him in case something he did triggered a spiritual response. That's how she first learned to frame a shot, how to look for the next three steps of a scene.

However, this was not a normal investigation. Instead of taking pictures, she was now being led away from the crime scene by an actor and his badass wife. As they walked through the hallways of Sterben High, carefully sidestepping Mrs. Bobby's body and the bear carcass, Lucy could swear another shadow was following them. A shadow too masculine for any of the women in their group and too slender for Chris's bulking frame.

The same shadow she recognized from the iris of Chevy Hunter's eye that just dragged Principal Hansen into hell.

Tip #8:
Honesty is the best policy.

IF LIVING WITH HER mother was equivalent to the darkest ring of hell, then staying with Chris and Kierra during her father's investigation was Lucy's purgatory. All of the Hansens were still missing so Mike Vitalis had focused his investigation on finding the brothers. After Lucy told him everything Principal had confessed, he theorized that bringing the brothers to justice would appease the spirit so the Hansens couldn't be dead yet. But in order to for the brothers to be brought to justice, Mike would need to find all of them first.

All of it resulted in long days and nights at Chris and Kierra's house for Lucy since Mike no longer trusted Lucy on her own. It wasn't so bad at first. Lucy spent the first couple days photographing the immaculate home, capturing Chris as he did the housework and practiced his monologues for potential auditions. She even helped him rehearse a particularly tough scene. But the novelty wore off and Lucy found herself sneaking peeks at her father's notes when he fell asleep at his desk, hoping for new insights on how to defeat the poltergeist so they could return to normalcy.

Finally, on day four of Chris and Kierra lockdown, Natalie came over to work on "school stuff" with Lucy. As school was still on an indefinite hiatus since all of its teachers fled town upon Mrs. Bobby's death, "school stuff" meant their own investigation into stopping the poltergeist. Lucy knew that continuing her involvement with her father's investigation was a risk, but, after seeing her father's lack of progress, she knew she had to keep investigating. Her current plan was just to slip whatever new information they discovered into his notes and hope for the best.

But, to Lucy's surprise, when she opened the door to greet Natalie, she met Georgia's eye first. Natalie could only shrug as Georgia waved enthusiastically at Lucy.

"Hi again!" Georgia said. "Natalie said I can crash your study group since Mara's trying to protect the town and Mrs. Hansen left to go live with her mom after Mr. Hansen disappeared and I don't like being alone after being nearly murdered that one time."

"It isn't a problem at all," Lucy said. "A good support system is necessary for trauma recovery."

"Oh no! I wasn't traumatized," Georgia said. "I just have nightmares about it and freeze up whenever I think about it so I like being around friends so I don't think about the life leaving John's eyes as much."

Lucy's only response was to open the door a little wider. The girls made their way to Chris and Kierra's dining room table. Georgia sat down and pulled out a weathered hardback copy of Shakespeare's *Cymbeline*. Natalie only gave the title a curious look before pulling out a SAT prep book she had hollowed out to hide her investigation notes into. Not paying attention to either friend, Lucy focused on unlocking her tablet and pulling up all of the photos she had taken during their investigation. She swiped between two pictures.

"I knew it," Lucy said. She showed the tablet to Natalie. "The shadow I witnessed in Principal Hansen's office is the same shape of the shadow that was in Chevy Hunter's eye."

After checking out the photos, Natalie looked over her purple framed glasses at Lucy. "I thought it was already pretty obvious that Gilly is the poltergeist behind both paranormal activities."

"That's not what I'm referring to," Lucy said. "I'm referring to the fact the poltergeist is becoming more tangible than a glimmer in an impressionable boy's eye. If all it wished was to remove the Hansen brothers from their nepotist power, then it wouldn't be as visible as it is now."

"But then what else would it want?" Natalie asked. "We know the Hunters didn't mean to hurt Gilly, but maybe they did anyway? They were the last ones to see him and Chase said his older brother was close to Gilly."

"It might explain why the poltergeist chose to reveal himself to Chevy," Lucy said. "An innocent life for innocent life."

"Just like Hamlet!" Georgia perked up. "You know like why Hamlet had to avenge his father's murder?"

Lucy nodded. "Yes, exact-"

"Did somebody say Hamlet?!" Chris asked, poking his head into the doorway. When Georgia nodded, Chris bounded into the room with a skip in his step. "Murder most foul, as in the best it is; but this most foul, strange and unnatural-"

"Haste me to know't, that I, with wings as swift, as meditation or the thoughts of love, may sweep to my revenge!" Georgia said, clapping her hands.

Chris and Georgia continued to bounce Shakespeare off of each other as their audience remained unimpressed with the interruption.

"Anyways..." Natalie said, returning her attention to Lucy. "When is your dad visiting the Hunter farm?"

Lucy sighed. "The Hunters still won't allow him on their property."

"What?!" Natalie exclaimed. "But Chase said-"

"Chase has been very apologetic, but it appears his parents and older brothers have something more severe to hide than a poltergeist," Lucy said. "Not that Chase directly admitted it, but I could only infer from their continued resistance to our visitation."

"Wait, are y'all talking about the Hunters?" Chris asked.

The front door opened and slammed shut. Still in her scrubs from Lebenville Medical, Kierra came walking into the dining room with several grocery bags on each arm.

"Alrighty I didn't know what you girls wanted for snacks so I got some veggie trays, six kinds of chips, and some cookies too!" Kierra said as she unpacked the bags. "But don't eat the cookies until after you get most of your homework done, okay?" Her eyes fell on the book in Georgia's hand. "Ooo! Shakespeare! Babe, you love Shakespeare."

"Aw babe, that's so sweet you remembered I love Shakespeare," Chris said, holding his chest. "But honey, the girls were talking about the Hunters!"

"What about the Hunters?" Kierra asked.

Lucy and Natalie shared a panicked look. Chris might be nice enough to not reveal their true study group intentions to Lucy's dad, but Kierra was ruthless. If she found out they were actually working on stopping the poltergeist, she would probably find a way to ship Lucy off to New York herself.

"We....need to get on their farm," Natalie said. "For...Lucy's portfolio!" She snapped her fingers. "Yes! Lucy has been taking pictures of the town and the only place she hasn't shot is the Hunter farm."

"Well that makes sense," Kierra said. "No one's been on the Hunter farm in decades."

"They're private people," Chris said. "The whole family didn't even come to our wedding, which was a shame. Chevron and I were in theatre together back in high school."

"With Jonathan Gilbert?" Lucy asked.

Chris made a face. "Who?"

"Honey, she means Gilly," Kierra said. "Remember? We saw his gravestone the night the Morrison boy was murdered."

"Oh! Gilly!" Chris said. "Tremendous guy."

Natalie and Lucy kept their mouths shut as Kierra continued unpacking her groceries onto the dining room table, blissfully unaware of her husband's remark.

"Doesn't Chevron owe you a favor, honey?" Kierra asked. "Or was it Chadron?"

"Babe, we barely knew Chadron," Chris said. "But yeah, Chevron *did* owe me a favor from the senior show's after-party."

"Well maybe you should call him up to cash in on that favor," Kierra said. "Chevron was always nice to us. He would let us on their farm for Lucy's pictures if you asked."

Surprisingly, Chris frowned. "Well, love, I was planning on using that favor to cast him in a production of *Rosencrantz & Guildenstern Are Dead* or even a showing of *Waiting for Godot* if he wanted. He was always so great in comedies."

Pursing her lips, Kierra gave a disapproving look to the groceries before turning to Chris with a forced smile.

"Well, *sweetie*, isn't helping out our neighbors more important than-" Kierra stopped herself.

Noting his wife's hesitation, Chris furrowed his eyebrows. "More important than *what*, sweetie?"

Kierra gave a curt smile. "Nothing, babe."

Only Georgia was ignorant to the severity of Kierra's statement. Natalie shot Lucy a worried glance. The perfect young couple stared at each other, the tension rising with every passing silent moment. Finally, with a solemn expression, Chris lifted a single index finger to his wife.

"Babe?"

"Yeah?" Kierra answered.

"We...." Chris said. "...*almost* had our first fight!"

Kierra let out a cheer as Chris leapt out of his chair to hug his wife. They embraced tightly before Kierra pulled away to let out a sigh.

"Let's never do that again!" Kierra said. "That was awful!"

"I know, sweetie!" Chris said. "I just want to go back to what we were doing before we nearly had a fight."

"Me too, honey," Kierra said. "....what were we doing before we almost had a fight?"

Natalie raised her hand slightly to interrupt the couple. "You were about to use Chris's favor with Chevron Hunter to get us on the farm so Lucy could take pictures."

Once again, Chris made a face. "I mean....that's not what I want to use my favor with Chevron for, but..." He looked down at his smiling wife. "Someone very smart and beautiful and badass told me it's more important to help out a neighbor and if it makes her happy, then I'm glad to do it!"

"Awww, babe," Kierra said. "You're the best future date to the Oscars ever."

"No you are!" Chris said.

Lucy took a picture of the couple in their embrace.

"The firsthand testimony of a young couple extensively sustaining the honest love of their honeymoon period against all odds is equally admirable and nauseating," Lucy stated. "I can declare, with certainty, that I aspire to no such activity with my own life."

Natalie thought about it. "I mean...maybe after I get my PhD. Like, I recognize other people might be able to balance marriage and medical school, but for me-wait, no." Amused, Lucy took a picture of her friend's incredulous face. "We need to *focus*. Chris and Kierra, do we have permission to go to the Hunter farm?"

"Of course!" Kierra said. "We'll have to go with you guys, of course. With all of this ghost stuff going around, we promised your parents we'd take care of y'all."

"This is going to be so fun to catch up with Chevron and Chadron!" Chris said. "Tremendous fellas. I'll go call them up now! Keep studying until then!"

"I better go make some cookies so we have something to give our hosts!" Kierra exclaimed. "Feel free to eat up the snacks!"

Once Kierra and Chris left the room, Natalie smiled at Lucy.

"This is great!" She whispered. "And I've finally gotten enough evidence from my studies to be able to perform our own ghost hunt! Well, poltergeist spirit settling..." Her eyes lit up as she reached into her backpack. "I even got my dad to make us our own Rem-Pod so we can detect energy disturbances! Wanna see it?"

"No, I've seen my father's," Lucy said. "I'm sure yours is similar or perhaps newly molded or even more handmade in fashion....but I'm sure it maintains efficiency despite designs ulterior to my father's personal preference."

There was a long moment as Lucy continued to cycle through photos she's examined a hundred times over, Natalie's eyes watching her the entire time.

"Are you worried about your dad?" Natalie finally asked. When the corners of Lucy's lips twitched, Natalie sighed. "We'll be *fine*. We haven't died yet-"

"Yet is the imperative word," Lucy said. "This is a dangerous situation we're willingly embracing. What further jeopardizes our lives is the deception that we've utilized in order to escape the security my father has ensured for us."

Natalie rolled her eyes. "C'mon, Lucy. *Everyone* lies to their parents."

"I do not," Lucy stated cooly. "Nora told my father and I enough lies to satisfy a lifetime. I do not intend to increase that capacity, especially if it risks innocent lives in the process."

As Lucy looked up at the door Chris and Kierra exited through, Natalie turned to look at Georgia who was heavily engrossed in her novel. The disparity in their choice of what deemed a risk to an innocent life caused the girls to look at each other in surprise.

"Oh! Were you-" Natalie asked, pointing to the door.

"I thought it was apparent that I was talking about-" Lucy said.

"Oh yeah! For sure that makes *total* sense," Natalie said. "But I just wasn't worried about Chris and Kierra. I mean, Kierra is a badass. Georgia is your stereotypical white girl in distress. If anyone's gonna die from this thing, it's probably gonna be her."

Lucy had no reasonable argument against Natalie's accusation. It was true that Kierra proved herself to be a worthy opponent against the paranormal and it was also true that Gilly had targeted Georgia before. But if the poltergeist formerly known as Gilly still had two brain cells to rub together, he'd recognize that hurting Georgia would invoke Murasaki's full wrath. It was obvious Murasaki would be willing to do anything to protect Georgia.

It wasn't obvious if the same could be said for Lucy and Natalie, especially if they were doing something as stupid as heading headfirst into a possible poltergeist trap with innocent lives.

Within the half hour, Chris had finished up calling in his favor with Chevron and Kierra had packed up her freshly baked cookies. The three girls and the happy couple all packed into Kierra's Subaru. The drive to the very outskirts of the town was surprisingly pleasant as Chris and Kierra merrily led the girls in Disney sing-a-longs and remained grossly in love. Lucy took several candids of everyone, relishing in the joy of it all. Her last batch of photos were very bleak, much like the outcome of the town if they couldn't stop the poltergeist soon, so she was happy for the change in mood.

However the joyful ride turned solemn as Kierra drove them up a long driveway surrounding by acres of dead corn stalks. Even though logic told Lucy that the harvest had ended months ago and thus it was reasonable for the remaining stalks to be dead, a cool chill that wrapped around the curve of her spine told her that there was more death to the land that couldn't be seen. It was a feeling refuted by the glowing farmhouse in the middle of a clearing within the cornfields.

The farmhouse was a massive three story estate with dark blue trimmings around fresh white paint. Plump pumpkins were placed in tasteful locations around the property, complementing the red and brown leaves gracing the oak trees outlining the clearing. To Lucy's surprise, there was a small armada of luxury vehicles in the form of a Porsche, a Lexus, and a Chevy SUV parked in the driveway leading up to a matching white and dark blue barn. In fact, Lucy noted that the only item of age to appear on the property was Chase's rusty blue truck which was parked near the luxury vehicles without an issue.

As Kierra pulled up around the circle driveway, Chase came strolling out of the front door with his thumbs in his pocket. He offered them all a friendly wave as Kierra parked the car. As everyone exited the vehicle, Chase strolled down the porch steps to greet them. He reached his hand out to Chris, preparing to shake his hand.

"Nice to see y'all found us just fine!" Chase said. "I know Google Maps has trouble with-"

Before he could finish his introduction, Chevy came bursting out of the front door in a flurry of excitement. His eyes locked onto Lucy as he rammed himself into the railing around the porch, a wide smile on his face.

"Hi Lucy!" Chevy shouted. "I've been thinking about you a lot!"

Georgia stifled a giggle as she and Natalie turned to see Lucy's reaction, not missing the hint of pink touching the usually stoic photographer's upper cheeks. She lifted her hand.

"Hi Chevy," Lucy said. "It's nice to see you too."

"Are you here to see the poltergeist?!" Chevy shouted. "Are you gonna get rid of him?!"

Chris and Kierra both looked curiously at Chevy. Sighing, Chase turned around to face his little brother.

"Chevy, I told you I'd handle it!" Chase shouted. "Get back inside and help Mom with the bakin' before I tell all these nice people how you wet the bed two nights ago when you forgot your pull-ups!"

Blushing hard, Chevy sprinted back into the farmhouse. Once the front door was slammed shut, Chase turned back to the group with an apologetic smile.

"I'm sorry about that, folks," Chase said. "Little brothers have quite the imagination, you know? He thinks the poltergeist threatening the town could be on *our* property. It's crazy, right?"

Chris and Kierra both relaxed, with Kierra offering her husband a pat on the shoulder as she did so.

"Too crazy! That ghost seems more occupied with the town than with you guys," Kierra said. "But I do have my gun in the back of my car in case something does go wrong. Can't be too safe these days, you know?"

"Yep! Your second amendment rights are totally safe here!" Chase laughed nervously. "Come on now, let's head inside. Momma's got some pie baking in the oven for y'all."

Excited by the prospect of being some of the first outsiders to step inside the Hunter household in over a decade, Chris and Kierra walked ahead with a skip in their step. Chase allowed a couple of feet of distance between them before stepping in front of the girls, crossing his arms over his chest in the process.

"Y'all are here for the poltergeist, aren't you?" He asked.

"No!" Natalie said. "We're here for Lucy's portfolio, ain't that right Georgia?"

Georgia nodded nervously. "I'm like totally not scared at all of being murdered by the same guy who killed John!"

With a smirk, Chase turned to Lucy. "Are you really here for your portfolio?"

Natalie burned a hard look into Lucy, pressing Lucy to answer correctly, as Lucy hesitated and moved her feet from side to side.

"I....cannot deny the allegations set forth upon me," Lucy said. "We are indeed here to settle the poltergeist's spirit without my father's approval or knowledge of the situation." When Natalie sighed, Lucy straightened. "It should also be noted that Chris and Kierra also have no knowledge of the full situation beyond the excuse we provided for your family."

Chase nodded. "I appreciate your honesty, Lucy, and I appreciate y'all choosing Chris and Kierra to help you out. Out of everyone else in Sterben, they would be the most understanding of our situation."

"What situation?" Natalie asked.

"Come inside for a slice of my momma's pie," Chase said. "And don't tell anyone else in town of what you find out."

There were many situations Lucy had witnessed in New York that might apply to the Hunter family. Maybe they were cannibals who ate Jonathan Gilbert's body. Maybe they were part of a cult that somehow offended or enticed Jonathan Gilbert in his life. Maybe they were rich enough to be passive to the pain and plight of a dying boy just on the edge of their property. Maybe they were a group of loners who got caught up in a crime they didn't commit and continued to live their life of loneliness due to the guilt they shared over owning a part in Jonathan Gilbert's death.

Or maybe they were Democrats.

As soon as they walked into the home, Lucy could see a rainbow flag draped on the wall above the family couch. Chase led them further into the well kept house, revealing walls covered with pictures of the family posing with various Democratic politicians among pictures of the boys in their football uniforms throughout the years. On a bookcase in the corner of the living room, Lucy noted there was an entire shelf dedicated to Hillary Clinton's books.

More importantly though, there was a distinct smell of fresh apple pie in the air. It was a sweet nectar that gave the already cozy home an even warmer feel. The kids walked into the dining room to see Chris and Kierra already sitting at a table with slices of pie in front of them, steam curling above each piece to reflect the treat's tastiness. A woman with dark brunette hair and a fitting business suit was next to them, smiling as she added a dollop of vanilla ice cream to the couple's slices.

On the other side of the table sat three burly men with the same hazel eyes and golden hair as Chase, all wearing the same stern expression as they stared at the young couple with folded arms across all of their chests. The only clear differences between the three were the color of their plaid shirts and the amount of facial hair each of them graced. The oldest had a full beard that matched his golden hair streaked with graying blonde hairs, the second oldest had a goatee, and the third graced clean stubble along his jawline. In unison, the three Hunter men all glanced up at the new arrivals as Lucy, Natalie, and Georgia walked into the room, each raising a bushy eyebrow as they did so.

Chase smiled. "Lucy, Natalie, Georgia, this is my paw, my oldest brother Chadron, and my second oldest brother Chevron. Paw, Chadron, and Chevron, this is Lucy Vitalis, she's new to town, and Georgia Peaches, she's from Lebenville. You should already know Natalie Hendrix."

None of the men stood to greet the ladies. Keeping their stern expressions, they all nodded again in unison towards the girls.

"Pleasure to meet you ladies," Paw said.

"Chase has told us all about ya," Chadron said.

"It's an honor," Chevron said.

Natalie and Georgia both shared their own form of greeting for the older Hunter men as Lucy snapped a picture. Naturally, none of the Hunter men reacted to the picture. The woman in the business suit put down the bucket of ice cream and approached the ladies with a warm smile and outstretched hand.

"I'm Charlotte, Chase's mom," The woman greeted, shaking each girl's hand enthusiastically. "Welcome to our home! It's so nice to finally meet some of my boys' friends. Go ahead and sit down! I'll get Chevy to bring out your slices of pie."

"Oh no worries, Mrs. Hunter, I've got it!"

All of the girls' eyes widened as a unarguably attractive black man came strolling out from the kitchen. His simple maroon pocket t-shirt barely fit against his rolling muscles. Even Kierra, so committed to Chris, put her hand on her chest at the sight of him. He was confident in his step, holding three new slices of apple pie with ease. The handsome man even offered the girls a gracious smile as he placed their slices of pie in front of them.

Mrs. Hunter let out a happy sigh. "You're such a big help, James! What would we do without you?"

"Oh no, it's really no problem at all!" James said. "Does anybody want some whip cream for your pie?"

Chris lifted his hand.

"I'll take some!" Chris said. "But I can go grab it-"

"No it's fine!" James said. "You guys sit and chat. I know it's been a while since Chevron has seen anyone from his high school so I'm sure you have a lot to catch up on."

With a rare departure from his stoic expression, Chevron smiled. "Thanks ho..." Chevron's smile fell as his eyes immediately fell onto their guests. "James."

James acknowledged the second oldest Hunter son with a sad smile and short head nod, patting Chevron on the shoulder as he walked past and into the kitchen. With a mouth full of fresh apple pie, Natalie swallowed quickly and shook her fork at the Hunters.

"Okay first off, *wow* this pie is amazing," Natalie said. "Second, who the *heck* was that?"

"Yeah he's, like, the most gorgeous man I've ever seen," Georgia said. "No offense, Chris."

The actor smiled heartily. "None taken!"

Paw and Chadron each turned towards Chevron, expecting an answer from him. With stern eyes not really matching anyone else's, Chevron shrugged.

"Family friend," He grunted.

Lucy nodded towards his left hand. "Do all of your family friends share a silver band on their ring fingers with you?"

Chevron clenched his left hand into a fist, hiding the ring.

"Family heirloom," He stated.

"Omg I, like, don't want to be the one to break this to you, but..." Georgia leaned over the table towards Chevron. "I, like, totally think your family friend has a crush on you."

Natalie and Lucy each gave Georgia a flat look. Chevron regarded Georgia's statement with a snort.

"Like I said, he's just a family friend," Chevron said.

"Who happens to live with us," Paw said.

"Full-time without having to pay rent," Chadron said.

As Paw and Chadron shared an amused snort at Chevron's expense, Natalie swallowed another bite of her pie before shaking her fork around.

"Alright this isn't some sort of sunken place scenario, right?" Natalie said. "Because if it is, then, despite the excellent pie, I think I need to *get out* if you understand what I'm saying-"

"No, no!" Chase said. "That's not it at all! James is...just a super cool dude who helps out around the farm a lot." He made a face. "That...that doesn't sound right."

"Is this why haven't you guys left the farm in over a decade?!" Natalie shouted. "Is it because of James?"

Lucy nodded. "I agree with my friend. Unless you can provide an ulterior motive for your chosen social isolation, we must assume your *family friend* is the reason."

Charlotte scoffed. "We would *never*-" Shaking her head, the Hunter matriarch remained composed. "I can understand where your allegations have bearings, but no. We're not intentionally staying away from Sterben because of our son and his...family friend. We just...don't know how the rest of the town would accept my....career choice."

There was an uneasy tension around the dinner table now. None of the Hunters made eye contact with their guests. Natalie stared long and hard at Chase, waiting for his explanation. The only one who appeared nonplussed at the situation was Georgia who was happily eating pie as if nothing was wrong. Finally, Chase relented under Natalie's never-ending glare and let out a deep sigh.

"Mom's the Finance Director for the, uh," Chase said, offering a nervous glance to his friends. "...Kansas Democratic Party."

As Lucy and Georgia remained calmly eating their pie, Natalie let her jaw drop before returning her attention to the rest of the table.

"*That's* the reason why you guys never leave the farm?" Natalie asked. "Are you seriously telling me you guys seriously haven't left in over a decade just because you're Democrats?!"

"'Fraid so," Paw said.

"We identify as very strict liberals," Chadron said.

"That kind of reputation can tarnish a name in a small Republican town like Sterben," Chevron said.

Natalie took a bite of her pie. "Why? It's not *that* big of deal if the town found out-"

The three Hunter men snorted in disbelief at the young girl.

"How long have you lived in Sterben?" Paw asked.

"Great-grandma got burned at the stake," Chadron said.

"They called it witchcraft, but we know it's 'cause she read Robin Hood out loud to the kiddos at the library," Chevron said.

Shaking their heads, the men reached for their cups of water at the same time.

"Damn McCarthyism," They all mumbled in unison.

Georgia clapped excitedly. "Oooo! I can, like, totally relate. They wanted to burn me at the stake too!"

Kierra turned to her husband. "Babe, did you know the Hunters were Democrats?"

"Oh...yeah," Chris said. "That's why Chevron owed me a favor. I, uh, caught him and Gilly....uh, discussing *gun control rights* at the senior show's after party and I promised to not tell anyone about it."

As Chris hastily stuffed his face with pie, avoiding his wife's hard stare, the three elder Hunter men all let out a unanimous grunt.

"Good man," Paw said.

"We always liked you two," Chadron said.

"It's a shame we missed the wedding," Chevron said.

"But it was harvest season," Paw said.

"Yes sir, the harvest always comes first," Chadron said.

"It's our livelihood, ya know," Chevron said.

Kierra sighed. "It's okay! If we ever get married again, we'll be sure to schedule it so you guys can make it!"

The three men nodded.

"Sounds like a plan," Paw said.

"We'll be looking forward to it," Chadron said.

"Always loved a good wedding," Chevron said.

Finishing her pie, Lucy calmly folded her hands under her chin and looked between all of the Hunters.

"Speaking of unnecessarily cryptic family secrets and nostalgia, Jonathan Gilbert and Chevron were friends?" She asked. "Was there any cause for malevolence between them? Anything that could, hypothetically speaking, curse Jonathan Gilbert's mortal soul to your land?"

The three Hunter men shook their heads in unison.

"Nope," Paw said.

"Gilly had a bit of an anger issue though," Chadron said.

"Only towards Sterben though," Chevron said.

Shaking her head, Charlotte Hunter let out a soft hum.

"Jonathan was a bright kid, but, oh how do I put this, he never felt *appreciated* in Sterben," Charlotte explained. "While it's a success now, the drama club wasn't exactly the most popular thing to be a part of when it first started. Chevron only avoided the bullying because Chadron was the captain of the football team."

Chris looked up from his pie to offer the Hunter matriarch a confused look.

"I wasn't bullied either though," Chris said.

"Oh honey," Kierra said, giving a gentle pat to Chris's bicep. "That's because everyone was scared I would beat them up, remember?"

Chris shrugged. "That makes sense. You *are* a badass."

Shaking her head, Charlotte ignored the couple and let out a heavy sigh. "Poor Jonathan didn't have anyone. Even his parents rejected him. We did the best we could to make things better for him. He was always a welcomed guest in our home. That's actually the reason why he was still near our property when-"

To the girls' surprise, Charlotte Hunter choked on her next words. Her bottom lip quivered violently. Shaking her head, she managed to fight off the tears with a deep breath. Kierra rubbed the Hunter matriarch's back as a show of empathy. The three Hunter men nodded.

"Gilly was like a fifth son to us," Paw explained.

"A good guy," Chadron said.
"A damn shame," Chevron said.

Disregarding the solemn air in the room, Lucy stood to her feet. Everyone stared up at her, curious on why she felt compelled to commit such an abrupt action. She opened her mouth, but withheld her revelation upon seeing the full members of her audience. Fighting back a smile, she pursed her lips and placed a hand on her camera.

"I...pardon the rude interruption, but I must complete my photography portfolio before the sun sets," Lucy stated. "Georgia, Natalie, and Chase, I'd be honored if you joined me. Chris and Kierra, you may stay and continue your verbal tour of nostalgia without our interruption."

"I'll grab Chevy!" Chase exclaimed, standing up from the table. "He knows some good spots to take photos."

Recovering from her breakdown, Charlotte wiped the tears from her eyes. "Be sure he uses the potty before you go out though. You know how nervous he gets around pretty girls."

"Check his diaper too," Paw said.

"Paw, he's on Pull-Ups now," Chadron said.

"Nah he's off them again to impress some girl at school," Chevron asked.

Chris leaned into Kierra. "Isn't their youngest thirteen?"

As Kierra subtly nodded, returning her attention to her slice of pie, Natalie and Georgia got up from the table as well and followed Chase and Lucy to the kitchen to grab Chevy. Their only interruption on their mission was James who was busy watching a pie in the oven and needed a photographer for an event his company was holding. Once Lucy was able to vaguely pledge to help take photos, the kids were free to explore the farm.

A safe distance away from the farmhouse, Natalie turned to Lucy who was occupied with photographing the house.

"Alright, what did you get so excited about in there?" Natalie asked.

Lucy snapped her photo before turning to the group. "Well while everyone had continued to mourn a soul too lost for this world, I had inferred the reason why the poltergeist had decided upon not only the Hunter farm as its hosting ground, but why he revealed himself to Chevy. Not only that, but it might be a key to how we can stop him."

"He did *what* to me?!" Chevy asked.

"Revealed himself, pay attention," Chase stated.

Chevy's bottom lip twitched. "I was-"

"Shh!" Natalie and Chase shushed at the same time, turning to Lucy.

Georgia lifted her hand. "Wait I'm, like, totally confused, so the bad ghost thing who murdered John is *here*?"

"Yes," Lucy said. "To have the strength he does, the poltergeist would need to have somewhere to return to and recover after each attack. Most choose their grave. We had assumed he had chosen Hunter farm because the Hunters were somehow involved in his death-"

"Which we weren't!" Chase exclaimed.

"-but we had missed the most obvious reason," Lucy said. "Gilly felt like this was his home in his previous life. This was where he was loved. Of *course*, this is where he's going to feel safest in his death, especially for the age he was when he died."

"Then why did he reveal himself to Chevy?" Natalie asked.

"I have two theories based on my father's previous investigations," Lucy said. "One, Chevy just happened to be the first living soul the poltergeist witnessed following the Hansen brothers' failure to oblige their tradition."

"The Hansen brothers?" Chevy asked, hopelessly confused.

"Or two, he was the youngest of the Hunter family and thus the one least likely to remember Gilly in his previous life," Lucy explained. "It was an attempt to resurrect Chevy's memory of Gilly so that he may strengthen his own power."

"That makes sense," Natalie said. "It also explains why he's been growing stronger as more of the town has been forced to remember him."

"Wait were y'all talking about Principal, Mayor, and Officer?" Chevy asked.

Chase rolled his eyes. "Yes! Again, pay attention."

"But-"

"Now how do we find the poltergeist?" Chase said, turning to Lucy. "I want it off the farm before-"

"But Chase-" Chevy pulled on his older brother's sleeve.

"-*before* it does more harm to the town," Chase said, snapping his arm away from his little brother and gritting his teeth in annoyance. "We may have a complicated relationship with Sterben, but-"

"*Chase!*"

"*What*, Chevy?!" Chase shouted back. "What is so dang important you gotta interrupt my conversation?"

The youngest Hunter boy jabbed his thumb behind him to the greater farmland.

"The Hansens are on the property," Chevy stated.

Natalie and Chase whipped their heads to him.

"*What?!*" They both exclaimed in unison. Natalie and Chase shared a look, surprised at their synchronization, before returning their attention to Chevy.

"Why didn't you tell us sooner?!" Chase asked.

"I did!" Chevy said. "Remember when I asked how much pie Mom was baking?"

"Not this again," Natalie groaned.

Licking his lips, Chase retained limited patience. "Yes, Chevy, I remember."

"Well I was wondering if I could bring some slices to Principal, Mayor, and Officer," Chevy said. "But then you told me she was only baking enough for Chris, Kierra, Lucy, Natalie, and Georgia and when I asked if she could make more, you told me not to be so needy and go vacuum the living room before they all showed up."

Barely resisting the urge to roll his eyes, Chase could only sigh at his little brother.

"Alright, you see where I'm coming from, right?" Chase asked. "About how you asking about inconsequential things may provide you with inconsequential answers?"

Chevy shrugged. "How else would I tell ya? It's not like I could just say the leaders of Sterben are tied up in the old shed where I tracked the fox and found the not-dead ghost guy."

Frustrated, Chase shook his fists in front of his brother.

"Yes! That is *exactly* what you say!" Chase said. "Now take us there as fast as you can or I swear I'm gonna pummel you into next Christmas!"

With wide eyes, the younger brother sprinted off into the cornfield, following a thin dirt path. Chase took off after him. Acting delightfully unaware of the potential danger they were headed towards, Georgia ran after them with a smile on her face. Natalie promptly followed as well. Lucy walked slowly, snapping photos of her friends running through the cornfield and of the serene property. If she could, she would stay in that moment forever. At least she would stay in it for as long as it took for her father to arrive and assist in their conquest.

But, then again, the longer they waited, the more danger the Hansen brothers could find themselves in. With a worried sigh, Lucy followed her friends down the narrow dirt path. She still had her holy water and salt from earlier in her bag, but they were supposed be used for self-defense. They were definitely not intended as a purposeful offense against malevolent spirits. That wasn't her job; it was her father's job.

Finally, the gang reached a small dilapidated shack at least a mile away from the farmhouse. At one point, it could've been a home for workers paid to cultivate crops on the massive plot of land. But, with the rise in technology and drop in available wages for human bodies, it was clear that the shack had been abandoned decades ago. Splintered wood and empty window panes were the only artifacts to remain of the former shelter. Despite the apparent disuse of the shack, there was an ominous force around it that stopped Chase, Natalie, Georgia, and Lucy in their tracks. They all waited in a line horizontal to the shack, staring at it.

Chevy, of course, walked straight up to the door without hesitation. He turned back around to face the group only when he noticed no one else followed him.

"Aw c'mon, guys!" He said. "Don't be chicken."

With a wide, teasing smile, Chevy entered the shack. The four teens looked between each other, almost daring the others to go in first before themselves. Finally, Natalie pulled out her REM pod, a cute little homemade thing, and aimed it at the building. All of the lights flashed up at once, emitting a chorus of beeping.

"It tests out," Natalie said. "Not only that but that's clearly a door similar to the one at the Wilson's, except..." She took a deep breath. "More visible."

"What does that mean?" Georgia asked quietly.

"Once we enter this shack," Lucy translated. "We're on spirit territory."

She lifted the camera to her eye. Before she could even think to touch the shutter button, the viewer went dark. Checking her camera, the entire thing had turned off and was impossible to turn back on. This caused her stomach to flip. Not only was Lucy and her friends about to tread into the poltergeists' home, but now her camera wasn't available. She couldn't think of a worse fate than the one they were willingly subjecting themselves to.

Before any of them could take another step forward, Chase linked his arms with Lucy and Natalie. With another shaky breath, Natalie linked her remaining arm with Georgia. It lifted Lucy's spirit a little to know that no matter what happened, they would take it together as a team. Even if this team only consisted of a budding photographer, a law-orientated farmboy, a future biomedical engineer, and a Shakespearean airhead, Lucy was grateful to have them on her team and as friends.

Confidence bubbling through all of them now, the four all strode to the front door with ease. When they arrived, all four teens tried to enter the one person doorway at the same time and bumbled into each other.

"Oof! Excuse me," Georgia mumbled.

"Sorry ladies," Chase mumbled at the same time.

Without thinking, Lucy, Chase, and Georgia aimed for the door again and caused the whole chain to crash within themselves again.

"*Guys,*" Natalie shouted. Everyone turned to her. "We all can't go in at the same time."

"I believe that much is now obvious," Lucy said. "However, I will concur with everyone's latent opinion that it would have appeared cool if we did."

Everyone mumbled their agreement with Lucy before separating their linked arms to enter the door one at a time. Allowing her friends to enter the building first, Lucy took a moment to adjust her hat and tie her long blonde hair into a low bun at the nape of her neck. As she did so, she uttered a prayer her father taught her as a child to try and allow safe passage into the spirit's home. In the depths of her heart, she knew it was a folly effort as the poltergeist was too powerful for such a simple prayer, but it provided her some comfort as she walked through the doorway.

Once she stepped inside, Lucy barely had time to recognize the whites of the tied up Hansen brothers' eyes before Chevy Hunter got possessed.

Tip #9:

Leave exorcisms to the professionals.

IT WAS A RATHER HORRID affair, as most possessions are. Lucy had only witnessed one firsthand before this moment. A rather pretty psychic had tried to impress Mike by hosting a séance to call forth the spirit he was investigating at the time. Just like the psychic, when Chevy Hunter got possessed, the first indication was wide surprised eyes before his neck snapped back rapidly. Everyone in the room screamed. When Chase rushed forward to his brother, Lucy held him back. She knew what came next and no one could touch him during it or risk losing the mortal life.

With unblinking eyes, Chevy Hunter's head continued to get jerked around, all of the bones in his neck cracking as it did so. He hunched forward, letting his tongue dangle loose out of his mouth, before abruptly standing up right. As all of the bones in his spine popped backwards one at a time, Natalie and Georgia both made a face. Chase was in shock, staring at his younger brother with wide eyes and a slack jaw. Lucy straightened herself as the possessed Chevy Hunter relaxed, stretching out his neck and rolling his shoulders.

"*Damn* that was nasty." A deeper voice echoed out of Chevy. "I mean, possessing Mayor for those five seconds was child's play compared to-" He paused his stretching to pat down his hips and butt. "Am I...wearing a diaper?! How old am I?!"

Chase stepped forward again. "Chevy...?"

"No." Lucy stated.

The youngest Hunter boy looked up at Lucy, a mischievous glint in his eye as he smiled at her.

"You've always been so brilliant, Lucy," Possessed Chevy said. "No wonder this kid was so madly in love with you."

"*What* is going on?!" Chase shouted. He shifted instantly into a defensive stance. "Chevy, snap out of this or I'll-"

Possessed Chevy lifted a hand and Chase flew backwards, slamming into the wall behind them. As his limp body slumped to the ground, a layer of dust fell from the ceiling. With a short gasp, Natalie promptly ran over and examined his injuries. Possessed Chevy was too occupied examining his new hands to pay any attention.

"Glad to know that still works," Possessed Chevy said. "One of the only good things about being *dead*, to be honest."

Natalie looked up from Chase to Lucy. "He's knocked out."

Still facing the possessed boy, Georgia lifted a finger. "Okay so I, like, totally recognize your voice, but I can't really place it."

Blinking incredulously, Lucy looked over at Georgia.

"I must confess, I believed the identity of the spirit possessing Chevy Hunter to be apparent even for your lackluster deduction abilities," Lucy said. "Given the circumstantial evidence and the fact we only know of two spirits in this town with the capabilities of possession, your own personal attachment to one of them should reveal-"

"Ah!" Possessed Chevy lifted an index finger. "As much as I enjoy hearing you talk, I want to hear it from these assholes."

In the chaos of Chevy's possession, the teens had nearly forgotten about the captured Hansen brothers. The poltergeist had not. He pointed his finger to the three Hansens tied up to their own wooden chair in a row along the wall. All of the duct tape ripped away from their mouths at once. Principal and Officer each made a face to show their discomfort, but tears came to a newly bare-lipped Mayor's eyes.

"My-my moustache...." Mayor whined. He looked up at Possessed Chevy. "Give it back!"

"Give me back my life, how 'bout dat?" With a conniving smile, Possessed Chevy twirled his finger and Mayor knocked his head back as if he got punched, his top hat flying off. When the mayor slowly moved his head back to the front, looking dazed, a small amount of blood trickled from his nostrils. Officer Hansen tried to scoot his chair away from his brother.

"Oh not-uh!" Officer shouted. "I don't like blood! Principal, trade me places!"

"No way, man," Principal said, visibly attempting to shift his body away from his brother despite the constraints. "*You* deal with him."

"No!" Officer exclaimed.

"Guys I think I'm bleeding," Mayor said.

Possessed Chevy walked to the Hansen brothers, folding his arms over his chest. It was sort of funny seeing a young boy like Chevy staring down three adult men, but at the same time Lucy recognized he was currently being possessed by a vengeful poltergeist so it wasn't actually *that* funny. She and Georgia gravitated together as Natalie continued taking care of Chase.

"Alright boys," Possessed Chevy said. "The first one to say my name gets to suffer the least."

"We'll never talk!" Mayor said.

"Yeah!" Principal affirmed. "We made a brotherly oath!"

"Gilly!" Officer cried out. "You're Gilly! We killed you! By accident!"

The possessed Chevy smiled and shot finger guns at the police officer. "Ay! Good job! You win the grand prize of eternal damnation!"

With a clap, Gilly brought forth a ring of fire void-circle similar to the one that Principal Hansen encountered in his office. However, this one was placed underneath Officer Hansen's seat. The police officer fell through it, screaming the entire way. Once he had disappeared, the hole closed upon itself. Principal and Mayor looked down at the spot their brother disappeared into, looked up at each other, and then bounced violently in their chairs while screaming at the top of their lungs.

"Help! Heeeellllllppppp!" Principal screamed.

"*Mike! Miiiiiiiiikkkkkkkkeeeeee!*" Mayor shouted.

"That fancy ghostbuster you hired to get rid of me?" Gilly snorted. "He's not coming. I've got him on a goose chase with that Japanese lady looking for *you* clowns. I've got the whole town thinking you ran away, unable to face me head-on."

Mayor made a face. "Pfffff like anyone in town would believe *that*."

Lucy, Georgia, and Natalie all glanced between each other. Even Principal avoided his brother's eye. Mayor let his jaw go slack.

"Are you kidding me?" Mayor asked.

"Previous behaviors warranted the reaction," Lucy said.

"Yeah, like, even Mrs. Hansen told me before she left that if that Officer ever showed his face again, to tell him to not bother looking for her because she's not interested in a coward who left her behind," Georgia said. "Oh! And that she left some frozen pizzas for me in the freezer and if those run out, then I can have some peanut butter and jelly sandwiches."

"I even thought you guys abandoned me," Principal said. "It wouldn't be the first time. I mean, how many times have you visited me in my office over the past nearly decade?"

"That was *your* choice! Officer and I had a city to run," Mayor argued. He nodded at Natalie. "You! Smart girl! Tell me why everyone thinks I'm a coward."

Natalie looked up from her work on Chase with wide eyes.

"Are you kidding?!" She asked. "Chase needs a doctor, Chevy's being possessed by a poltergeist, Officer Hansen is in hell, and you want a self-esteem boost from me, but you can't even remember my name?! Hell no!" Shaking her head, she returned her attention to the unconscious Chase. "This town, man."

Lifting his arms, Gilly smiled smugly in Chevy's body. "See, Mayor? Apparently once you start running, you never stop. You wouldn't happen to know anything about running away, would you?"

Mayor gritted his teeth. "No I wouldn't!"

"That's right!" Principal exclaimed confidently. "We definitely would not know nothing about running away when we should not have in order to save our reputation and livelihoods!"

"Shut up, you idiot!" Mayor said.

"What?!" Principal said. "All I said was that we *didn't* do that. I didn't say we did do it even though we did. I said we didn't so you can't be mad at me."

With a wicked smile, Gilly snapped Chevy's fingers and turned back to Lucy and Georgia.

"Can I count that as a confession?" He asked.

The girls shook their heads in a clear refusal. Gilly shrugged Chevy's shoulders and turned back to the Hansen brothers.

"Well I gotta send you both to eternal damnation eventually," Gilly said. "Whose first?"

As the Hansen brothers blathered for their innocence, Georgia leaned into Lucy.

"We should, like, stop this right?" Georgia whispered.

"Would you like to try?" Lucy asked. "My only supplies are meant for spirits equivalent to that of a weaker soul, not one with the capabilities of condemning the living to an eternal fate."

"Yeah but, like, your dad and Mara can," Georgia said. "Right? We should, like, get them here."

"Cell phones don't work," Natalie whispered as she stood to her feet. "I already tried calling for Kierra."

"Oh, Kierra's a badass," Georgia said. "Good choice."

Natalie looked at Georgia with stern eyes. "While I agree, she's also a nurse and Chase requires medical attention."

"One of us will have to leave the shack to make the call," Lucy said. "Preferably without alerting the poltergeist so we can contain him to this location until the right person, and spirit, arrive."

"Ooo! Me!" Georgia said, waving her hand up. "I wanna call Mara!"

Lucy and Natalie gave each other a look before shrugging at Georgia.

"Yeah that works," Natalie said. "It at least gets the vulnerable white girl out of the way."

Excited, Georgia clapped her hands softly. "Yay! No one's gonna die this time!"

"Aside from the kind yet dim-witted Officer Hansen, of course," Lucy said. "And, assumedly, Principal and Mayor if we cannot get my father here in time."

As the girls were forming their plan, Gilly possessing the body of Chevy Hunter had somehow arranged it so that the remaining Hansen brothers were back to back. Both of them were ugly crying as the fourteen year old boy rested his hands on his knees and kept smiling widely, the previously innocent face of Chevy Hunter looking menacing. Mayor huffed in a lip quivering sob as he leaned back into his brother.

"Princey, I'm sorry," Mayor whined. "This is all my fault. I never should've listened to Mom. I should've died before Officer and you."

"No, Mayor, I'm the older brother," Principal said. "I should've told you Mom was an egomaniac narcissist obsessed with our family name. I should die first."

Gilly let out a massive groan. "Alright, this isn't fun. I've been planning all the ways I was going to mess with you assholes for nearly a decade and now that I'm here....it's just kind of sad." Principal and Mayor whimpered and nodded their heads. "Plus, I feel *kind of* sadistic about it since the poor body I'm occupying is an innocent fourteen year old boy who would never do this in his life."

"You're absolutely right, Gilly," Mayor stated, nodding his head.

"Yeah," Principal said. "Ford would probably let us go....just so you know."

Lifting Chevy's eyebrows, Gilly stared at Principal.

"Ford? That's what you think this kid's name is?" Gilly asked, incredulous. "Is your next guess Toyota? Maybe Honda?"

Mayor leaned back into his brother's ear. "Try Subaru."

"Jeep!" Principal said. "That was his name! The youngest Hunter boy was Jeep!"

Shaking his head, Gilly tsked at Principal's ineptitude. "You know...I was *so* close to letting you guys go. But then I remembered...." He leaned into the brothers. "You're both assholes who can't even remember your own residents' names. Not only that, but you were both totally okay with letting me die on the side of the road."

The brothers attempted to share a glance before looking back up at the boy.

"So...if we remember the kid's name," Mayor asked. "You'll let us go?"

"I don't know." Gilly tilted Chevy's head and smirked. "If you hit a fellow classmate in an accident, will you call the appropriate authorities....or your parents?"

Before Principal and Mayor could reply, Gilly snapped his fingers. The same void hole that ate Officer Hansen appeared under the remaining Hansen brothers. They both went down screaming and crying. As soon as they disappeared, Gilly twirled his index finger and the void hole closed. He turned back to the girls with a sigh.

"My apologies for the-" Chevy's eye squinted to the space in between Natalie and Lucy. "....where did the pretty girl from Lebenville go? The one I should've killed for trying to make out on my grave?"

The two girls looked to the space. Sure enough, Georgia Peaches was gone. Neither of them had heard or seen her sneak out. It wasn't *quite* how they wanted the plan to go, but it was the only one they had to work with now.

"Oh shi-" Natalie darted a look back up to the poltergeist and shifted her curse word. "She was...never here?"

"Bologna sandwich!" Gilly shouted aggressively. He jolted up, touching his throat as he did so. "Hm. Not the word I was looking for, but I guess Chevy still has some influence on those things. Whatever, just move out of my way and-"

Keeping her eyes locked onto the possessed boy, Lucy flipped open her messenger bag and pulled out a pepper spray canister. She pointed it at him and he threw his hands up, squinting at Lucy. As the poltergeist possessed boy remained in place, she used her other hand to pull out a crucifix. Lucy handed it to Natalie before reaching back into her bag to pull out a fresh Bible. She handed this to Natalie as well before reaching back *again* into the messenger bag to pull out a salt pellet gun. Natalie looked from the bag to Lucy, silently questioning the contents her friend had decided to keep in her bag. Lucy noted her friend with a swift side-glance that barely took attention away from the poltergeist.

"What?" Lucy said. "Did you really believe I kept textbooks in there? Particularly given my current attendance record at the school?"

"Fair point," Natalie said.

The girls looked back to the poltergeist.

"Now, malevolent spirit, there are two ways we can put you to rest," Lucy stated. "One is negotiation, but given your aggressive tendencies, I'm assuming you'll choose the more difficult option. However, your purpose *has* been fulfilled. All of your murderers have been vanquished so your unjust murder has been put to justice and now it's time for you to go free."

Once the poltergeist had time to register Lucy's words, he laughed. He placed his hands down at his side, not even flinching when the girls stepped forward with their weapons of choice. Chevy looked between both of them, Gilly's judgement resting behind the usually kind eyes.

"Oh man. And here I thought you guys had it all figured out," Gilly said. "I mean all of the clues were right there. Plus, it's *you* guys. If anyone in this town was going to figure it out, it would be you two."

The girls glanced at each other again, with Natalie lifting the crucifix and the Bible higher.

"What is he talking about?" She asked.

"He doesn't believe his death was the largest injustice to his life," Lucy explained. "There is another injustice that tethers his soul to this earth."

Further relaxing into Chevy's body, Gilly shot finger guns at Lucy.

"Ah! You're killing it!" Gilly said. "As much as I *hated* those assholes who left me to die alone on the side of a road, the Hansen brothers were not my main priority. Fun to see cry, yeah, but I didn't deny myself the pearly gates for them."

It was rare to find a living soul, let alone a dead one, that wouldn't count death as the largest inconvenience on their life. Even in the rare instances, the soul was often deluded and corrupted by a physical imbalance of chemicals in the brain. Every human deserves their life, no matter what they personally believe. It must take a hatred beyond comprehension and logic to despise something more than something that ends your own life.

Natalie's face dropped. "The town. He's talking about all of Sterben."

"Wow! Great work!" Gilly clapped Chevy's hands together. "You are a truly intelligent woman. Both of you are, so I'd be *very* appreciative if you would help me with my plan to destroy Sterben piece by piece!" Getting very excited, Gilly raised his fists into the air. "I want every native Sterben resident to realize just how miserable and soul-crushing this town truly is!"

"And your form of education is through murder, torture, and abuse of your paranormal abilities?" Lucy asked. "Given your current record, you might be a more effective educator than our recently deceased principal."

"To be fair though, Principal Hansen never actually taught anything," Natalie said. "You could literally say the capital of Kansas is Topeka and it would be more than what he ever taught us."

Gilly rolled his eyes, looking like a child attempting to play adult in Chevy's fourteen year old body. "You don't *get it*. You guys aren't natives.

You've seen the outside world and you know how much better it is." He pointed towards the door. "The rest of them? They don't! They think Sterben is the best life can get. They're all *content-*" He spat the word out like venom. "-with their six man football teams and their lack of culture or restaurants and so anything that challenges them is a threat they must diminish."

Considering the villain's monologue, Natalie nodded slowly. "Okaaaay, but you realize that murdering the entire town isn't the solution right? It's about shifting the infrastructure with small acts of kindness, community out-reach-"

"Are you aware that the theatre program you began is actually being re-ceived quite well in Sterben now?" Lucy said. "That is a great example of community outreach! See? You did something very well for Sterben without committing genocide."

"Too bad the theatre program can't continue until we stop the murder-happy poltergeist that's been terrorizing the town for the past two months," Natalie said. "So if you could just go bye-bye, that would be great because I'm getting *really* tired of your-"

"*Arghhhhh* you don't get it!" Gilly whined. "You don't! You just *don't*. It's about this stupid town and everything it stands for! I've been locked into the borders of this dumb place for nearly a decade now! It's like this whole stupid town is on a loop. Nothing is ever going to change in Sterben. Ever. Sterben sucks. It's awful. There's nothing redeemable about this place. It smells like cow crap, the nearest Walmart is in Lebenville, and-"

"-and you are not eligible to decide its fate." Lucy stated cooly.

Gilly gave her a cold look through Chevy's wide hazel eyes.

"And you get to decide mine?" Gilly asked.

Lucy's breath stuttered.

"Your disregard for the human life within the town makes you compara-ble to the Hansen brothers, if not worse given your body count," Lucy said. "If you agree with their fate, then you have decided your own."

Empowered by Lucy's words, Natalie held out her crucifix and Bible with a bit more confidence. Gilly stared at the girls in disbelief, letting out a short laugh as he stepped to the side and rubbed his mouth. It was getting in-creasingly more obvious how Gilly's strong personality didn't belong in sweet Chevy Hunter's body.

"I...I had this *whole* plan," Gilly said. "It was the perfect plan. We all take down Sterben together, rise from the ashes, and then...then I get to live my life again. Not only that, but I get to live my life with the best family ever. The only family that ever cared about me."

"That's Chevy's life," Natalie stammered. "You're stealing Chevy's-"

"Yeah I *know* whose body I'm in!" Gilly shouted. "I wouldn't choose to be thirteen again for the life of me, but Chevy can be easily missed. A loaf of bread has more use and personality than him. The only good part about this kid was that he understood my pain."

Natalie blinked. "The pain of being dead or...?"

"The pain of this entire town crushing down on your soul," Gilly said. "The pain of having all of your goals and accomplishments be diminished by one weakness-"

"You need a diaper too?" Natalie asked.

"No! Just-" Gilly shook his head. "You get it okay? Chevy was under-appreciated, I was under-appreciated, he was in love with Lucy, I'm...mildly infatuated."

Groaning, Natalie tapped the crucifix on her forehead. Lucy remained stone faced, giving no reaction which way or the other for Gilly's feelings.

"My *dude*," Natalie said. "Can you, like, not?"

"I'm sorry, but I was a ghost and she looks like one. You have no idea how hard it is for a teenage ghost to date in this town, let me tell you," Gilly said. "Not to mention, our shared appreciation for the arts-"

"No." Lucy stated.

Gilly blinked. "I didn't ask anyth-"

"Your feelings are not reciprocated and your emotions do not entitle me to change my position," Lucy said. "Now that is transparent, please understand that my subsequent actions are not a consequence of these facts and are instead an attempt to prevent potential peril."

Without hesitation, Lucy shot her salt pellet gun at Gilly. It hit him square in the middle of Chevy's forehead and he let out a shout as he stumbled back. She continued to shoot her salt pellet gun at him, emptying the chamber into his chest, shoulders, and arms. Walking forward, Lucy tossed the salt gun to the side and lifted her pepper spray canister. Once Gilly looked back up, she pressed her index finger onto the top of the canister's button.

Instead of the prickling heat of pepper spray, a cooling mist of water spritzed out of the canister in a flurry. Natalie perked up an eyebrow until Gilly let out an agonizing scream, covering Chevy's eyes with the lower palms of Chevy's hands. Holy water. Once the canister had emptied with a hiss of empty air, Lucy threw that to the side as well. The Gilly possessed Chevy was still rubbing his eyes, screaming and shouting as he did so. Lucy turned to Natalie.

"I may have deluded the truth in that statement," Lucy admitted. "While I was intending to prevent potential peril, I also acted out of anger for his treatment of my father and Sterben."

"Glad to hear it." Natalie let out a heavy breath. "Now what? Where's Georgia? Where's your dad?"

"Uncertain," Lucy stated. She grabbed the Bible from Natalie's hand. "We must perform the exorcism ourselves. Your parents took the class, yes?"

"Father O'Shannon basically just said Mass and told them to come to him if they needed an exorcism!" Natalie said. "How do we perform an exorcism by ourselves?!"

"Carefully so we don't summon something from the poltergeist's world by accident," Lucy explained. "Try to avoid Latin and anything from the *Exorcist* film series."

Natalie darted a nervous look to Lucy. "Because of the film's curse?"

"No," Lucy said. "It's just in poor taste."

Once Gilly was able to find his bearings and recover from the holy water attack, Natalie lifted her crucifix and took a shaky breath. Gilly met her eye.

"What are yo-"

"The power of Christ compels you!" Natalie shouted, the crucifix shaking in her hand.

Sighing, Lucy shook her head. "That's from *Exorcist.*"

"Well I don't know anything else!" Natalie whispered back.

Gilly didn't react at all to Natalie's attempt at a exorcism. He even twiddled his fingers in front of his face to confirm she had no effect on him.

"Yep. Still in this body." Gilly stuck Chevy's hands in the jeans pockets and sighed. "Ladies. Again, I *really* don't want to hurt you. We would all make a great team if you gave it a shot."

Cracking open the Bible to a bookmarked location, Lucy used muscle memory to bring her index finger to a highlighted section and looked down. "For he said unto him, come out of the man, thou unclean spirit."

"The power of Christ!" Natalie shouted in accompaniment, shaking the crucifix in the poltergeist's face. "I'm not afraid of no ghosts!"

The poltergeist gritted his teeth and squinted at the girls. "Ooo I got a shiver out of that."

Natalie perked up. "Really?"

"Absolutely not," Gilly said.

"...Chevy?"

At the weak voice, Gilly's face went white. The girls turned around to see Chase slowly waking up, rubbing his head as he did so. He squinted in between the girls at his little brother. To their surprise, Gilly remained frozen in the spot, staring blankly at Chase. His jaw went slack as he continued to stare at the older Hunter brother. For a moment, his hazel eyes glazed over back to their naive glint.

"....Help...."

Before the girls could register that it was Chevy's voice, not Gilly's, that came out of Chevy's mouth, the shack door blasted open. Both girls reached their arms over their heads, Natalie to protect herself and Lucy to save her hat. The debris hadn't even cleared by the time a grid of neon green lasers encompassed the room. Chase looked around, stunned at the spectacle, as each line of lasers poured over every inch of the room.

Following the lasers was Mike Vitalis in a heavy hazmat-like suit, holding the two-handed machine that was the source of the lasers. He shifted the weight of the machine to one side as he used his other hand to move the visor covering his face upwards. To Lucy's relief, his eyes weren't angry. Determined, concerned definitely, but not angry. There was a chance he would forgive her then.

"Get out of here, kids!" Mike shouted. "Clear the area!"

Natalie moved to scoop up Chase in her arms, letting him put all of his weight on her shoulders as she hobbled both of them out of the shack. Lucy followed them with the same swiftness, more afraid of her father's wrath than Gilly's actions. When they reached the outside world, something slammed into all of them. Natalie and Lucy were both relieved to realize it was only Georgia hugging them, not an attack.

"You guys are alright!" She shrieked. Pulling away, Georgia pouted. "I thought you guys were gonna be dead!"

"You *should* have died."

They all looked to the serious voice. Murasaki was glaring murder at the entirety of the group, particularly focusing on Lucy. Her hands were filled with a green smoke that trailed into a charcoal color as she faced it at the group. Unwillingly taking a step back, Lucy ran into Natalie and Chase, causing Natalie to nearly drop Chase in the stumble.

"I'm-I'm..." Lucy couldn't finish.

"Chase!"

Charlotte Hunter came running forward, grabbing her third oldest son away from Natalie and wrapping him in a bear hug. He dug his face into her shoulder as Chadron, Chevron, James, and Mr. Hunter followed her, all looking from Chase to the shack.

"Where's Chevy?" Paw asked.

"He went with y'all, right?" Chadron asked.

"Where's he at?" Chevron asked.

There was a flash of light followed by a sharp bang from within the shack and everyone stepped back. The only people that stepped forward were Chris and Kierra who had finally caught up with the group. Kierra was holding her trusty rifle in her hands while Chris carried her first aid kit. Once she gave one look to Chase though, she forced Chris to trade with her so she could take the first aid kit to the Hunters. Chris held the rifle awkwardly as Kierra tried to convince the Hunters to part with Chase so she could examine him.

Lucy's heart hammered hard against her chest. This was real. They were in real danger. Chase needed medical attention, the Hunters had no idea what the fate of their youngest son was, and her father....her father was dealing with the threat alone. Georgia had revealed Murasaki was casting a protective force over the humans outside of the shack in case Gilly escaped the fight. She was not helping Mike.

This would just keep happening too if Mike couldn't stop the poltergeist. Gilly would do this to everyone in Sterben. Lucy and Natalie had failed to stop him and even made it worse by supplying a vessel he could use to travel the human world with ease. All of the powers of a poltergeist with all of the privileges of a living soul...there was rarely a worse paranormal threat. There was another flash of light followed by a loud bang that shook the shack. Lucy clutched her camera straps.

Her father was right. Sterben was different.

That's why she was overcome with gratitude when her father came out of the shack alive. His face downfallen and his hazmat suit was smoking, but Mike Vitalis was alive. Lucy tried to rush forward to greet him, but was interrupted by the entire Hunter family. Charlotte pushed Chase to his protective older brothers and stormed over to Mike with fury in her steps.

"Where's Chevy?!" She screamed. "Where's my boy?!"

Mike removed his helmet so he could meet Mrs. Hunter's eye. "I-I'm sorry. He's...gone."

"Gone?!" Charlotte screamed again. "What do you mean, *gone*?!"

This was a hard moment for the second best paranormal investigator in the world. Mike Vitalis hated informing families of bad news and this was the worst news of all for any family to hear.

"A powerful poltergeist has possessed your son's body and during my attempt to exorcise the spirit, he vanished with the boy," Mike said, exhaling a heavy breath. "Again, I cannot reiterate my-"

"Sorry, hold on." Charlotte held up her index finger. "A *poltergeist*? Like from the 80's movie?"

Mike stalled for a moment. "...sure. If you want to reduce what is occupying your son's body to a cheap Hollywood villain, then yeah. Sure."

There was a quiet moment as the Hunters registered the situation. Then, all at once, Charlotte, Paw, Chadron, and Chevron Hunter all burst out laughing. It was a bubbling laughter, rich in a mocking tone. Looking tired in the face, Chase could only offer an apologetic glance to Lucy and Natalie. Once Charlotte was able to get a free breath in, she shook her head at Mike.

"Mr. Vitalis..." Charlotte Hunter had tears in her eyes matching her smile. "There's no such thing as ghosts!"

"My wife's right," Paw said.

"Chevy's as possessed as Grandma on a Friday," Chadron said.

"As a Hansen on any other day of the week," Chevron said.

All of the Hunter men laughed again, slapping each other on the back as they did so. Charlotte continued to laugh as well before she walked over to Mike and gave him a gentle pat on the shoulder.

"Listen, I appreciate you humoring my youngest like this," Charlotte said. "When he's done playing in his little fort, tell him he can come up for a slice of pie."

"He plays in there for hours," Paw said.

"He's even got an imaginary friend," Chadron said.

"Better than a closet," Chevron said.

The Hunter men let out another hearty chortle. As literally everyone in the area aside from the Hunters all spoke up at once to try and correct the Hunters on their belief, Charlotte led her boys back up the hill to their farmhouse and ignored all of them by waving her hand jokingly in their direction. Chase stayed behind with Kierra, just looking at his family in disbelief. Once they had disappeared out of view, he turned to the rest of the group.

"To be fair," Chase said. "They haven't been in town for a while so they missed the whole 'Gilly is a poltergeist' thing."

"Gilly? Jonathan Gilbert?" Chris asked. "He's the evil ghost haunting Sterben?"

"Oh sweetie," Kierra said. "I thought it was obvious after he took over your show. I mean, he *always* tried to upstage you in high school."

"Oh gosh, you're right! You're so smart, wifey," Chris said. "But still, it was Gilly?!"

"Yep!" Natalie said, interrupting the couple. "He also sent the Hansen brothers to the pit of hell and is going to try and destroy the city now."

"No spirit of human origin can hold that power," Murasaki said.

"We saw it with our own eyes!" Georgia exclaimed. "There was this big scary hole and, like, when they went down it they sounded like a cartoon. You know, like, *AHH*HHHH*hhhhh*..."

Everyone stared at Georgia until she finished her reenactment. Out of the group, Murasaki stared at Georgia with the most disbelief. A soft shade of red tinted Georgia's cheeks and she politely stepped back, avoiding Murasaki's never-ending gaze. Breaking the awkward silence, Lucy nodded.

"I can confirm the actions of the poltergeists as noted by Georgia," Lucy said. "He did exhibit powers outside of expectations-"

"Stop, Lucy." Exhaustion weighed down Mike's words. He rubbed his face and looked back up at the group. "Folks, I will escort you to your respective homes. I promise we will not lose another human soul to this spirit."

Chase Hunter stepped forward. "Sir, with all due respect, what about my brother? Where is he?"

"We'll discuss that at another time," Mike said. "For now, let's-"

"That's my little brother we're talking about, sir!" Chase shouted. "My family may dismiss him and your claims, but I won't. I want my little brother back and I want answers *now*!"

Kierra stepped forward and pushed the furious Hunter boy back. "Calm down, sweetie, Mike's doing his best."

"Yeah! Mike's the best!" Chris said. "Aren't you, Mike?"

"Second best," Mike said. "Once again, the quicker we evacuate the land, the safer we will all be."

The hike away from the shack was grim. Chase was still fuming, a reserved anger Natalie later confirmed that he had only previously exhibited when the Lebenville referees called the football game unfairly in Lebenville's favor. Chris and Kierra followed behind him, looking at each other with worried eyes before holding each other's hands. The rest of the girls walked in a line with Mike Vitalis taking the rear, ensuring everyone else's safety.

After they safely dropped Chase off at the farmhouse, with Mike providing him some wards and information on what to do if Chevy showed up again, Chris and Kierra offered to take Natalie and Georgia home. Mike allowed them to do so, but only if he were able to follow them and they allowed Murasaki to accompany them.

With Kierra's five person car filled, that left Lucy to join her dad in his truck. As she climbed into the passenger seat of her dad's truck, she tried not to think of what would come next. Her father was visibly upset when she had intervened on his attempt to save Principal Hansen...what would he say if he knew she tried to exorcise a powerful poltergeist by herself? Not only that, but she lost three human lives and Chevy Hunter's body in the process. Mike Vitalis would be *furious* at any one of those facts she committed let alone all of them combined.

That's why it was so surprising when he remained quiet.

They both watched in silence as Chris and Kierra dropped Natalie off at the her house. She waved sadly to Lucy from her front porch as the Hendrixes exited the house, greeting their daughter with open arms. Lucy managed to twiddle her fingers at her friend before Mike continued following Chris and Kierra. The silence continued as Georgia exited the vehicle at the empty Hansen residence. She remained frozen at the end of the pathway leading to the home, staring at it, until Murasaki finally exited the vehicle and accompanied Georgia to the house. Once the woman and spirit were safely inside the building, Chris joined his wife in the front of the car and they drove towards home.

Clearing her throat, Lucy fiddled with her camera strap as she avoided looking at her father in their short car ride returning home.

"You know, Georgia is quite infatuated with the jibakurei," Lucy said. "It's humoring because it appears as though she is unaware that-"

"Luce?"

"Yes?"

"You know I've gotta send you to live with your mother now, right?"

There was a sharp ringing in her ears. She swallowed the lump growing in her throat and shook her head. "No-no! No you don't have to! You can lock me in the house if you have to-"

"Luce-"

"In the bunker!" Lucy shouted. "I'll let you have my camera for the rest of my life and you can lock me in the bunker and-and-"

"*Lucy*!" Mike shouted, the cab of the truck shaking with his voice. "You *know* this is the last thing I wanna do. *God* knows I would only willingly give you to that woman if your life depended on it and goddammit it does." His bottom lip quivered. "Sterben is too dangerous. For you. For everyone."

"And you don't think Nora is a threat to my life?!" Lucy shouted. "The woman cares more for her own ambitions than her daughter and you should know that!"

"But at least she has Diesel and Diesel would make sure you were taken care of," Mike said. "He'll send you to a good school, get you in touch with all of the best curators in New York so you can show off your photos, update your equipment when-"

"I don't care about any of that-"

"Well I do, okay?" Mike said. "I want the best for you. Not only that, but I want you to stay alive. So if sending you to your mother in New York gives you both of those things, then goddammit I should've done that before we even moved to this godforsaken town."

Lucy remained quiet as they pulled into the driveway of their tiny little house. For all of her life, they were the team. Even when Nora was still active in their life, it was her father making her smile, her father going out of their budget to gift her first camera, her father teaching her how to look for the beauty in the mundane. She still remembered when he first took her to take pictures in Central Park, her father laughing as he struggled to keep up with how fast she ran around taking photos on her baby Kodak digital camera.

Now as they exited the vehicle, Lucy looked at her father's face and realized she couldn't remember the last time he laughed. Was it before the poltergeist got stronger? Was it before they even moved to Sterben? Was it even as far back as before they hit financial trouble, her father taking ride sharing jobs just to meet bills? No. It was on the road to Sterben in the moving truck. Her father at the wheel, Lucy entertained him by playing a road trip game of "Unfortunately, Fortunately" with him through a bland patch of I-80.

"Unfortunately, we're broke," He said.

"Fortunately, you got a job," She said.

"Unfortunately it's in the middle of nowhere Kansas," He said.

"Fortunately, it's in a town that literally translates to 'death' in German," Lucy said. "So you should be in lots of business."

He had laughed hard back then, having to stop himself from swerving off the side of the road. Lucy missed that. Lucy missed when she could make him laugh, when they were a team. Now? Now with a powerful poltergeist on the loose, occupying the body of a fairly innocent thirteen year old who still wore diapers and causing Lucy to move back in with her awful mother, this was no time for laughing.

Tip #10:
Love isn't a valid excuse to die.

LUCY WAS ALLOWED TO stay in Sterben long enough to attend Chris and Kierra's wedding. According to the couple, Sterben had gotten too glum in the past couple weeks. Losing Chevy Hunter and the Hansen brothers to the poltergeist was the final straw. So Chris and Kierra decided to put their leftover wedding decorations to good use and hold another wedding to lift everyone's spirits. What was most impressive was that they had managed to plan the whole thing within 12 hours, hand-delivering invitations as soon as the sun rose the morning following the incident at the Hunter's farm.

Although Mike had wanted Lucy to leave as soon as possible, he couldn't let her leave after Chris and Kierra confessed the Vitalises were the first stop on their route. Not to mention, attending their second wedding was the least Mike and Lucy could do. Lucy was even glad for it as helping Chris and Kierra decorate their backyard for the wedding allowed her to procrastinate on packing for New York. It had also bought her an extra day to figure out a way to get out of leaving Sterben.

Unfortunately, the placement of various ribbons and flowers at Kierra's discretion was more captivating than Lucy could predict. By the time she had arrived at the ceremony the next day with her father, trading out her traditional black dress ensemble for a white dress and white flat brim hat, Lucy had resigned to her fate. She spotted Natalie sitting in a row of chairs with her parents, wearing a semi-formal orange dress with a twisting design embroidered into it, and smiled as Natalie waved her over. Turning away from Natalie's beckoning, Lucy looked up at her father, who had dug out a dusty gray suit to wear for the wedding.

Acknowledging his daughter's sad eyes, Mike nodded towards Natalie. "You can go sit with her. We've got the car ride to Wichita to spend time together."

Lucy smiled before bumping her father's shoulder. "Thanks, Dad."

She rushed over to her friend. Natalie stood to her feet and approached Lucy, giving her a big hug when they met.

"I can't believe you're moving!" Natalie spoke into Lucy's shoulder. They pulled away and Natalie adjusted her glasses. "Do you think you'll be back after your dad stops Gilly?"

"I don't know," Lucy admitted. "Our plan was always to move back to the city once Dad completed his job here."

"Oh..." Natalie frowned. "Well let's at least get our own row so Georgia and Murasaki can sit with us. That way you can kind of hang out with your Sterben friends one last time."

Lucy could only offer a meek smile as Natalie led her to the empty row of chairs in front of her parents. The girls sat down and smoothed down the skirts of their dresses as they did so. There was a moment of silence as they took in the scene, admiring the mix of white lace, maroon, and white gold decorations. It was a warm and delicate look, matching the late fall Kansas landscape while maintaining the warmth of the summer. Near the callalily arch Chris and Kierra intended to get married under again, the middle school band was attempting to play some soft romantic tunes with an oboe, a handful of clarinets, one rusty flute, and a off-tune violin.

Pointing at the ribbons lining the sides of the aisle, Natalie leaned into Lucy. "The maroon and white gold are new. The white lace is from the summer though, from their....last wedding. Just a few months ago." After a moment, Natalie snorted and shook her head. "This town is ridiculous sometimes."

"This town has the same amount of expected eccentricity as other towns with a similar demographic and location," Lucy said. "Although, no other town I'm aware of has a poltergeist attempting to demolish it resident by resident."

"Yeah it's a real bummer you're going to be missing out on that," Natalie said. "But you know, it's weird — is Gilly counting *all* Sterben residents or just the natives? He seems to really have it in for the natives, but that seems unfair to everyone else in town."

"It also appears unfair to those who arrived in Sterben after his demise," Lucy said. "Then again we're discussing the spirit of a overly-dramatic teenage boy. We're lucky he didn't burn down the town when I rejected his advances."

The girls giggled as a shadow appeared in the corner of their eyes at the end of their row. They looked up and relaxed when they met Georgia's eye. She smiled and waved at them, her long blonde hair tied up in a wrap around braid around her head that matched her flowing off-shoulder light pink dress. Behind her was Murasaki, dressed the same as always but with her cat Okiku in her arms. The gray kitty had a pretty black bow on him and looked very pretty indeed. More importantly, Okiku knew he looked pretty.

"Mind if we sit here?" Georgia asked.

"We saved them for you guys!" Natalie said.

Georgia slid into the seat next to Lucy with Murasaki taking the seat next to Georgia, refusing eye contact with Lucy and Natalie. Unaware of Murasaki's rudeness, Georgia smiled at the girls.

"You guys look, like, really cute," Georgia said. "But, like, Lucy isn't it bad luck to wear white to a wedding?"

"Is it?" Lucy asked. "I believed it to be worse if I had worn black and I own no other colors."

Georgia perked up. "Oh that's okay then! If I ever get out of house arrest, I'll, like, totally let you raid my closet in Lebenville for next time!"

As Lucy's face fell, Natalie turned to Georgia. "You didn't hear? Lucy's leaving after the wedding. She's going back to New York."

"What?!" Georgia said. "Omg, that's so sad."

"Your father is staying, correct?" Murasaki questioned.

"Yes," Lucy answered. "He's coming back after dropping me off at the airport tonight."

"Good," Murasaki said. "Your departure is welcome. Your father's is not."

Natalie shot a glare to Murasaki. "Even if he did leave, I thought it was *your* job to protect Sterben. He was only hired when you failed."

A chill ran through the air as Murasaki straightened, offering Natalie only a mean side glance. "I have yet to fail. I even deliberately withheld my arrival until the entirety of the population had arrived at this location."

"The...entirety?" Natalie asked. Both her and Lucy looked around. The space of Chris and Kierra's backyard was hardly filled. Pockets of people mulled around, talking quietly amongst themselves. Mike had the entire back row to himself as he awkwardly looked through the program. Had that many people abandoned the town or, worse, died?

"I still think you look really pretty," Georgia said to Murasaki, blushing slightly and ignoring the downsized Sterben population. "Okie looks really pretty too!"

The cat purred happily in Murasaki's arms as the spirit lightened up, petting her beloved cat as she gushed in his direction.

"He *is* a pretty kitty!" Murasaki cooed. "Aren't you a pretty kitty? Aren't you?"

Okiku purred.

"Speaking of your duty, we were just discussing the finer points of the poltergeist's threats against Sterben before your arrival," Lucy said. "Murasaki, in your opinion as Sterben's head jibakurei, do you believe he will not rest until all Sterben natives or residents in general are in hell?"

"Yeah, also specifically, do you think he means residents that lived in town before he died or what?" Natalie asked. "All of this is pretty important to my-*our* well-being."

She reached over Lucy to give Georgia a reassuring pat on the shoulder. Murasaki sighed and almost rolled her eyes at the situation.

"Mortal souls are always in peril when a poltergeist claims dominance in an area," Murasaki said. "But if he claims his soul cannot rest until all of Sterben has perished, then I would believe his words."

"Yeah but there's no way he should be powerful enough to do that," Natalie said. "According to all of the books I read, he's performing acts only a demon should be able to."

"Oh? You read some books did you?" Murasaki asked. "Then you must know *everything* about lost souls."

Natalie noted the spirit's sass with an eye roll. Lucy turned to her friend.

"He *did* claim he's been locked into Sterben's city limits for the past nearly decade," Lucy said. "Perhaps that offered him some time to practice his powers?"

"A soul is only locked into a certain location if it chooses to remain willingly or is cursed," Murasaki said. "Given his hatred for this town, both in life and death, I would assume the latter."

Georgia sat up straight and looked around wildly.

"Omg are there, like, witches in Sterben too?!" She asked. "There's, like, *so* much going on in this town!"

With a soft sigh, Murasaki shook her head as she scratched behind Okiku's ears. "Curses do not have to be summoned through the occult. For mortals, a curse could be the guilt of a broken promise or the weight of cruel words taken to heart."

Natalie perked up and looked over to the spirit. "So, let's say, a respected teacher told Gilly he would die as he lived, in Sterben....would that be a curse?"

"A fulfilled prophecy, despite being unintentional and unexpected, and delivered in anger would be just cause for a curse," Lucy said. "Am I wrong, Murasaki?"

The Japanese spirit lifted her chin. "No. You are not."

"So...we break the curse and he goes away?" Natalie asked. "That's how it works, right?"

Murasaki snorted, giving Okiku a little scratch under his chin as she did so. "If you believe you can break a curse when you can't even exorcise a spirit, then by all means try for it."

Natalie and Lucy shared a look before turning back to Murasaki, who continued to ignore the girls' prying stare.

"Are you making fun of us?" Natalie asked.

"Well I'm not trying to encourage you," Murasaki said. "So I supposed you could say that I-"

The spirit stopped speaking and straightened herself in alert. Okiku poked its sleepy head up, twitching his ears around. At the exact same moment, the middle school band all let out a gasp of breath in their instruments before looking to the back of Chris and Kierra's yard. The audience muttered excitedly between themselves as they too turned to where the middle schoolers were staring. Natalie, Lucy, and Georgia couldn't resist the curiosity and turned to see the disturbance as well.

At the end of the aisle was the entire Hunter family, James included. Chase and James were the only ones who appeared awkward and aware of the entire town's eyes on them. Paw, Chadron, and Chevron all wore their hair parted the same way with matching navy blue suits and light blue ties. In a formal light blue dress, Charlotte lead her family down the aisle, smiling at her neighbors who gaped at them. Paw, Chadron, and Chevron all filed into a row across from the girls with James following Chevron into his seat.

While his mom claimed the row in front of her family, Chase ran over to the girls and slid into the row in front of them, roughly claiming the chair in front of Natalie. He wore a navy blue tie with a light blue plaid shirt and the sleeves rolled up to his elbows.

"Ladies, I need to warn y'all," Chase whispered. "Yesterday-"

"Picture time!" Carol Carroll came running up, iPhone in hand, to their rows. "It's so good to see all of you teenagers hanging out and not doing drugs. Say 'Chris and Kierra'!"

She lifted her iPhone to take a photo. As everyone else managed a smile, Lucy subtly moved Georgia in front of her to cover herself from the picture. Georgia didn't seem to notice and Lucy was able to escape the un-welcomed photo. When Carol Carroll put the iPhone down, Lucy tapped Georgia's shoulder to indicate she was in the way and Georgia sat back again, acting like nothing happened.

"Thank you, Carol," Chase said. "Now-"

"So Chase," Carol said. "It's been nearly a decade since your folks left the farm, huh?"

"Over a decade," Chase said. "Anyways-"

"Do you think they'll give a word for the paper?" Carol asked. "Also, who's that handsome man with your brother? New worker for the farm?"

Carol Carroll didn't seem to notice how Chase tensed, just like she didn't notice her presence was unwelcome among the teens.

"James is a family friend," Chase said. "But *anyways*, ladies-"

"Lucy Vitalis!" Desperate for attention, Carol Carroll ignored Chase's exasperation. "I notice you don't have your camera with you....did Chris and Kierra not ask *you* to take pictures for their wedding?"

Disbelieving the adult woman's behavior, Lucy blinked slowly. "They did offer, but unfortunately I do not consider my photography to be suitable for their expectations, particularly given my mood."

"Oh?" Carol Carroll puckered her lips. "How *interesting*. It looks like they got the best photographer in Sterben to take their pictures, didn't they?" She waved her iPhone around.

"...for their expectations, absolutely." Lucy said.

Satisfied with her proof that she was better than a teenager, the middle-age Carol Carroll left to talk to the remaining Hunters. As soon as she left the row, Chase turned back to the girls.

"Alright, again, we don't have much time," He said. "I tried to text y'all yesterday, but he caught me. I've been on lockdown ever since."

"Who caught you?" Natalie asked.

"Hello friends!"

They all looked to the new voice. Chevy Hunter stood at the end of the row. He wore a navy blue suit too big for his tiny frame that matched Paw, Chadron, and Chevron's suits. With a menacing smile, Chevy Hunter looked the same as he always did to people who didn't know the truth. But to people who did know, he was an unwelcome intrusion. As Chevy approached Chase in his row, Okiku hissed and green smoke drifted off of Murasaki's fingers. Chase ran his fingers through his hair in an attempt to subtly cover his face from Chevy.

"Him," He whispered. "I was trying to warn you about him."

"Of course you were, dearest big brother!" Gilly echoed through Chase's body. "After all, wasn't it you that smudged my room with smoked sage so I couldn't enter it? Ah man, what a prankster, huh?"

When the poltergeist moved to playfully rustle Chase's hair, Chase swerved to avoid contact. He put his hand up defensively in an attempt to block off Gilly.

"For the last time, don't touch me," Chase said. "You ain't my brother."

Gilly shifted Chevy's feet awkwardly, obviously not happy with Chase's reaction but unable to do anything about it. Instead, he turned to Lucy and smiled brightly.

"Lucy, you look gorgeous!" Gilly said. "I mean, you look good in black too but white at a wedding? Very bold. I admire it."

"The boldness was unintentional and your comments have me regretting my wardrobe choice," Lucy said. "I thought I had made it clear my opinion of you and your infatuation with the idea of me."

"Yeah but you know, with the wedding and everything, I thought you'd give me a chance to change your mind," Gilly said. "If not tonight, then some time in the future. If I lay low for a bit, I'm sure they'll open the school again!

I mean, I have the intelligence of a fresh high school graduate so I'm sure I can get Chevy up a couple grades so we can have classes together-"

"Omg you didn't hear, did you?" Georgia exclaimed. "Lucy is-"

"-not going to school!" Natalie interrupted. "She's taking online classes with me."

"Really? That's super nice!" Georgia said. "Especially since Lucy's going-"

"Georgia." Murasaki snapped her head to Georgia. "Stop talking."

Georgia obeyed with a soft head nod and pink cheeks. Chevy's eyes darted between Lucy and Georgia, Gilly questioning their weird interaction. It was obvious to the not-socially oblivious girls that telling the malevolent spirit of a hormonal teenage boy that his crush was going very far away to a place he could never go was a bad idea. They were all already skating on thin ice around Gilly; they didn't need to swim in the ice cold waters of hell with him too.

Thankfully, their salvation came in the form of two massive figures appearing at the end of the row behind him. Gilly turned around to face both Mike and Chris. Chris was dressed in a black suit with a maroon tie and white gold vest, looking well groomed for his second wedding. Mike indicated towards Chevy.

"I told you the poltergeist was here," Mike said. "If you want, I can eradicate him now but it'll interrupt your wedding. Escorting him off property may or may not also disturb your wedding, depending on his mood. It's your call, Chris. Consider it a wedding present."

Facing Mike, Gilly snorted. "You can't get rid of me, old man."

Rubbing the back of his neck, Chris twisted his face. "Aw man. I'm no good at decisions like this. I'll go ask Kierra-" He snapped his fingers. "I can't. It's bad luck to see the bride before the wedding."

"Well technically, you're already married," Natalie piped up. "So you're not ruining anything there."

"I would also argue that having a poltergeist at your wedding is worse luck than not," Lucy said. "But, as my father said, it's your choice."

Realization crossed Chevy's face, a dangerous notion given the fact he was currently possessed by a trickster spirit.

"Chris, c'mon man!" Gilly's voice dropped into a gentle tone more suitable for Chevy. "It's me! Your old pal, Gilly! I missed your last wedding...this is the *one* chance I'll get to see it. Please let me stay?"

For an added measure, Gilly abused Chevy's innate childlike features to give Chris puppy dog eyes. Biting down on his lower lip, Chris offered an apologetic look to Mike before turning back to Gilly.

"I mean....that's a great point," Chris said. He shrugged at Gilly. "Just don't ruin the wedding or anything, okay? It's Kierra's second big day and I want it to be as special as the first."

With a mocking smile, Gilly put Chevy's hands up in surrender. "A truce it is then!"

As Gilly and Chris shook hands on it, smiling and laughing, Mike immediately pointed at Lucy.

"Do you mind skipping the reception?" He asked.

"A little."

"Too bad," Mike said. "Thank God your things are already in the truck."

Running his hand through his dark hair, Mike Vitalis stormed off. Only Lucy seemed to notice that her father had skipped his row to head back to their house. Chris finished exchanging kind words with the poltergeist attending his wedding and headed up to his spot near the callalily arch. Still holding his smile on Chevy's face, Gilly turned back to the group.

"Oh man," Gilly said. "I told you guys Sterben natives were morons."

Everyone shortened their look into a glare. With a disgusted snort, Chase shook his head.

"Mistaking generosity for a lack of intelligence is a fool's folly," Lucy said

"And you really think you could be better than Chevy?" He asked.

"Ah, whatever!" Gilly waved Chevy's hand dismissively in his critics' direction.

Natalie furrowed her eyebrows at the poltergeist. "You're a jerk!"

"Yeah!" Georgia said. "Lucy deserves, like, way better than you!"

With a smug smirk, Gilly indicated towards the crowd at the wedding. "Who else could she possibly go for?"

"No one," Natalie said. "Because she's an independent woman dedicated to herself and her photography."

As Natalie and Lucy high-fived without breaking eye contact with Gilly, Georgia matched Gilly's smug smirk.

"Yeah!" Georgia said. "And like it doesn't even matter because she's moving back to New York after the wedding so, like, there's like a million people in New York she can fall in love with instead! In New York! Not here! Because she's not going to be here in, like, however long this wedding is!"

All of the girls, minus Georgia, groaned out loud and shook their heads. Chevy's face was completely downtrodden, the result of his entire future crumbling before his eyes. Chase gave only a simple nod.

"Good for you, Lucy," Chase said. "Can't say I blame ya, given the situation in Sterben, but I'll miss y-"

"No." Gilly stated. "You're not leaving. You can't leave."

Lucy exhaled slowly. "I refuse to provide an excuse to appease your toxic ideology of our relationship. My departure is a result of your actions and you must accept your consequences as any fully functioning adult should."

"Okay but Lucy, I'm not toxic, okay? I'm a *nice guy*." Gilly spoke through Chevy's lips, but his eyes burned with a fury Chevy could never summon. "If you just gave me a chance-"

"Oooo don't believe him, Lucy," Georgia cooed. "John said he was a nice guy and then he forced me to make out with him and then he died."

Murasaki snapped her head to Georgia. "Who is this John?"

"Never mind John Morrison! His entire family were moronic sportsball-loving jerks and he deserved what was coming to him," Gilly said. "Lucy, can't you see my murders are justified?! I'm the good guy here! I'm killing the losers who made this world a worse place!"

"What about Betty Bells?" Natalie asked. "She was just a sweet old lady with dementia."

"I was aiming for the entire trailer," Gilly said. "They were making fun of you, Lucy, and I stopped them! See?! I'm a good guy!"

"My mother and her husband were on that trailer," Lucy said.

"More reason to bury it alive!" Gilly said, letting out a laugh.

With an unamused expression, Lucy turned to Natalie. "Why that does it. I believe his adoration for the murder of innocent lives has overturned all of my previous feelings of apathy and disgust for this boy."

Still keeping her cool expression, Lucy turned back to Gilly. "I will inform you that wishing my mother death is a popular opinion and puts you in common company with many people. Your distaste for her, nor your insistence to protect me from things that were never a bother on my life in the first place, will not win any affection from me."

The tension between Gilly and Lucy as they glared at each other could freeze steel. Lucy was challenging him to further question her authority. Gilly was stunned, his idea of Lucy Vitalis as a person shattering with every passing moment. The longer he stared, the more his idyllic image of her chipped away, transforming her sweet face into a fiercely independent woman who could handle no as an answer. Lucy continued to see Gilly as she always saw him: a disillusioned teenage boy veiling his dark intentions with an innocent boy's face.

"I'm alone...again," Gilly said. "It makes sense. I was alone in my life, so why shouldn't I be alone in my-"

"Oh my god, would you shut up?" Natalie said. "You weren't alone. You just rejected all of your support systems to fulfill your self-narration that you're some sort of martyr for your demented cause."

Chase pointed at Natalie as he looked up at Gilly. "She does have a point."

"Yeah and, like, there's a really simple solution if you, like, really wanna be happy," Georgia said. "Just, like, don't kill any more people and quit thinking you're better than other people and...hold on..." She thought about it a little bit longer. "Yeah that's, like, it."

Everyone murmured in agreement with even Murasaki nodding her head softly, never lifting her dark eyes away from the poltergeist, and her cat purring happily in her lap. With pursed lips, Gilly lifted an index finger to interrupt everyone.

"I have an even simpler solution," Gilly said. He put down his finger. "I destroy this entire town and bury all of you losers with it."

The gang went quiet. Chase darted a look to his family across the aisle.

"Well you can't kill me," He said. "Mom will see right through you if you do."

"Ah, that's the thing, I don't really have a use for your family any more without Lucy," Gilly said. "So I'm going to kill them too."

"You've called a truce on this holy ground," Murasaki stated. "You may not commit any acts of terror according to your word."

Gilly snorted. "Sweetheart...I'm a poltergeist. Rules don't apply to me."

Standing to her feet, Murasaki dropped Okiku to his feet. The cat hissed at the malevolent spirit. Gilly took a step back in Chevy's body as Murasaki's palms glowed white, straight black smoke spiraling down her hands in a pitfall of death. Her eyes took on a shocking green, the space around her eyes sinking into her skull. As soon as Gilly realized what was happening, his face shifted. He was no longer holding a smug smirk but rather wide eyes and a soft face. Reaching behind him, Gilly knocked over several chairs behind him in an elaborate show for attention.

"M-m-mom!!!" Gilly shouted, sending his voice an octave higher to match Chevy's voice. "Mom! Help! The scary lady is threatening me!"

Murasaki maintained her stance even as Charlotte Hunter ran over in a rush. She glared at the Japanese spirit and shook her finger.

"You stop that right now, young lady!" Charlotte shrieked. "That's an order!"

Surprisingly, Murasaki obeyed. The black smoke and glowing green eyes disappeared in a flash, leaving a disheveled Japanese woman in an aged kimono glaring at Chevy Hunter. Sighing, Charlotte Hunter took her youngest son by the shoulder.

"You okay, kid?" She asked.

"I'm-I'm okay, Mommy," Gilly whimpered. He hugged Charlotte's waist. "I'm just glad you're so brave."

Beaming, Mrs. Hunter ran her fingers through Chevy's hair in a loving touch. She then snapped her head up to glare at Chase.

"And what were you doing?!" She shouted. "It's your job to protect him, Chase!"

Chase's eyes fell flat on the body of his younger brother. "Don't remind me."

"I'll remind you, alright!" Charlotte shouted again. She pointed an angry finger to her now-empty row across the aisle. "March, you two! The wedding's about to start any minute now and I don't need you two causing any more of a scene."

Gilly gladly walked ahead with a skip in Chevy's step. Chase pulled himself up from his seat, digging his hands into his pockets as he followed his former little brother out of the row. Charlotte marched in line right after them, proud of her unquestioned authority. Natalie and Lucy both turned to each other, each intending to consult the other for their plan on how to stop Gilly. But before they could speak, the middle school band all let out a resounding cacophony of noise meant to resemble a wedding march.

The entire town of Sterben stood to attention, Lucy, Natalie, Georgia, and Murasaki included. Okiku even sat back on his little hind legs near Murasaki's feet. Everyone's heads turned to look back at Chris and Kierra's backdoor. When the sliding glass pane opened, a large majority of the crowd gasped. Kierra came sauntering out holding a bouquet of callalilies that matched the arch her husband stood under. Her dress was camo-colored with a hunter's orange trim and a large ruffled skirt. Even though most New York fashion blogs would call her dress an atrocity, Kierra looked absolutely gorgeous in it.

She walked down the aisle, attempting to match the middle schooler's sorry beat to the traditional wedding march. Kierra was overflowing with happiness as she looked towards her husband who gazed upon her with tears in his eyes, acting as if they haven't seen each other in nearly a century. When she finally reached the callalily arch, Chris removed his wife's veil and gave her a small kiss on the forehead. Kierra's cheeks grew red as she let out a soft giggle.

A small old man with wisps of white hair behind the ears was under the calla lily arch as well. Smiling proudly at the happy couple, he turned to the audience. "Please be seated."

Everyone took their seat. Lucy and Natalie immediately looked over to Gilly in Chevy Hunter's body to gauge his reaction. He remained calm as he looked upon the married couple and their elderly priest. The girls shared a worried look before returning their attention to the wedding.

"Dearly beloved," Father O'Shannon said loudly. "We are here today to witness the testament of love against trying times, to hear the truth behind God's greatest gift, and...to later drink copious amounts of alcohol later tonight at Chris and Kierra's expense."

The older crowd cheered at this while Chris and Kierra laughed. Despite everything, Lucy could actually feel some of the tension in her chest loosen. She had her doubts earlier when she was helping decorate the venue, but now she could see the magic behind Chris and Kierra's insane idea. Taking the time to relax and celebrate happiness really could lighten a dark mood. She untwisted her fingers in her lap.

"Now we already know these two young fools have already wedded themselves in the eyes of God, but the happy couple has taken the time to write their vows...again," Father O'Shannon said. "Just don't accidentally summon a bear and the ghost of a playwright this time, Chris."

The crowd laughed again, ignoring the fact the referenced bear and ghost of a playwright killed two women in the process. Kierra pulled out a notecard from her bouquet and smiled at her husband before reading it out loud.

"Pumpkin," Kierra said. "You are the Eric to my Ariel. The Romeo to my Juliet. The Anthony to my Cleopatra."

Georgia leaned into Lucy. "She, like, realizes she's naming *tragic* Shakespeare couples, right?"

Frowning, Lucy softly shook her head as Kierra continued her vows.

"You are the best of the best of the best," Kierra said. "Thank you for always having my back when I cover your front, for putting on great shows when I attend, and not flinching too much when I practice my stitches on you."

"That's....not good practice," Natalie whispered.

Kierra smiled widely. "As your wife times two, I promise I will always be your date to the Oscars...times two."

Kierra beamed as Chris wiped away a tear, prompting the audience to coo at their affection. He then took his wife's hands and inhaled deeply.

"Kierra, my love," He said. "How shall I compare thee to a summer's day? Love alters not with his brief hours and weeks, but bears it out even to the edge of doom. If this be error and upon me prov'd, I never writ, nor no man ever lov'd."

There was a sniffle to Lucy's side. She turned to see Georgia full on crying. Using her thumbs, Georgia attempted to clean her running mascara from her bottom eyelids.

"It's just, like...." She sniffled again. "....so beautiful."

Chris beamed at his wife.

"From the Night at the Movies themed prom night in high school to every Academy Awards from now to beyond our deaths," Chris said. "I pledge that I will always take you, Kierra, the love of my life, to the Oscars. Forever and always."

As everyone else in the crowd let out a sob or cooed at the couple's true and honest love, Father O'Shannon lifted his chin high.

"Now unless anyone has any objections," He shouted. "I dub this husband and wife, husband and wife.....again."

Everyone cheered and clapped for the happy couple. Chris and Kierra moved to kiss each other as husband and wife times two.

"I've got an objection!"

The cheering and near-kissing halted. Chris and Kierra and their audience turned to the voice. The body of Chevy Hunter was standing on his chair, but it was Jonathan Gilbert's voice who had objected. Next to him, Chase Hunter was pinching the bridge of his nose in frustration.

"Idiot," Chase said. "Only the official witnesses on the marriage certificate can formally object within *legal* reason. Anyone else and any other reason isn't legally binding and is just being rude. God you're such a moron-"

"Chevy!" Charlotte seethed as she pulled on her son's suit. "Get down from there! You're embarrassing us-"

"I am not Chevy Hunter!" Gilly boomed. "My name is Jonathan Gilbert and Sterben, Kansas is about to meet my reckoning!"

Lightning came crashing down in two strokes behind the callalily arch. Chris, Kierra, and Father O'Shannon all flinched at the action. As crimson red clouds rolled into the sky, Kierra threw her bouquet at Chris's massive chest.

"Dang it, Chris, you let the poltergeist into our wedding?!" Kierra exclaimed.

Chris shrugged. "I thought you wanted our old classmates here!"

"You're just too nice sometimes, babe," Kierra said. She then stormed forward and pointed an accusing finger at Gilly in Chevy Hunter's body. "Jonathan, my husband times two may let you upstage him at all of his shows, but I'm not him. You're going to pay for upstaging my second wedding!" She then whipped around to Chris. "Babe, Imma need my second wedding present early."

Chris turned white. "But honey-"

"*Now*, sweetie!"

Hitching up the skirt of her camo wedding dress, Kierra took off down the aisle. Everyone muttered nervously amongst themselves as Chris followed her, ripping off his tie in the process. Gilly looked proud in his stolen body, smiling smugly as the middle school band hurried to play the ending wedding song. The clashing noises of instruments gave the scene an eerie feel to it, one matched by the continually rolling red clouds in the sky. Lucy, Natalie, Georgia, and Murasaki all stood to their feet.

"Malevolent spirit," Murasaki shouted. Using the tips of her fingers in place of a sword, Murasaki mimicked a traditional Battōjutsu stance to initiate the green smoke on her fingers. "Stand down or face hell."

"No!" Charlotte stood to her feet and shielded Chevy's body from the spirit. "You can't hurt him! He has my son!"

Gilly snorted at the protective mother. "Chevy? Oh no. I'm sorry. He can't come to the phone right now. Why? *Because he's dead.*"

With a wave of the poltergeist's hand, Charlotte Hunter went flying into her two oldest sons, husband, and James. All of them toppled together in a massive dog-pile. The rest of Sterben screamed and ran away. All too happy with the development of the situation, Gilly clapped his hands together.

"Let's have a little more fun," He said. "How about...all of the ghosts this hellhole has amassed in its pitiful life? That sounds fun."

Intertwining his fingers, he abruptly cracked the knuckles in Chevy's fingers. A giant crack emerged in the earth behind the callalily arch. Father O'Shannon had barely managed to look back before the crack widened, eating him alive. As fast as he fell into it, a wave of opaque white spirits came rushing out from it. Eyes wide, Lucy grabbed a hold of Georgia and Natalie. Natalie promptly led them out of the row and all three girls ran in the opposite direction of the ghost wave.

Murasaki took a stance mid-aisle, Okiku standing in pounce position next to its owner. Moving her hands intricately, she managed to form a green smoke screen large enough to hold the ghost wave away from the retreating Sterben residents. When Gilly noticed, he turned with Chevy's hand outreached to the spirit. But Chase came up from behind and tackled the polter-geist, more than happy to pummel the body of his younger brother into the earth.

Natalie looked back to see Chase and Chevy wrestling on the ground. She stopped running and held her friends back too.

"We need to help Chase!" Natalie shouted. "Gilly's going to tear through him."

Lucy's eyes darted around the scene. "Natalie, grab a chair. Georgia, grab some of this ribbon with me. We can hold him back."

Her friends obeyed. Natalie grabbed the nearest folding chair and ran to-wards the younger Hunter boys as Lucy and Georgia ripped the ribbons off. The Hunter family got to their feet as Natalie approached. They all interrupt-ed her path.

"How can we help?" Paw asked.

"We brought the family truck," Chadron said.

"But not the family guns," Chevron said.

"Except for these babies!" James said, flashing his impressive biceps to Natalie. Chevron's cheeks dashed pink.

Still holding her folding chair, Natalie looked around. "Um....try to get the people out of town? Before the big scary ghost wave gets them? Or Gilly does?" When the Hunter family stared at her, she threw her arms up in sur-render. "I don't know! I'm only sixteen! It seems like a good idea!"

The Hunter family all looked between each other. Charlotte rolled up her sleeves.

"Well you heard the woman, boys!" Charlotte shouted. "We're evacuat-ing the town! Call in all of the favors you got to do it."

Paw, Chadron, Chevron, and James all looked at each other before turn-ing back to the Hunter matriarch.

"Yes ma'am!" They all shouted in unison.

All of the Hunters, and James, ran off with Charlotte barking orders be-hind them. Lucy and Georgia caught up to Natalie with armfuls of maroon ribbon. Looking back at the Hunters, Lucy turned back to Natalie.

"Where are they running to?" She asked.

"They're going to go evacuate the town," Natalie said. "Now what am I doing with the chair?"

Lucy made a face. "Evacuate the town? That's a better job for Chris and Kierra, if they ever show up again. With their effortless teamwork and brute strength from years of farm-work, the Hunters are more suited for taking on this ghost wave if Murasaki fails."

"Ooo I agree!" Georgia said. "That's, like, a bad move on their part."

Gritting her teeth, Natalie held her chair up towards her friends. "I! Am! Only! Sixteen! Now tell me what I'm doing with this chair before I slam it *against your head.*"

Stepping back, Lucy noted Natalie's stress level with a soft nod of her head. "Right. You're going to hit Gilly with the chair when Chase inevitably fails against him. Then Georgia and I are going to tie Gilly up with the ribbon."

"*That's* your plan?!" Natalie exclaimed.

"Well, in case you've forgotten, I am *also* only sixteen," Lucy stated. "This is the best I have when facing hell on short notice."

Nodding, Natalie turned back to the wrestling brothers. "I can relate."

There was a cat's hiss to the side of them. The girls looked to see Murasaki struggling under the weight of her green smokescreen, barely managing to hold back the ghost wave. It had grown massive, completely overtaking half of Chris and Kierra's backyard. Some parts of it had even grown into Lucy and Mike's backyard, but there was an invisible barrier around the bunker that kept the ghost wave away from it. Okiku circled his owner, hissing when it could and mewing worryingly in between.

With the ribbon still in hand, Georgia pointed to the bunker. "Hey we should go there!"

"After we contain the poltergeist," Lucy said. "He's going to take down the town if we don't. No bunker can withstand that damage."

"Oh no!" Natalie shouted. "Chase is losing!"

Sure enough, one Hunter boy finally got bucked away from the other. When he landed a few feet away from his brother, Natalie ran over with her chair raised over head with a shout.

"This is for Sterben!" With a battle cry, she slammed the folding chair onto the brother's back and he fell back to the earth. Lucy and Georgia ran forward, untangling their ribbon as the fallen brother let out a groan. When he tried to get back up, Natalie let out another battle cry and slammed the chair onto his back again.

"Ah! *Dang* it, Natalie!" Chase shouted from the ground. "It's me!"

"Oh!" Natalie dropped the chair behind her and got to her knees to help Chase back up. "Sorry! I thought it was your brother!"

"I could only hope as much," He grunted.

Georgia looked around. "Then where's-"

A strike of lightning fell from the sky and struck Murasaki. She writhed in pain, falling to her knees but maintaining her green smokescreen. A handful of spirits escaped over the top of the barrier. Gilly was off to the side, standing with his hand outstretched towards Murasaki. Lucy bent down and picked up Natalie's folding chair as Natalie pulled Chase to his feet. She tightened her grip on the metal chair.

"Alright Georgia, on the count of three," Lucy said. "One, two-"

Another strike of lightning and Murasaki let out an agonizing scream, Okiku mewing worryingly next to her side.

"Mara! Okie!" Georgia shouted. She abandoned her ribbon and Lucy's side to run to the Japanese spirit.

"Three!" Lucy shouted.

She ran forward, careful not to let her long white skirt trip her up. When Gilly turned to face her, she swung the chair across his face. It made direct impact and he stumbled to the ground. Lifting the chair above her head, Lucy brought it down onto Gilly. As soon as it hit his shoulder, she dropped the chair due to the painful vibrations across her palms. Rubbing her hands, she turned to direct Georgia's ribbon tying.

But Georgia was at Murasaki's side, rubbing her back encouragingly and keeping her lips to the spirit's ear. Lucy's face fell as the side of Gilly's foot made impact with her ankle. She fell to the ground and as soon as she found her bearings, started to crawl backwards away from the poltergeist and towards *any* new weapon she could get her hand on. Gilly got to his feet and walked slowly towards his victim, his smile once again menacing against the contrast of Chevy's sweet face.

"You let me be alone again, Lucy," Gilly taunted. "If you had just returned my feelings, saw what I saw-"

"I have seen what you have seen and I am disgusted," Lucy said. "Your disvalue of human life is atrocious as your reasoning is for it."

"You did look so lovely for a wedding," Gilly said, ignoring Lucy's words. "Too bad you're now at a funeral."

Gilly waved Chevy's hand and Lucy suddenly found herself in the same black outfit when she first arrived in Sterben, when she first captured Gilly's image in Chevy Hunter's eye.

"That is a *violation*," Lucy shouted. "I have the right to choose my own outfits just as I have the right to choose my own life! You have *no* right to dictate any of that!"

Lucy kicked her boot up, hoping the heel of it would make impact with his groin. But the poltergeist caught her ankle before she could. Gilly smiled at her.

"You're cute when you're angry," Gilly said. "Maybe if I curse you to the same afterlife I've held, you'll change your mind about me."

Just as he lifted his free hand towards Lucy, a bullet embedded itself into his shoulder. Gilly let go of Lucy's ankle and automatically reached for his new wound. She scrambled to her feet and ran back to her friends. Chase was still in pain as Natalie hoisted his arm over her shoulders to hold his weight. Behind her friends, Lucy could see Kierra reloading a shiny new sniper rifle that was balanced on her patio dining table. Still wearing her camo wedding dress, Kierra had removed the veil and let her blonde hair run loose in the wind. She put her eye back to the scope of her new weapon.

"That's the *last* time you ruin my wedding, Gilly!" She shouted. "By the time I'm done with you, you're going to *wish* my husband was as mean as me!"

Chase, Natalie, and Lucy all looked at each other.

"What a badass," They all said in unison.

As Kierra lined up her next shot, Chris came out of their house with a rifle case in one hand and a piece of a false wall from an old show with the other. When Kierra gave a shot at Gilly's knee, Lucy recognized what the bride was doing for them. She turned to Natalie.

"You should get Chase behind Kierra!" Lucy said. "I'm going to grab Georgia. We can find my father and-"

"We'll figure it out later, just go!" Natalie shouted. She started lugging Chase towards Chris and Kierra. Chris noticed them and ran forward, glad to grab Chase's other side to help the teens get to safety faster. Lucy ran to Georgia who was holding onto Murasaki without the spirit noticing. Okiku and Georgia both turned to Lucy with desperate eyes, the former mewing softly in worry.

"She's not going to make it." Georgia's voice was surprisingly solemn. "This is too much! Where's your dad?"

"Arriving shortly, I'm sure," Lucy said. She grabbed her friend's upper arm. "C'mon! We've gotta head back before Gilly-"

"I can't leave her!" Georgia ripped her arm away from Lucy's grip. "Maybe you don't think I can love her, but I do! I care about her!"

"For the last time, she is a thousand years old spirit who cannot feel the capacity to love a mortal soul," Lucy said. "To keep it simple, you are digging your own grave."

"I don't care!" Georgia said. "If I dig my own grave, then I want it next to Mara's!"

"You are no better than Gilly with this absurdity!" Lucy shouted.

"And you're....a jerk! Just like him!"

Georgia stuck her tongue out at Lucy before turning back to tell Murasaki how good of a job she was doing. It was unclear whether or not the spirit heard the encouragement. Murasaki was still hard at work holding back the phantom ghost wave that was threatening to destroy the town. Now Lucy could see ghostly faces being pressed against Murasaki's green smokescreen, screaming for release from their pain.

The sight terrified Lucy and she stepped back in shock. Against her feelings for Georgia's safety, Lucy then turned and ran to the makeshift barricade formed around Kierra by Chris, Natalie, and Chase. Almost all of it was formed by old pieces of Chris's stage shows, but now he was pulling out pieces of furniture from their house to supplement the barricade. Lucy arrived as Chris set a wooden chair on top of the pile.

"Just like Les Mis!" Chris shouted cheerily. He then ran back into the house for more supplies.

Pushing a fake rock into place, Natalie's eyes went wide at the sight of Lucy arriving solo. "Where's Georgia?!"

"She's refusing to leave the spirit who is refusing to leave her duty!" Lucy shouted, waving an exasperated hand in Georgia's direction. "If she-"

"*Duck!*"

The intensity of Kierra's warning caused everyone in the vicinity to hit the floor. A splatter of bullets hit the barricade with a few of them flying past and into Chris and Kierra's home. Once it was safe, Kierra got back up into position and continued to shoot at the poltergeist with her brand new sniper rifle.

Standing back to her feet, Lucy shot a wide eye glance at Natalie. "When did the poltergeist receive a gun?!"

"He hasn't!" Kierra shouted. She fired off another round. "He's been catching my bullets and sending them back whenever he wants. At least it's distracting him from doing any damage to anything else, *duck*!"

Everyone obeyed again and more bullets whizzed through the cheap stage prop barricade. Digging his shoulder into a wooden beam holding up the structure and threatening to fall, Chase glanced up at Lucy with an electric drill in hand.

"At least she ain't hurtin' Chevy anymore," Chase stated. With a grunt, he drilled a screw into the support beam before looking back up again. "I don't believe a word that murderer says. He didn't kill Chevy. He can't. Chevy's got too much heart."

"*Duck!*"

Chase didn't even budge as another rain of bullets shot through the structure. He continued to drill into the support beam, his eyebrows furrowing at his work. Chris exited the house and dropped the entire dining room table on the patio. He then worked on breaking off the legs of the table.

"Maybe if we make some crosses out of these things," Chris grunted as he managed to rip one leg out. "We can get some ghost protection going on here."

"The only ghost protection you're going to get at this point is in my bunker."

Everyone turned to the serious voice. Mike Vitalis stood valiantly just outside of the makeshift barricade. He was out of his dusty suit for the wedding and instead wore a silver exoskeleton that reflected the glint of the blood red sky above them. Lucy looked at it with disdain. It was a gift from her mother after her wedding to Diesel; a show of both her newfound money and the higher position within the paranormal world she acquired through this marriage, a position Mike Vitalis had worked for his entire life.

Until this point, the exoskeleton was also a show of Nora Edmund's ignorance of the true nature of Mike's work. It sat in a heavy chest, collecting dust, for the past five years. But now, here Mike Vitalis wore it proudly, taking it out on its first test run with blind trust that his ex-wife wasn't the immoral narcissist she appeared to be 95% of the time. The only thing that was at risk if the suit failed was the entire town of Sterben and all of the lives within it.

Lucy's gift was an expired roll of film.

Mike pointed to the battle scene laid before him. "I'll help the jibakurei close the rift between this life and the afterlife. When that happens, I need every mortal soul in the area to head to the bunker for when I take down the poltergeist."

Eyes wide, Natalie pointed towards the ghost wall. "That's what that's called? A rift? I've just been calling it the scary ghost wall thing from hell."

"Honestly, me too," Lucy stated quietly.

"Just don't hurt Chevy, sir!" Chase shouted. "He's in there, I know he is, sir."

Mike nodded. "I'll do my-"

"*Duck!*"

Everyone ducked and more bullets sprayed across the barricade. The bullets made tiny pings against Mike's exoskeleton suit. Lifting his metal arm up, Mike didn't say another word and ran towards the firefight, his suit slowing him down significantly and causing the earth to tremble beneath each step. There was a skip in Lucy's heart as she realized there was a chance this was the last time she'd see her father....and she said nothing.

"Alright children," Chris said. "As Mike was giving orders, I completely ignored him and tore apart this lovely walnut table with my bare hands." He indicated to the scraps of wood at his feet now. "Let's add it to the barricade to protect my beautiful wife!"

Natalie and Lucy got to their feet. Grabbing scraps of wood, they did their best to push it into the homemade barricade. What couldn't fit into a space, they held it to the wall and Chase ran over with his electric drill and bolted it into whatever spot they held it in. It was a good system that worked for the two minutes where Mike set-up his new suit to help Murasaki. Then there was a bright flash of light, a recess from the ominous light of the blood colored sky. When it cleared, Kierra put her eye to the scope on her sniper.

"Oh no!" She gasped. Pulling away from the scope, Kierra turned to her husband. "Murasaki is knocked out! Georgia's trying to carry her up here and Mike's stuck on ghost wall duty alone!"

"I'm on it!" Chris shouted. "Cover me, sweetheart."

"Forever and always." Kierra fired off her rifle, acting nonchalant at her badass-ness.

Without hesitation, Chris leapt over the patio table and sprinted towards Georgia. Murasaki was truly out cold with Georgia doing her best to drag the spirit's unconscious body towards the barricade. But her face was determined, as was Okiku's as the cat protectively ducked between the girls' legs, mewing for help. Sterben's lead actor was swift to reach the ladies, lifting the unconscious Murasaki with ease and carrying her in both arms.

"Duck!"

All of the teenagers behind the barricade obeyed Kierra's command as usual, ducking and covering their bodies the best they could from Gilly's attack. But the normal spray of bullets never arrived. Instead, a feathered fowl came flying over the barricade, smacking into the side of Chris and Kierra's house before flopping onto the ground. All of the teenagers perked their heads up curiously as the bird wiggled back over to its webbed feet, fluffing its wings back up as if it didn't just smack into the side of a house.

"Oh." Chase said, deflating. "I get it. It's a duck."

"A duck?" Natalie asked. "Is he just messing with us or-"

Before Natalie could finish her sentence, the duck exploded. The blast was enough to send Lucy, Natalie, Chase, and Kierra flying through their own barricade, demolishing crucial parts of the makeshift structure. As soon as they found their bearings, they picked themselves back up to discover just a handful of new scratches and bruises on their bodies. Kierra was the first to get to her feet, immediately resetting her aim on the poltergeist with the scope on her sniper rifle. Chris, with Murasaki in his arms, and Georgia, with Okiku in her arms, reached the group.

"We've gotta head to Mike's bunker!" He shouted. "It's too dangerous out here!"

Kierra fired off another round. "I agree with you, babe. Everyone, make a break for it! Chris and I will cover."

Nodding, Chris ran ahead of the teens to lead the way to the bunker with Murasaki still in his arms. Kierra took the rear, maintaining a constant aim on Gilly and occasionally shooting towards him to keep him on his toes. She tried to keep pace with the rest of the group, but given her position, she fell behind. The poltergeist swiftly noticed and redirected his attack. After Gilly raised both hands with bent fingers, roots from the massive trees nearby shot up from the earth. Kierra barely had time to lift her gun towards them before they wrapped around her legs, forcing her to fall and drop her weapon.

As soon as Kierra let out a surprised shout, Chris stopped the group. Whipping around, he noticed his wife tangled in the tree roots. Without another thought, he passed Murasaki to Chase who had to adjust to handle the sudden weight.

"Go, kids!" Chris shouted. "To the bunker! Kierra, I'm coming!"

Chris broke off in a dead sprint to his wife. Kierra tugged at the roots around her legs, not even having the chance to notice the confused duck flying in an arc straight towards her. But Chris, however, did. At the exact moment the duck should've hit Kierra, Chris leapt forward and grabbed the duck mid-air. He held it close to his chest as he somersaulted away from Kierra. When Chris landed on the ground, the duck exploded. Chris finished his roll to reveal a gaping burn hole through his wedding suit and grave injury on his chest, a flurry of feathers as the only remains of his attacker.

Kierra gasped. "Chris!"

A little too late, Kierra finally broke free of the roots that held her in place. Grabbing her sniper rifle, she ran over to Chris and knelt beside him. After examining his injury, she swiftly took his hands, tears in her eyes.

"Babe, you're dying," Kierra said. "You're not going to make it to-"

"-to the Oscars? I know," Chris said. He removed a wisp of blonde hair away from his wife's face. "But every day felt like the Oscars with you, love."

More tears came to Kierra's eyes. "Actually I was going to say 'the hospital', but that was too sweet and now I feel kind of dumb." She held his hands to her chest. "You took a duck for me, babe."

"I'll take a duck for you forever and always, babe," Chris said. "You're my wife times two."

"And you're my husband times two!" Kierra said. "I love you so much, sweetie!"

Before Chris could say anything, she bent over and they shared a kiss, one last final kiss worthy of a glorious finale for the most loving power couple of Sterben, Kansas. When they parted, Kierra smoothed down Chris's hair.

"Am..am I still your date to the Oscars?" Chris asked.

Kierra beamed. "Forever and always, babe."

Chris smiled. "Well...babe." He coughed before looking up at his wife with teary eyes. "I'm going to the big Oscar in the sky now. I-I-I..." Swallowing hard, he tucked a loose strand of her blonde hair behind her ear. "I love you."

With one last choking gag, Chris closed his eyes before his head relaxed unnaturally back into the ground. Kierra waited a moment, hoping her worst nightmare hadn't come true. Then, with a menacing scowl, she dropped her dead husband's hands and picked up her gun. Standing to her feet, Kierra stepped over Chris's body and adopted a powerful stance in her camo wedding dress. She cocked the sniper rifle to attention as she glared at the amused poltergeist with all of the hatred of a woman scorned.

Kierra lifted the scope to her eye. "Get ready to die once and for all, motherfu-"

Quack.

Looking down to her feet, Kierra made eye contact with the very confused duck that waddled up to the skirt of her dress. It cocked its head at her, almost apologizing for its presence. Kierra let out a slow exhale.

"Oh shi-"

The duck exploded and Kierra's body landed with a dull thud next to her husband's similarly lifeless body. The newlyweds were dead. It took less than two minutes. Behind the destruction, Natalie, Chase, Lucy, and Georgia all witnessed Chris and Kierra's dramatic deaths with wide eyes and slacked jaws. Finally, Natalie let out a choked laugh of disbelief and shock.

"....ducks," Natalie said. "Exploding...ducks....killed Chris and Kierra."

"...as it appears, yes, exploding ducks have...diminished Chris and Kierra's life," Lucy said.

"Okay but..." Natalie turned to Lucy. "....*ducks.*"

"I didn't expect it," Georgia said, lifting her hand.

"No one did, Georgia!" Natalie exclaimed. "They were *ducks*. Ducks don't kill!"

"Ladies, as much as I wanna keep debating the murderin' capabilities of ducks, let's not waste Chris and Kierra's sacrifice," Chase said. "We need to get to the bunker *now*."

Gilly was too busy gloating to himself over how his exploding ducks actually worked to notice the gang head straight to the Vitalis's bunker. The teenagers were too busy scrambling to enter the building and lock themselves in to notice how the poltergeist's attention shifted to the exoskeleton-clad Mike Vitalis, who was too occupied with successfully closing the rift to notice Chris and Kierra were dead. Their deaths meant his cover was exposed and he was now defenseless against a murder-happy poltergeist.

A murder-happy poltergeist who was more than glad to use innocent lives to take other innocent lives.

Tip #11:
Don't be a hero.

WHEN MURASAKI CAME to, the teenagers competed in a tournament of rock, paper, scissors to see who would tell her the bad news that Sterben was in hell.

"Okay but, like, I don't see how paper can beat rock," Georgia said. "A rock can, like, tear paper if you throw it through it."

"Well something's gotta beat rock," Natalie said. "The rock can't just beat all of them."

"How about a jackhammer?" Chase asked. "See? All you gotta do is take your index and middle finger, put them together, and-" He gave a hard look to the hand gesture he had now created as Natalie's cheeks darkened. "You know what? I ain't even going to finish this idea. This was a bad idea."

"Rock remains undefeated then." Lucy was in the far corner of her father's bunker with her black hat tipped over her face, attempting to sleep away her emotional pain. "It triumphs over the paper and the scissors and laughs about it."

With Okiku purring merrily on her lap, Murasaki waved her hands to silence everyone. "I do not care for this children's game. Just tell me where I am and if the poltergeist is defeated."

Natalie, Georgia, and Chase all glanced at each other to challenge the other to speak first.

"Well, first off, we're in Lucy's dad's bunker," Natalie said. "There! I answered the first one so you guys have to answer the rest."

"Chris and Kierra are dead!" Georgia clapped excitedly. "Ooo this is fun! Your turn, Chase!"

With a defeated sigh, Chris ran his fingers through his hair. "And my brother ain't been saved yet. The poltergeist still has a hold on his mortal soul and I'm...I'm the big brother who let him have it."

173

Standing up from his spot on the bench, Chase tried to pace in the limited space. Mike Vitalis's beloved bunker did well in its duty, but it was far from luxurious. The only light source was a single tungsten bulb illuminating the single room, barely even lighting the blue paint crudely painted on the walls and the religious symbols that adorned it. There were flat planks of wood sticking out of the walls a few feet off the ground, acting as benches for people to sit or sleep. Above their heads following the bench's path was shelving lined with canned goods and basic essentials. Below the bench Lucy had claimed were crates filled with knotted blankets and a basic first aid kit.

Natalie stood as well, offering Chase a comforting pat on his shoulders. "Hey! Don't be so hard on yourself. No one's been able to stop Gilly yet."

"Yeah but, if we didn't follow Chevy to that shack, if I had been a little faster and didn't let him beat me up..." Chase shook his head. "I'd still be a big brother."

Murasaki sighed. "I should have never been saved. I should have been left behind in the wake of my failure. My soul would be condemned to a tree, something more worthwhile of protecting Sterben than my own body."

Georgia gasped. "Don't say that, Mara! You're, like, totally better than a tree!"

"If you had returned with me, Georgia, Chris and Kierra may have had the time to return to safety," Lucy stated. "But you stayed and sacrificed their lives in the process."

"Lucy! Be nice to Georgia!" Natalie exclaimed. After taking a moment to close her eyes, Natalie put her hands in a praying motion near her chest and inhaled deeply. She then opened her eyes to face her friends. "Okay, guys, this is a bit...*stressful* for everyone right now. We're all saying things we don't mean."

"Oh!" Georgia said. "I thought I meant that Mara was better than a tree."

"Georgia, just-" Natalie held an index finger up to Georgia. "Okay. We had some communication issues out there. Lucy, I'm sorry I said I would smack your face with a chair. You know I would never."

Lucy nodded. "I am aware."

"And Chase?" Natalie said. "I'm really sorry about your brother, but I'm also really sorry for actually smacking you multiple times with a chair."

"Understandable," Chase said.

"So, like, guys!" Natalie exclaimed, facing the rest of the bunker. "When we get out of here, we just need to communicate better on how to stop Gilly and I think we can do it! We're a great team!"

With a snort, Lucy leaned back into her spot. "The next time we leave this safehouse, Sterben will be in hell and we will be the last living souls in the town. My father cannot handle him alone."

"Is that what you're throwing a fit about?" Natalie asked. "Are you scared for your dad?"

"I have fears for this entire town!" Lucy exclaimed, sitting up again. "Yes I fear for my father's life as he is the only person fighting against a poltergeist with seemingly unlimited power and yet we sit here in a glorified coffin, awaiting our own deaths at a teenager's discretion." Her eyes were wide and desperate. "We cannot change our fates. Heroism is a fool's glory. Only the meek survive."

She sunk back into her seat, more than happy to ignore all of her friends' prying stares by moving her hat back down to her face. Lucy knew better than anyone that if her father couldn't defeat an enemy, no one else could either. There's only so much someone can do against an agent of hell and they all had already fully exhausted their efforts. The more at peace they were with their deaths, the more likely they could move on in the next life and stay dead.

"What is this?" A new voice exclaimed. "I thought this was a comedy, not a tragedy!"

Everyone turned to the source of the new voice, with even Lucy lifting her hat to look, and they all gasped. Georgia was the most excitable, tapping her heels together in a poor attempt to handle her energy.

"It's-" They all spoke in unison.

"*Theghostofwilliamshakespeare!!!*"

"-The Ghost of William...Shakes...peare...." Natalie, Lucy and Chase all puttered out after Georgia's enthusiastic response. It took another moment for Georgia to realize her friends' annoyance.

"Oh, were we doing a, like, in-sync thing?" Georgia asked. "That's my bad."

"Nah it's fine," Natalie said. "I mean, it would've been great if we did, but we didn't so...it's fine."

The Ghost of William Shakespeare nodded as he spread his arms out. "Tis I! The greatest playwright of all time!"

"Debatable," Natalie muttered.

Georgia whipped her head around to Natalie with a menacing glare. "You shut your mouth, he's a genius."

"I appreciate the gratitude, noble mistress." The Ghost of William Shakespeare bowed his head towards Georgia. "Were you not the lass that sparred wits with me earlier? At the showing of my favorite work?"

Georgia gasped and clutched her chest. "But here's the joy: my friend and I are one! Sweet flattery!"

Lucy gave Georgia a flat look. "Are you ignoring the reality that he summoned a bear that purposefully killed Teri and Jeri?"

"It wasn't his fault!" Georgia exclaimed. "It was Gilly's! He made Shakespeare do it! Gosh, did you guys, like, not even listen to him when he was talking?"

Shaking her head in disbelief, Natalie turned to the Ghost of William Shakespeare. "What are you even doing here?"

"Ay well after some rough deals with a handful of witches, none of which happy with my interpretation of them," Shakespeare said. "The Bard has found himself wandering this earth, long after his death, and, to much his surprise, long enough to witness his own wife rise to her own fame on the stage."

"Okay, first off, that's not your wife. It's a completely different woman," Natalie said. "Second, I sort of meant what were you doing *here* in the bunker meant to prevent spirits like *you* from entering it?"

"Ahhhh! Yes, tis a story most humorous," The Bard said. "When the tortured soul, the one who lost his life too soon, unleashed the other spirits along with me...for some must watch, while some must sleep...so runs the world away."

Chase groaned. "Georgia, can you translate?"

"He ran away because he was scared," Georgia said. "How is this not obvi-"

"We get it! Sterben's education system is inferior to Lebenville's," Natalie stated, annoyed. "Quit rubbing it in our faces."

Georgia blinked at Natalie. "...is Shakespeare taught in school? That's great! I've been petitioning the Lebenville school board-"

"Okay, shush, you're done," Natalie said.

The Ghost of William Shakespeare shrugged his spectral shoulders. "In my moment of weak, while I sat with the intent to ne'er show, what do I hear but words most false, words most foul." Floating up to a standing position, the Ghost of William Shakespeare shook his finger as he paced the free bunker space. "Boldness may not be my friend, but it shall be yours. By how much unexpected, by so much? We must awake endeavor for defense; For courage mounteth with occasion."

Leaning into Chase, Natalie kept her voice low. "Are we actually getting a pep talk from William Shakespeare right now?"

"I have no idea," Chase said. "Our Shakespeare unit was *Lion King*."

"'Tis a wise man who once said," The Ghost of William Shakespeare continued, unaware of the kids' confusion with his language. "Cowards die many times before their deaths; the valiant never taste of death but once. Doth thou know whost said that?"

Georgia's hand shot straight up. "Caesar! Act two, scene two of *Julius Caesar*!"

"*I* said it!" The Ghost of William Shakespeare exclaimed valiantly, ignoring Georgia. "Me, the coward, and looketh upon my soul, for I am just a shadow of your world. Curse the witches!"

"They were Marlowe fans, huh?" Georgia asked, nodding with an all-knowing confidence.

Murasaki held up a finger. "I am also an undead spirit, but I am far from a coward."

"Dost thou speak the truth?" The Ghost of Shakespeare asked. "Did my silent ear not hear, a comparison to a tree, for your feet remain as rooted as one?"

All the jibakurei could do was purse her lips, unable to fight the Bard's claim.

"You cannot blame her hesitation to approach the poltergeist once more," Lucy said. "We have faced him countless times and he remains victorious."

"We fail!" The Ghost of Shakespeare shouted excitedly. "But screw your courage to the sticking-place and we'll not fail. He hath borne himself beyond the promise of his age, doing, in the figure of a lamb, the feats of a lion, and that's a valiant flea that dares eat his breakfast on the lip of a lion. But the smallest worm will turn being trodden on, and doves will peck in safeguard of their brood."

The group stared at the ghost, Georgia with tears in her eyes and the rest in miffed confusion. After a long moment when it became apparent the Bard had finished his monologue with no intention to translate it into the group's vernacular, Chase raised an earnest hand.

"So, like..." He looked around to gauge everyone else's reactions. "...Shakespeare's Mufasa and he's telling us to go back to Pride Rock, right?"

Natalie nodded nervously. "Yeah that's what I got from it."

Chase relaxed. "Oh thank God."

Standing to her feet, Lucy took a deep breath. "The Ghost of William Shakespeare is right. We are fleas to the lion or...whatever, but we must fight or we will end up as pathetic as him in our afterlife."

The Ghost of William Shakespeare made a face. "I-I'm not...*pathetic*."

Ignoring The Bard, Lucy continued. "Unfortunately, we are all too aware that any physical altercation with the poltergeist ends in defeat. Does anyone have any other ideas on how to defeat the spirit?"

After a moment of contemplation, Natalie snapped her fingers and smiled. "The curse! Gilly's locked into Sterben, right? Plus his whole thing is about destroying Sterben....so we just need to get rid of Sterben! Remove the constant from the equation and the variables fail!"

Murasaki snorted. "Not under my watch, I assure you."

"I hate to break it to you, but the town's already getting destroyed under your watch," Natalie said. When Murasaki furrowed her eyebrows at the girl, Natalie swallowed suddenly. "...no offense, ma'am."

Georgia raised her hand. "I, like, don't know if you guys, like, know this, but Lebenville's been trying to expand into Sterben for, like, years now. You guys have the best farmland!"

Natalie and Chase shared a look of disgust before shaking their heads.

"Not happening," They said in unison.

Lucy dropped her hands at her friends. "Are you *serious*? I thought we've discussed the futility of your rivalry with Lebenville and agreed it was insolent."

"Yeah but...I think I'd rather die at the hands of an unhinged poltergeist than live in Lebenville," Chase said. "Any good thinking person would."

"Can we put it to a vote?" Natalie asked. "Because I think Murasaki would also agree that selling Sterben to Lebenville would be a *bad idea* given that her purpose is to protect Sterben, *not* Lebenville."

Ignoring Natalie' heavy hints, the jibakurei shrugged. "This land was here before Sterben was and thus I shall remain with or without Sterben. My vote remains neutral."

"C'mon Mara!" In a surprising move, Georgia leaned forward and put her hands on top of the spirits' own folded hands. Murasaki looked between Georgia's hand placement and her wide eyes. "*Please* vote in favor of extending Lebenville! It would mean I could, like, visit you more often and that means a lot to me."

The spirit had a rare glint of vulnerability in her eyes as she looked upon Georgia. To be fair, Georgia Peaches was fighting with an excellent pair of puppy dog eyes. Okiku stared up at the two women, letting out a soft mew as he looked between them. Finally, with Georgia's hands still on hers, Murasaki let out a shallow sigh.

"I vote...in favor of the Lebenville plan," Murasaki said. Georgia let out a squeal and the spirit kept her face neutral. "It is our best chance to save this land and I do not particularly enjoy the idea of spending the rest of eternity with fellow undead spirits."

Okiku let out a scolding mew as it butted Murasaki's legs with his head.

"I did *not* vote for Georgia's favor!" Murasaki whispered to the cat.

"That's not what Okie said!" Georgia sang.

"Do not-" Murasaki composed herself, restraining her anger to appear calm. "Do *not* talk to my cat about my affairs."

Okiku responded by purring merrily against Georgia's legs.

"Alright." Chase let out an exasperated sigh. "Democracy has spoken."

Natalie snorted. "Well, *too bad* we have no way to communicate with Lebenville. Paranormal zones don't have cell or internet service, remember?"

Shaking his head, Chase grunted and put his fist to his mouth to prevent from speaking. The rest of the bunker stared at him. He banged his free hand against the rickety bunker wall to try and stop himself. Furrowing her eyebrows, Natalie cocked her head to the side, questioning his actions. Finally, Chase removed his fist and looked down at the floor with a heavy exhale, clearly ashamed of himself.

"The Mayors of Sterben and Lebenville have a direct hotline in their offices that circumnavigate traditional internet and cell service," Chase explained. "It was established during the '60's."

"For the Cold War?" Natalie asked.

"Nope," Chase said pointedly. "Hippies."

"Omg that's, like, perfect!" Georgia exclaimed. "We just have to go to your guys' mayor office and call up Mayor Fox's office to extend Lebenville! It's perfect."

"Is it perfect?" Natalie asked, gazing at Georgia over the top of her purple framed glasses.

"Why, with courage then!" Shakespeare said, clapping his spectral hands together. "What cannot be avoided, 'twere childish weakness to lament or fear, we race forth, to grasp at our own pace!"

"In other words..." Lucy turned to her friends with a soft smile. "We are all going to die."

Tip #12:
Believe in the impossible.

STERBEN WAS IN HELL. At least, it appeared to be. The skies were still filled with blood red clouds that rolled over each other in demanding waves. They gave an orange tint to the already bleak Kansas landscape. A dusty scent of smoke drifted through the air, offering weight to the hazy aura surrounding the distance. Sterben's already poorly paved streets were empty and destroyed, victim to a hormonal teenage boy with access to hell.

However, none of this scared the team as much as the ducks.

All of them hid behind an abandoned minivan, surveying their enemy. The ducks were numerous, circling the entirety of the block surrounding town hall in a capacity that would make land mines jealous. All in all, the ducks didn't look any different from normal ducks. They even fluttered their wings and popped their heads around as any normal duck would do. Just to double check, Chase tossed a twig at the fowl. It bounced off of one of their heads and the duck barely twitched at it. A few seconds later, the duck exploded and the gang had to hide behind the van again to make sure they weren't sprayed with a handful of feathers.

"Alright, the duck thing was maybe funny once," Chase said. "Now this is just ridiculous."

"While the humor of the situation is subjective, the efficiency in the ducks' purpose cannot be ignored," Lucy said. "They *are* responsible for Chris and Kierra's lives."

Natalie flipped through her notebook. "The only thing I got for this is…. 'don't feed ducks bread.'" When she noticed Chase and Lucy staring at her, Natalie shrugged. "I saw it on the internet and thought it would be a good thing to remember. This notebook isn't just for our paranormal studies, you know. I have a life outside of this."

Straightening, Georgia faced the group with the grace of a natural leader and enthusiasm of a cheerleader. "Okay so, like, then what we should totally do is get, like, a ton of bread and feed it to them! That way they'll get, like, bogged down with the carbs and go to sleep and not explode!"

"It is a tale...full of sound and fury, signifying...." The Ghost of Shakespeare said. "...nothing."

Deflating, Georgia sighed. "You're, like, so right. That's, like, way too elaborate. I don't even know where we can get enough bread for these ducks."

The Ghost of Shakespeare nodded knowingly. "For the gods know I speak this in hunger for bread, not in thirst for revenge."

"You'd rather eat bread than get rid of the poltergeist that forced you to kill two women?" Natalie asked.

"No!" Georgia snorted. "He's talking about-"

"Let bygones be bygones," The Bard stated quickly.

As Georgia gave her undead hero a questioning look, Natalie scanned the scene.

"Alright, so we know it takes a couple seconds for them to explode," She said. "So I think...if we time it right, we should just be able to run through them. We just can't slow down or turn around."

"I can provide some protection from the blasts," Murasaki said. "But the woman of science is correct in that we cannot retreat once we begin the assault. The risk is too high."

"The explosion will also alert the poltergeist to our whereabouts," Lucy said. "While I would appreciate the poltergeist diverting his attack from my father, it is not ideal for our personal safety."

"Then I will also stay behind to ensure the malevolent spirit does not reach you," Murasaki said without skipping a beat. "Shakespeare will join me as the dead cannot be killed twice."

"Perhaps, my lady shall consider, here, my position stays?" The Ghost of William Shakespeare offered.

"No," Murasaki stated.

"Well..." Chase swallowed hard. "In order for this to work, someone's gotta go first to test the theory. To establish a constant, right?"

Blinking rapidly, Natalie turned to Chase. "Uh...yeah? That's....actually right."

"I've been payin' attention," Chase said. He offered a small smile to Natalie before turning back to the ducks. "Anyways, the constant. I think I should be the one to go first. I let Gilly possess my little brother and-"

"God bless thee, brave man!" The Ghost of Shakespeare tried to clap his hand on Chase's back. Instead, his hand repeatedly went through the young man and Chase shivered every time it did. "O'er-rauhot, o'er wroght, I always say! Go forth, embrace thy destiny with the fullest of confidence."

Swallowing again, Chase nodded nervously. He gave a look to Lucy and Natalie who each offered their own silent encouragement to the task ahead of him. It took another silent few seconds of deliberation before Chase opened the minivan's door. He crawled through the middle of the minivan and exited through the sliding door on the opposite side. With his feet landing on the asphalt on the other side of their barrier, there was a tense moment as Chase stared down the ducks, trying to find where he should place his footing. A single duck quacked at him.

"Go wisely and slowly," The Ghost of Shakespeare whispered not so quietly towards Chase. "Those who rush, stumble and fall."

Nodding slowly in delayed comprehension, Chase turned back to the ducks. "...thanks Mr. Shakespeare."

In preparation, Georgia crawled into the open space Chase had left in the middle of the minivan to watch his task. Murasaki lifted her hands, allowing wisps of green smoke to lift off of her palms. With a deep breath, Chase made eye contact with the duck who quacked at him. He then took a leap and landed to an open space next to it. Natalie let out an instinctive shout and grabbed onto Lucy's arm.

When nothing happened, everyone relaxed. Chase turned around and gave a relieved smile to the group. "It's alright! Just be sure to not touch them and-"

The duck exploded and Chase jumped away, throwing his arms up to shield himself. Murasaki moved and her green smoke swiftly contained the exploding duck, keeping the blast contained. But it was too late as during his escape, Chase stepped on another duck. The duck and Chase both shouted out in surprise with Chase stepping backwards away from the duck he stomped on. As that duck exploded, with Murasaki containing that explosion as well, Chase nudged his heel into another duck.

As soon as Murasaki kept the third exploding duck from hurting him, Chase looked up at the girls. "Screw it! Just run, y'all! Just run for it!"

He broke off into a dead sprint towards town hall, ducks exploding along his path. Without hesitation, Natalie ran forward too. When she tried following Chase's path devoid of waterfowl due to the explosions, nearby ducks waddled over to chase Natalie. She screamed and ran faster, struggling to avoid the duck explosions and catch up to Chase. As the intricate pattern of ducks became chaos, Lucy ran to the front of the van and grabbed Georgia's wrist.

"Stay close to me!" She shouted.

Dragging Georgia out of the minivan, Lucy was sure to guide themselves through the wave of exploding ducks as safely as possible. Once Lucy and Georgia entered the mad dash to town hall, it was just an endless wave of exploding birds behind the teens. Murasaki was doing her best to keep the explosions away from the teenagers, but feathers still sprayed across all of them at one point or another. The ducks were relentless in their pursuit.

Finally, Lucy and Georgia's feet made it to the stone steps leading up to the front steps of town hall. The ducks continued to waddle towards their targets, occasionally exploding at random. One exploded near the massive Greek columns holding the building and caused the roof to shake. Chase and Natalie reached out to Lucy and Georgia to pull them into the front doors. Lucy accepted their offering and leapt through the doorway. Georgia remained on the front steps, staring out on the approaching wave of ducks.

"C'mon Georgia!" Natalie shouted. "Get inside!"

"But...Mara..." Georgia turned back to her friends. "I can't let her stay out here by herself. Will isn't as brave as her! He'll let her die!"

The ducks were enclosing on them, each explosion causing the building to shift in the foundation.

"Georgia, listen to me," Lucy said. "I understand you care for her and that is very important to you. But that isn't going to save you here. In this situation, you need to do what's best for you and trust that she can care for herself. Your life is as precious as hers and you deserve to live too."

After a moment too long of standing there and staring at Lucy, Georgia finally ran forward into Chase's outstretched arms. He pulled her into the building and Natalie shut the doors behind them. As soon as he let go of

Georgia, Chase unbuckled his belt and pulled it out of his pants. The girls ran to the mayor's office as Chase tied his belt around the handles of town hall's front doors.

The young ladies all ran through the front area of the mayor's office, careful not to slip on the files and papers they had left out from their previous visit. Lucy and Natalie both worked together to push open the massively heavy doors leading to the Mayor's Office, barely managing to open it wide enough for them to squeeze through it. As soon as they were all in, Chase running in while holding his pants up, Natalie and Lucy shut the doors behind them. They closed with a heavy clunk.

"It'll buy us some time, but not enough," Natalie said. "Where's the hotline?"

"The Mayor had a panic button under his desk for the police force," Lucy said. "Perhaps there's something similar for Lebenville?"

"Maybe it's this big red phone on the desk with the sticky note that says 'NOT A Toy!'?" Georgia said. "Ooo! There's a 'L' on the button!"

The remaining three teens bolted to the desk and scrambled around it. Lucy was the first to the phone and picked up the receiver before the Sterben residents could have last minute doubts. To her surprise though, it was Natalie who slammed her palm against the 'L' button. There was a single ring in the receiver placed on Lucy's ear before Mayor Hansen's Mac flashed to life. FaceTime appeared on the screen and the teenagers moved to accept the request from the unknown number.

As soon as they clicked on the little green 'Accept' button, a fresh face appeared on the Mac screen. She was unnaturally gorgeous with bright blue eyes and dark hair tied into a bun at the back of her head. Behind her, they could see the town of Lebenville through a massive window. The sky was a gorgeous shade of blue with the sun shining and cute suburban houses still intact. The Mayor of Lebenville was in the middle of signing documents when they had called.

"Alright Sterben." The Mayor of Lebenville finished signing a document before looking up at the camera and staring unamused at the teens. "Did you finally figure out your biggest landowners are liberals or what is this about?"

Chase looked around at the group to gauge their reaction before looking at the FaceTime screen. "Ma'am, we'll get straight to the point, we heard from a very reliable source-"

"Me!" Georgia jumped up and waved at the computer. "Hi Mayor Fox! It's me, Georgia Peaches!"

As soon as her eyes fell on Georgia, Mayor Fox went from stern to glowing enthusiasm within the blink of an eye. "Oh hi Miss Peaches! We *really* miss you over here. When does your house arrest end?"

"Oh I, like, totally don't know," Georgia said. "It was until they got rid of the ghost, but then Officer died or went to hell or something so like-"

"Y'all can talk about that later." Chase said. Mayor Fox's expression fell back to stern when Chase spoke. "Right now, we need to discuss Lebenville buying Sterben out and extending their borders onto us."

There was an explosion that shook all of the Sterben Town Hall, causing bits of the ceiling to fall on the teens. Natalie pushed Chase out of the way of the camera.

"Yeah, we don't like it either, but it's the only way we can be saved," Natalie said. "As you can see, we're kind of in *literal* hell right now."

"Is that what that gathering of red clouds is doing over your town?" Mayor Fox asked. "I thought the pollution of stupid was just abnormally heavy today." As Natalie and Chase let their jaws drop in disgust, Mayor Fox smirked and returned to her paperwork. "Unfortunately, the deal to expand Lebenville into Sterben is no longer available."

Even Georgia gasped at this revelation. "But, Mayor Fox! I thought that was, like, step four of the 'Make Lebenville Greater' initiative."

"It was when Sterben had anything to offer," Mayor Fox said. "But ever since this 'ghost' or whatever plague got into your borders, the land value has plummeted, almost all of your residents have abandoned the town...there's nothing of value left to Sterben."

"So, what, you're just going to let us all die then?!" Natalie shouted. "You're going to let Sterben be ruined by some supernatural force because you think it's worthless?"

"Yes." Mayor Fox didn't hesitate in her response. "If it were worth saving, I would save it. But I am aware from our medical team that there is already a successful evacuation effort underway in the town so thus I shall recommend you all leave and let the city rot as it would inevitably do so anyways. Now, excuse me, but I have work to do."

Mayor Fox wiggled her fingers at the camera before ending the FaceTime. Chase slammed his fists on the table.

"Gosh *dang it*," He shouted. "I hate Lebenville!"

"Yeah I've never seen Mayor Fox so mean before," Georgia said. "Gosh, I hope you don't think we're all rude like that."

Natalie let out a heavy sigh as she rubbed her eyes underneath her glasses. "Well...I don't know about you guys, but I *really* don't wanna die yet. I'm supposed to be a biomedical engineer!"

With a solemn nod, Chase rubbed the back of his neck. "Natalie's right. Hell, even Mayor Fox is right. Sterben ain't worth dying over at this point."

While Lucy could understand the logic behind Mayor Fox's choice, she could barely believe that she still made it. Her friends were once so determined to save their hometown that they ran through an army of exploding ducks for it and now they were surrendering. All because everything seemed hopeless to save it. All because someone else, someone who wasn't even there, determined it was hopeless. Lucy refused to stand for such injustice. Even if no one else wanted to, Lucy Vitalis was going to save Sterben. It was the least she could do for her friends.

"No," Lucy stated plainly. "There must be another way. Chase, you're intelligent with laws. Is there another way we can dissolve the borders of Sterben?"

"A municipal dissolution?" Chase asked. "Yeah, but it would require a town-wide vote, a final decision by the mayor, and approval from the state legislation so we can re-delegate our taxes to the county...unless..." Shaking his finger, Chase was deep in thought. "We can just change the name. On all legal documents, Sterben will register as a different town! And-*and* it only requires a town hall meeting vote! Anyone can attend town hall meetings!" His excitement swiftly deflated as a thought crossed his mind. "But...we need a mayor. Mayor always has the final decision, no matter what we do."

With an enthusiastic smile, Georgia threw her hand in the air. "Ooo! Ooo! I'll be Mayor! Just like Mayor Fox, but, like, way nicer."

Chase shook his head. "I appreciate the enthusiasm, Georgia, and I'm sure you'd be great, but you don't fit the requirements."

"What's the requirements?" Natalie asked. "I mean, it's Sterben. Mayor Hansen spent most of his time grooming that fake mustache of his."

"Well for one, you gotta be a Sterben resident," Chase said. "For two, there's a special stipulation in Sterben's law that automatically appoints the largest landowner in Sterben to the office of mayor if no one else can fill the position." Folding his arms over his chest, Chase shrugged. "I think it's from the old days when the town was just getting started and really had no authority, but-"

"Chase!" Natalie exclaimed. "The Hunters are the largest landowners in Sterben!" When Chase raised his eyebrow, Natalie looked over to Lucy for confirmation. Lucy gave a short nod and Natalie turned back to Chase with a wide smile. "You can be mayor!"

Not taking his stern eyes off of Natalie, Chase shook his head. "No. That ain't correct. It's the Hansens. The Hunters forfeited some of their land back in the 1800's to the Hansens, so even though we gained some more back when we married into the Bells, wait..." Chase fell deep in thought.

"If I recall correctly, the Wilsons have also bestowed their land onto your family," Lucy offered. "Their plot of land combined with your current holdings gives you an advantage against the Hansens."

"The words of the undead don't hold up in court, but y'all might be right," Chase said. "The Bells were the third largest landowners and if we got half of their land back in the 70's..." He looked up at the girls. "Can I have a calculator?"

The building shook violently, causing some of the ancient books to fall from the shelving around them. The teens gathered their balance and Natalie looked up at Chase.

"Let's just trust your family's got enough land for you to be mayor," Natalie said. "Do you need to be eighteen?"

"Kansas doesn't have any laws regarding the age of a mayoral candidate so even Chevy could be mayor if we wanted," Chase said. "Either way, I'll be eighteen in January so if we want to hold a formal election then-"

"Okay great!" Natalie clapped her hands together. "You're mayor! Congrats, Mayor Hunter! Now re-name the town so we can get out of hell!"

"Hold on now!" Putting his palms up, Mayor Hunter accepted his new position with an easy confidence. "I just told y'all we need a closed town hall meeting with a vote to do this. If this is how we're saving Sterben, we're following every step perfectly."

The girls groaned. There was another violent shake to the building, knocking more books off the shelves. Despite the imminent danger, Chase stood his ground, folding his arms over his chest. Looking between the heavy doors and the new mayor of Sterben, Natalie let out a heavy sigh.

"Alright Mayor Han-*Hunter*, Mayor Hunter," She said. "Let's get this over with....*quickly*, please."

Nodding, Chase walked over to his new desk with long strides. "Anyone have nice handwriting? We definitely need minutes."

"Me!!" Georgia said. "I'll take notes."

She dutifully skipped to Chase's desk. He sat down in the leather seat and scrambled through the mayor's desk, grabbing a pen and an empty piece of paper for Georgia. With a smile, Georgia took the materials and turned to Natalie and Lucy.

"This is fun!" Georgia whispered.

"Okay first item on today's agenda," Chase said. "A motion to re-name the town of Sterben, Kansas. All in favor say 'aye'?"

Natalie and Lucy couldn't say 'aye' fast enough, both of them even raising their hands in approval. Georgia lifted her pen in approval as well before jotting down a note on her piece of paper. Folding his hands on top of the desk, Chase turned to the girls.

"Now, given the limited size of this meeting, we will require a unanimous vote in favor of the new name," Chase said. "What should the new name be?"

At this, the teens balked. Looking between each other, all of them realized that they never planned to get this far. Only Chase seemed confident, awaiting his citizens' answers. Finally, Natalie turned to the new mayor with unsure eyes.

"St-Sterben...ville?" She offered.

Chase gave a short nod. "Okay. Make your case for it."

"Um....I have no idea?" Natalie said. "I just added a 'ville' to the end of the original name? Because I'm not very creative and currently panicking?"

"Ooo! Lucy's creative!" Georgia said. "What's your idea, Lucy?!"

There was a sharp bang against the heavy doors behind them, causing everyone to jump. Then the doors rattled precariously, the result of someone trying their hardest to break through the impossibly heavy gateway. Swallowing a new lump in her throat, Lucy turned to Mayor Hunter.

"We should rename the town after Chris and Kierra," Lucy said. "In honor of their sacrifice and devotion to their community and neighbors."

"That's a great idea!" Chase said. "What was their last name?"

Everyone looked between each other, waiting for the other to answer. Meanwhile, the heavy doors continued to rattle. Natalie had wide eyes.

"Are you kidding me?!" She exclaimed. "*No* one knows their last name?!"

"Do you?" Lucy asked.

"No!" Natalie said. "I never needed to."

There was another loud bang against the large doors.

"You know, like, Topeka once called themselves Google," Georgia said. "Maybe we could be, like, Yahoo. Oh! Or AOL. I love AOL."

When there was a bang against the heavy doors tremendous enough to knock all of the remaining books off of the shelving adjacent to the door, Chase threw his hands up. "We're running out of time! Georgia, write down all the suggestions on four separate ballots. We vote *now*."

Georgia did what was requested of her with happy enthusiasm. Her hands moved swiftly across four pieces of paper, her loopy handwriting remaining pristine across all four ballots. Mayor Hunter bounced his knee nervously, watching his new secretary work as fast as she could. Natalie and Lucy were both checking the rattling wooden doors behind them and at Georgia's work, trying to gauge which one would come first.

As soon as Georgia finished the final line on the last box of the last ballot, the heavy doors stopped rattling. Worried, everyone turned to the doors rather than their ballots. When it appeared safe, they all grabbed an individual ballot and looked at the options on it. Before anyone could even put their own pen to the paper, the wooden doors burst open with a splintering blast. Everyone instinctively shielded themselves from the damage, throwing their arms in front of their faces.

Looking bloody and beaten, the body of Chevy Hunter as possessed by Jonathan Gilbert stormed through the wreckage. When Lucy's eyes landed on the spirit, she let out a shocked gasp and felt weak in her knees. If he survived and stood before them....then her father...Lucy grabbed onto Natalie's shoulder. Her friend was more than willing to support Lucy's weight. Gilly matched Lucy's eye before spreading his arms out.

"Lucyyyyy!" He shouted, a scowl painted on Chevy Hunter's sweet face. "I'm home!"

"Mara…" Georgia whispered, her happy face falling.

Lucy's fear turned into rage as she pushed away her friend and stormed towards the intruder. "What did you do to my father? How did you get in here you sick-"

"Lucy, the vote!" Natalie shouted. "Just vote and it'll get rid of him!"

"Oh it'll be hard to vote when you're all *dead*," Gilly shouted.

Lifting Chevy's arm, Gilly smiled menacingly as planks of wood pulled themselves from the floor. Bolting over the desk, Chase ran towards the poltergeist, intent on tackling the creature. Before he could reach the body of his younger brother, two planks of splintered wood shot up from the floorboards and crossed into Chase's clothes, heaving the new mayor several feet upwards. As Chase squirmed against his unconventional restraints, Natalie's eyes went wide.

"No!" She screamed.

Before she could move towards Chase to help him, Gilly flattened his palm and sent Natalie flying back into Mayor Hansen's portrait. The oils from the painting melted into a nightmarish substitute for quicksand, absorbing Natalie's body into the image. Grimacing, Natalie worked to break free from the portrait.

"Oh c'mon!" Natalie shouted, clawing her nails into the oily colors to try and rip free. "This was a nice dress, you jerk!"

Lucy and Georgia tried to reach for Natalie to pull her out from her unusual entrapment, but they swiftly discovered that their feet were sinking into the wooden floor. Grabbing their legs, both ladies failed at pulling themselves free.

Georgia's face twisted in frustration. "Oh poisonous bunch-backed toad!"

Chase let out a grunt and reached his arms to the plank of wood lifting him from the back of his shirt. "Y'all….gotta vote! Don't worry about me! I was gonna concede the mayor's vote to that of the majority's anyways."

"You guys are supposed to be dead!" Gilly shouted. "Why won't you *die?*"

Hooking Chevy's fingers, Gilly looked frustrated as he summoned another plank of wood, sharpened at the end, to shoot towards Chase's throat. It slowed down, the tip of the plank barely grazing Chase's neck. Moving his hands from the plank of wood holding him up, Chase grabbed onto the plank directly below his throat and tried to push it away. Natalie's torso sunk deeper into the painting, her nails and fingers stained by the musty oil during her attempted escape. Lucy and Georgia were each about shin-deep into the floor, but remained closest to the desk where all four ballots remained. They shared a look.

"Hey Lucy," Georgia said. "Should we, like-"

"Vote even if it risks our lives in the process?" Lucy asked. "Absolutely."

"OMG that's a great idea!" Georgia said. "I was going to say that we should convince Chase to try and talk Gilly out of, like, possessing his little brother."

Lucy blinked. "...what?"

"You know? Like Oliver and Orlando in *As You Like It*?" Georgia asked. "After Orlando gets rid of the evil snake in the forest, Oliver's suddenly super nice to Orlando. Chase just, like, needs to get rid of Gilly and Chevy will be super nice again."

Lucy blinked again. "That....that isn't how exorcisms traditionally work, but I suppose we're in no position to worry about failure."

The girls were now knee-deep into the wooden floor. Natalie's twisted braids were now embedded in the painting, holding her head in place. If Chase's Adam Apple bobbed, it would touch the spike positioned near his throat. Lucy turned her head towards the new mayor.

"Chase! Speak to the spirit as if he were your brother!" Lucy shouted. "We will continue the vote."

"Why?" Chase choked out.

"There's a reason why he hasn't killed us yet!" Natalie shouted from her spot in the painting. "And it's not because the hormonal teenage boy suddenly went good!"

It took a moment for Chase to realize what Natalie was saying. Finally, Chase grunted as he turned back to Gilly, continuing to push the spike away as he did so. "Hey, *hey* poop for brains! Need your diaper changed yet?"

With beads of sweat intertwining with the bloodied cuts on Chevy's sweet face, Gilly scowled. "Poop for...?" Confusion crossed Chevy's hazel eyes before the poltergeist shook his head. "Stop trying to distract me while I'm trying to kill you!"

Lucy turned to Georgia. "We need to vote so that Gilly's spirit is cast out of Sterben forever."

"Good idea!" Georgia reached for her ballot. She then furrowed her eyebrows at the three remaining ballots and looked up at Lucy. "But...we need Natalie's vote."

The two girls looked up at Natalie who was now heavily sunken into the oil painting. Only her face, forearms, and shins remained. There was no way for the young scientist to reach her ballot and no way for her friends to reach her as they were sinking into the wooden floor at an alarming rate. Pursing her lips, Natalie flicked her forearms out in an attempt to shrug.

"Well, I don't mean to be a *pain*-ting for you guys," Natalie said. "But try not to *Dali* figuring out how to have me vote when I'm being Han Solo-d here, okay?"

Lucy's face fell flat. "Puns? At a time like this?"

Natalie smiled. "It's the only thing *O'Keefe*-ing me going."

"Boo!" Georgia said, giving Natalie a thumbs down.

As Lucy and Georgia returned their attention to their ballots, Chase was working hard to keep the approaching stake from stabbing into the front of his throat. Gilly furrowed Chevy's eyebrows, glaring in frustration as the older Hunter brother resisted the poltergeist's attack.

"I know what you're trying to do!" Gilly accused. "But your brother is dead! I killed him! Chevy Hunter is no more!"

"Alright calm down, edgelord," Chase said. "No one can kill Chevy's spirit that easily. The kid was relentless."

A massive flinch overtook the poltergeist, jerking the boy backwards. Recovering, Gilly looked at Chase with surprise in Chevy's hazel eyes. Shaking his head again, Gilly grit his teeth.

"STOP!" Gilly screamed, panic edging his voice. The walls of the mayor's office shook again. "You can't stop me! I have spent the past nearly decade honing my powers for this moment. I have taken down the second best paranormal private investigator in the world and I will take you down too!"

"No. You won't." Chase said, his voice holding a resting power behind it. "Because you're my little brother and for how much I pick on you, for how much you pick on me, you love me as much as I love you and I ain't leaving here until I get you back."

Gilly's confidence faltered. Tears came to Chevy's hazel eyes despite Gilly's scowl still holding on his face.

"You're....not-" Gilly shook Chevy's head. "No. No one loves me. I'm alone in this world."

As Gilly's hand tensed in his attempt to push the stake of wood into Chase's neck, Georgia and Lucy were now hip-deep into the floor with each of their completed ballots in hand. Natalie remained sunken into the portrait, now only her wrists and face were exposed. In a vain attempt to complete the vote, Georgia reached for Natalie the best she could. Natalie wiggled her fingers in that direction. The piece of paper was only off by at least a foot.

"Stop! You'll only hurt yourselves and waste more time," Lucy said. "Can we do a verbal vote? Like when we put the initiative into motion?"

"Isn't that, like, cheating?" Georgia asked. "Plus when we announce the change to the rest of the town, we should, like, totally have some written proof of it. I feel like that's more official."

Lucy nodded. "You're right. Written proof will also increase the strength of this plan working against the poltergeist."

"So how are we going to get the ballot to Natalie?" Georgia asked.

With a deep sigh, Lucy removed her flat brim hat to run her fingers in her white hair. Georgia's eyes went wide.

"I don't have a clue," Lucy said. "Do you think we could-"

"Your hat!" Georgia exclaimed. "It looks like a Frisbee!"

Blinking, it took Lucy a moment to register what Georgia was saying. "...we're not going to-"

"Oh, like, we're *totally* using it as a Frisbee!" Georgia snatched the hat from Lucy's hands and dumped Natalie's empty ballot with a pen into the inner lining of the hat. She then turned to Natalie. "Okay! We're, like, gonna throw this at you and you can catch it and fill out your ballot! Does that sound like a good plan?"

"Whatever you guys are going to do, just *Van Gogh* for it," Natalie said. "Time is *Monet,* after all."

"Okay! Three, two, one, *go!*" Georgia threw the hat. Both Natalie and Lucy shouted out in a panic. But then Natalie caught it. She looked in surprise at how Lucy's hat was now in her right hand before staring at Georgia with the same wide eyes.

"That was...." Lucy said. "Lucky?"

"*Lucky*?!" Natalie shouted. "That was a *miracle!* What the heck, Georgia?!"

Georgia shrugged. "You told me to go for it."

"You know...we'd be in a real *Picasso* of a situation if you didn't catch that." When Natalie's face fell flat, Lucy smiled. "You know? Like *pickle* but-"

"Yeah I got it."

As Natalie worked on filling her ballot, Chase barely dodged the wooden spike as it darted towards his throat by turning his head away from it. When the spike retreated, he looked down at his little brother with wide eyes.

"Chevy, I know you're in there!" Chase shouted. "You're stronger than this! You don't need to do this!"

"Stop pretending you care about him!" Gilly roared. "You don't care about him! You've always been mean to him! That's why he came to *me,* not *you.*"

"What are you talking about?! Of course I care about my little bro!" Chase shouted. "Remember how hard you cried when Chadron replaced your Elmo pull-ups with boxers?"

Chevy's hazel eyes widened as the memory flashed across Gilly's mind.

"No..." Gilly whimpered.

"He was just tryin' to get you prepared for high school, bud, but he was too mean about it," Chase said. "So do you remember how I covered Chevron's chores for a week so I could sneak away with you to get new pull-ups?"

Gilly twitched as he struggled to shake Chevy's head. The stake inched closer to Chase's throat again. This time, Chase didn't try to stop it. He just hung lazily off of his planks of wood as he looked down at his little brother.

"We...we got ice cream too," Gilly's voice said, quietly dropping in octaves.

Barely even realizing his plan was working, Chase smiled. "Yeah buddy, we did! And do you remember what I told Mom when we got back, when she asked where we went?"

With tears in his eyes, Gilly heaved in a heavy breath. "No. No, no no, no! I wasn't there! I...was....*wasn't* there."

"I told Mom we went out for a drive," Chase said.

"No," Gilly seethed. The tears were dripping from Chevy's eyes in heavy streams. "My name is Jonathan Gilbert!"

Chase continued, barely noticing how the planks of wood holding him up started rescinding back into their original spots. As he was brought closer to the floor, the stake of wood remained pointed at his throat. Gilly focused all of his power on that stake of wood, slowing down the girls' descent into the wooden flooring and oil portrait. Lucy and Georgia worked on pulling themselves out of the ground.

"I never told Mom you went back to pull-ups-"

"My friends call me Gilly!" Gilly shouted. His hand was shaking violently in front of him. "I am the most powerful poltergeist to hit Sterben!"

"I never told her about the bad nights when you still wet your sheets-"

"I was supposed to go to DePaul!" Gilly screamed desperately. "I was the best actor of my class! I was going to be on Broadway!"

"I didn't tell anyone-"

"I don't want to die!" Gilly screamed, his voice cracking on the last word. At this, Chase stopped his taunting. Even Lucy and Georgia halted their attempts to save themselves to look over at the scene. Chase's feet met the floor and he looked at his poltergeist possessed little brother.

But it was no longer an all-powerful poltergeist threatening to kill an entire town in front of them. Instead it was a scared teenage boy in an innocent boy's body. Tears and snot had contorted his face into a pathetic excuse for a villain. Despite all of the murdering and destruction the poltergeist caused, he was still a kid. A kid who was unfairly taken too early from life and never got the chance to redeem himself.

Unhooking himself from the wooden planks, Chase walked calmly over to the spirit. Gilly sniffled and stared sadly up at the older Hunter boy. The stake remained aimed at Chase's throat, more in defense than offense at this point. Not looking away from the poltergeist, Chase leaned down and put his hands on his knees to match his little brother's eye.

Softly, Chase shook his head.

"I don't care." Chase's nostrils flared. "Nobody messes with my little brother like that." His hazel eyes scanned Chevy's face, examining for any sign of weakness. "Because do you know who still washes your sheets after you wet the bed so you won't get in trouble?"

The air was quiet, tense. Gilly swallowed another large breath, struggling to survive against the twitching and the crying. "...no."

Chase smirked. "Well 'cause I do."

As Chase moved towards the poltergeist, the stake of wood went flying through the air. But Chase had ducked, aiming to grab his little brother. Pulling Chevy into him, Chase wrapped him into the biggest bear hug an older sibling could give. At the same time, Georgia grabbed the ballot from Natalie's hand and looked over it before smiling up in Chase's direction.

"Mayor Hunter, the motion has passed!" She announced. "With an unanimous vote of 3 to 0, Sterben, Kansas will now be known as....Sterbenville, Kansas."

The stake of wood previously aimed at Chase's head stabbed right into Mayor Hansen's painted forehead above Natalie. She let out an ear-piercing scream.

"Gosh *darn it!*" She yelled out. "I'm so done with this nearly dying nonsense! Just get me *out of here.*"

Noticing Natalie was still stuck in the painting, Lucy and Georgia ran over and tried to dig her out of what remained of the oil painting around her torso. Chevy relaxed in Chase's arms and inhaled a massive gulp of air. As soon as he caught his breath, Chevy hugged his brother back as tight as he could. Chase tightened his hold, digging his face into Chevy's shoulder.

"Chase..." Chevy gasped into his brother's shoulder. "How did you know he was trying to trick you?"

"I didn't," Chase confessed.

"Can we have some help?" Lucy asked, still holding onto Natalie's arm as she and Georgia attempted to yank the girl out of the painting. "We could use another pair of hands."

The Hunter boys ran over. Chevy and Chase were both unafraid to dig their hands into the dried oily substance, getting their nails and fingers stained by the dark paint in their attempt to free Natalie. With the girls yanking on Natalie's arms and the Hunters digging into the portrait, the group was able to successfully pull her out of the portrait. She landed roughly into Chase's chest and he held her until she found her balance. Once she did, she looked up and her cheeks darkened when she realized her savior's identity.

"Oh! Um...thanks Chase, Mayor! Mayor Hunter!" Clearing her throat, Natalie brushed some of the oil paint flecks off of her orange dress. "That was...great. You did great!"

"Aw it was nothing." Now Chase's cheeks grew red. "Less stressful than Election Day on the farm, ya know."

"Oooo!" Chevy Hunter cooed. "Chase has a crush on Natalie!"

The mayor's entire face went beet red and Chevy laughed. Chase smacked his brother's shoulder. "Shut up! I'm the mayor now, you know. You gotta treat me with respect!"

"The mayor of what? The Mayor of Poopsville?" Chevy asked.

For a moment, Lucy thought Chase would lash out at his younger brother again. But instead, Chase offered a proud smirk before clapping his little brother on the shoulder.

"You're getting the hang of it," He said.

"Okay, but more importantly, *what* was that with me in the painting and you guys in the ground?!" Natalie asked, facing Lucy and Georgia. "I thought I was going to drown in Mayor Hansen! My nightmares are going to be a wreck for *weeks*."

Lucy shrugged. "If it's any consolation, I think I got a splinter, maybe?"

"Ooo on like your shin or something? Me too." Georgia reached down for her legs. "Yeah that was really the worst."

Natalie rolled her eyes. "I can't believe white privilege is *still* at work even with the undead!"

Georgia let out a gasp. "Mara! I wonder if she's okay if Gilly got through her!"

"And my father!" Lucy exclaimed. "He had to get through my father before he got through Murasaki."

Without another word, the two young women bolted to the front door of the town hall. Natalie and the Hunter brothers followed their friends with Chase holding onto his pants as he ran after them. His impromptu belt lock was split in half with the door swinging partially open. Lucy burst through the door first and embraced the open Sterbenville air. Georgia joined her side and they scanned the scene before them.

The blood red clouds were clearing away, revealing a muted blue sky behind them. There were thousands of duck feathers scattered across the stairs and stone pathway surrounding Town Hall. A gust of wind shot by, whipping a few of them into a gentle spin. The air no longer smelt exclusively of smoke and sulfur. Instead, there was a crisp chill to the atmosphere with a hint of moisture to it all.

Across the flurry of duck feathers on the asphalt street were the small army of luxury cars from the Hunters' land with mud on their fancy tires, Chase's old blue truck, and the minivan they had all previously hidden behind. The Hunters mulled around their vehicles, looking nervous and unsure of the situation. Paw and Chadron both peered up at the sky, hopeful that they weren't imagining the red clouds disappearing. James and Chevron remained stoic around each other, only sharing a single glance before looking up at the sky as well.

Meanwhile, Charlotte Hunter was peering towards Town Hall with both hands shading her eyes. When she discovered Lucy and Georgia emerging from the building, her face lit up and she turned her head over to her boys.

"They're okay!" Charlotte shouted.

With a wide smile, she enthusiastically indicated for the girls to join them. Lucy and Georgia ran over to the family. As they approached the vehicles, they were surprised to see more guests from the wedding emerging from them, trusting everything was safe. Despite the newfound commotion, Charlotte strode over to the tail end of Chase's truck. Lucy and Georgia redirected their path and followed Charlotte.

"We're mighty happy y'all came out when you did," Charlotte said. "The town was ready to set the whole building on fire. Something about a sacrifice the Hansens had promised?"

Georgia and Lucy shared a look before looking back up at the Hunter matriarch.

"But wait..." Lucy stepped forward to match Charlotte's step. "Did you bring them all back to save us?"

"We did, but it wasn't our idea," Charlotte said. "It was everyone else who wanted to come back and save Sterben. We were just the transport and auxiliary support."

"Charlotte!" Paw shouted. "Boys are out!"

The mother stopped at the end of Chase's truck and smiled before turning to the girls.

"Just wait right here, ladies," Charlotte said. "I'm comin', Chandler!"

As Charlotte ran off, Georgia and Lucy shared a glance before looking back to the crowd gathering at the steps of Town Hall. Sure enough, everyone who had cared enough to survive Sterben long enough for Chris and Kierra's wedding had returned to the town. The middle school band, their parents, the Carrolls, and every other face Lucy was sure she had seen at one point or another during her adventure in Sterben was there again. They were all prepared to fight for their small hometown, despite the risk. Smiling, Georgia leaned into Lucy.

"Can you believe Mayor Fox called this worthless?" Georgia asked.

Pleasantly surprised, Lucy shook her head. "It appears Lebenville really is the worst."

As Georgia let out a giggle, a strong force slammed into the Lebenville native's body. Georgia took a step back to accommodate the intrusion before realizing it was just Murasaki hugging her tightly.

"I am glad you are okay, Georgia Peaches of Lebenville!" Murasaki pulled away and smiled at Georgia. "Not a scratch on you. Not bad for a mortal soul who faced a powerful malevolent spirit."

"Um....yeah!" Georgia smiled, her eyes unable to process what was happening. "Uh...Lucy survived too! Like, totally not a scratch on her too!"

Backing away from Georgia, Murasaki gave a simple head nod and attempted a friendly smile towards Lucy. "Yes...the girl dressed for death...it is...excellent to see you in full health as well."

When the spirit moved forward to give Lucy a hug as well, Lucy leaned away from Murasaki. "Yes. I am also happy I am in full health. No need for...embrace, oh."

Almost forcibly, Murasaki wrapped Lucy into an awkward hug. Her disheveled hair found its way directly into Lucy's face. The spirit gave off a cold aura and stank of a cruel combination of dust and fungus. Lucy barely managed to hold back a disgusted cough as she gave the jibakurei a gentle pat on the back.

"Okay. I deem the hug of excellent quality and it can now conclude," Lucy said. Murasaki pulled away and an unwilling shiver went down Lucy's spine. She straightened out her dress before looking back up to the spirit. "So you are still intact. Can I assume the same for-"

"The Bard? Tis true, the witches spell still cast," The Ghost of William Shakespeare said, floating to an annoyed Murasaki's side. "For the soul of true creative, cannot die, cannot err by the hand of thy enemy."

Lucy held back an outwards groan.

"I meant my father," Lucy stated. "Is he okay? Where is he?"

The Bard nodded knowingly. "It is a wise father that knows his own child. To you, your father should be as a god."

"I am aware," Lucy said. "Thank you for-"

"Luce?"

Turning around on her heel, Lucy turned to the voice. Mike Vitalis was alive. Out of his exoskeleton suit with a brand new black eye and a clean sling on his left arm, but alive. Happy tears glinted in his eyes as he let out a breath of disbelief at the sight of his daughter. Lucy treated herself to a wide smile and ran towards him. Despite his injured left arm, Mike gladly used his right arm to catch his daughter by her waist and hug her tightly. He spun around in a circle, letting her legs fly as he continued to hold his child against him.

Letting Lucy back down softly on the ground, Mike Vitalis smiled as he touched her face with his free hand. "You okay, kid? You're not hurt anywhere?"

"I'm better than okay!" Lucy exclaimed, continuing to smile widely. "I thought you were dead!"

"Well, it turns out Nora's gift does pretty good as a shield against malevolent spirits," Mike said. "Better that got hit than me, but the guy still had a helluva punch. He had seen the exploding...ducks, was it?"

"Yes," Lucy said.

"Typical poltergeist humor," Mike said, shaking his head. "Anyway, I had chased him down here to stop him and he got his good hit on me, but luckily your...ghost friends over here were able to save me." He nodded towards Murasaki and The Ghost of William Shakespeare. "Well, Lin-Manuel Miranda over there was hiding behind a minivan, but the jibakurei did a pretty good job taking care of me."

The Ghost of William Shakespeare looked aghast. "Whom ist this folly you speak of? I am the greatest playwright of all time-"

"Murasaki, you saved my father?" Lucy asked.

The spirit gave a short nod "He is a brave warrior and I will continue to require his help protecting this land, especially with the recent rise in unjust death."

Georgia let her jaw drop. "But...Mara, I thought you were going to protect *us* from Gilly!"

"I had trusted that you would be able to protect yourself," Murasaki said. "I was not about to risk an innocent life for lives that could care for themselves."

Beaming, Georgia took Murasaki's hands before letting go of them suddenly as she realized there were people around. Disappointment crossed Murasaki's face before it returned to its normally neutral state. Georgia cleared her throat.

"Well...thank you for that trust," Georgia said. "I, like, really really appreciate it."

"You'll continue to protect this land?" Lucy turned to her father. "But the job is done. Your services are no longer required here. Are we not moving back to New York?"

Mike let out a deep sigh. "Well, we could. But the jibakurei is correct. After all of this carnage....there's gonna be a lot of undead souls roaming the joint looking for peace. A paranormal private investigator is going to be required to help them find that peace." He lifted his eyebrows. "Unless, of course, you *want* to move back to New York then we'll start packing tomo-"

"Nope," Lucy said. "Sterbenville is perfect."

Mike made a face. "Sterbenville?"

"Excuse me, everyone!" Chase's voice boomed over the crowd. "Can I have your attention, please?"

He was positioned on the top step of Town Hall with Natalie close to his side. Chevy stood with the Hunter family, and James, with Charlotte holding her youngest son close to herself. All of Sterben's survivors looked up to Chase expectedly. To his friends, it was obvious that Chase was nervous. But to everyone else, he spoke with the confidence expected for the most popular senior at Sterben High School. Chase Hunter was a natural leader.

"Due to certain circumstances, aka a poltergeist roaming attempting to destroy the town-" This caused a polite laugh to ripple through the crowd. "-Mayor Hansen will be unable to return to duty. In his place, I have accepted the role of mayor in accordance to Sterben local law."

At this point, Lucy expected booing or, at least, some fighting, especially from local reporter and PTA mom Carol Carroll. But the woman actually cheered with others in the crowd, happy to see a good boy such as Chase Hunter in such a prestigious position. With a reluctant wave, Mayor Hunter smiled at his new citizens.

"Thank you for your support, uh..." He rubbed the back of his neck with one hand, using the other hand to hold up his loose pants. "I hope to continue to hold your support when I break to you my first piece of legislation, which was to rename the town of Sterben to Sterbenville in order to vacate the poltergeist that was cursed to inhabit this land."

As the crowd muttered nervously to themselves, Mike nodded his head.

"Hm. That's...actually very smart." He looked at his daughter. "You and your friends should help me on investigations more often."

"We tried," Lucy said. "You threatened to send me to New York every time we contributed to it."

"Yeah well you know I'm still trying to figure out this whole single parenting thing out," Mike sighed and took Lucy under his good arm. "I'll probably always be figuring it out."

"That's fine," Lucy said. "If it means anything, I believe you're doing an excellent job so far."

Mike smiled. "It means the world to me, honey."

He bent down to kiss the top of his daughter's head as a wave of hands rose in the crowd. With wide eyes, Chase pointed to the first hand in the crowd.

"When was this decided?"

"Uh....about a half hour ago," Chase answered. "My, uh...executive assistant has the minutes from the emergency town hall meeting. Georgia, mind joining me up here to announce the minutes?"

Everyone turned to Georgia Peaches. With all of Sterbenville's eyes on her, Georgia's cheeks flushed. She turned to Murasaki with happy eyes before running up the stone steps with a skip in her step. Natalie happily took a step away to make room for her friend. As Georgia took Chase's right hand side, another hand shot into the air.

"Carol Carroll of the Sterben Herald here," Carol Carroll announced. "Mayor Hunter, if I can even call you that, did you really appoint the Lebenville slut as your executive assistant without consulting the city council?"

More disgruntled voices in the crowd agreed with Carol Carroll as Georgia's face fell.

"Nope," Chase announced confidently. "I appointed the best person for the task to be my executive assistant. City council approval is not necessary for this position."

With a shy, but grateful smile, Georgia nodded at Chase. Chase matched her smile and nodded back before turning back to his crowd.

"Any more questions?" He asked.

There were many.

"How is she the best for the job?! She's from Lebenville!"

"Were there no other solutions to stopping the poltergeist?"

"Wasn't Mike supposed to stop the poltergeist?"

"When's the sacrificial fire?"

"Natalie, honey, are you okay?"

"Aren't we supposed to vote for you to be mayor?"

"Am I required to rename the Sterben Herald to the Sterben*ville* Herald?"

As more disgruntled questions and voices rose from the crowd, it was clear Chase was overwhelmed. Georgia looked closed to tears and Natalie was frozen in horror, staring out at the angry crowd with wide, disbelieving eyes. From the group of Hunters hanging out near the new mayor, Chevron shook his head and stepped out from his position next to Chadron.

"Aw hell," He said. Pointing at his little brother, Chevron continued to walk across his family. "You owe me, Chase."

Chevron made a straight beeline towards James. The "family friend" looked at Chevron with straightened shoulders. As all of Sterbenville looked on, Chevron Hunter, the second eldest son of the town's largest landowners, the younger brother of former football captain Chadron Hunter, and the older brother to the new mayor, took James's empty right-hand side. He waited until he was sure all eyes were on him rather than Chase. Then, with one swift movement, he took James's free hand, interlocking their fingers together.

Carol Carroll sucked in a loud gasp.

James's cheeks darkened at Chevron's act, but he looked overall pleased with the result. The top of Chevron's cheeks were the softest shade of pink as the rest of his face remained forcibly neutral. Meanwhile, Paw and Chadron scanned the crowd with mean eyes, widening their chest in a preemptive defense. Before the town could make their own full opinion about the situation, Mayor Chase Hunter moved to applaud his brother and James in a public show of support. But when he lifted his hands off of his hips, he unintentionally removed them from their job of protecting his loose waistline. This caused the new mayor's pants to fall to his ankles, revealing a pair of red boxers with pink hearts all over them to a large portion of the Sterbenville population.

All of the matters of the details of Sterben's change into Sterbenville, including the second eldest Hunter boy's reveal, were swiftly forgotten in lieu of laughing at the brand new mayor's fault. All Chase could do as his town laughed at him was shrug and pose proudly as Carol Carroll took pictures of the incident for the paper. It appeared that the poltergeist, as a whole, and the devastation he caused were all but forgotten in exchange for new, happier memories.

If Lucy knew anything for certain, she knew new was a great thing to be.

Tip #13:

Invest in therapy.

IT TOOK A LITTLE OVER a week for Sterbenville to settle into its new name. Mayor Hunter was very adamant in his community rebuilding initiative and, luckily, his citizens were as just as devoted to fixing up their town. With teamwork skills only fit for small town residents, the people of Sterbenville were able to repair the broken roads and redo some of the lost landscaping in no time. People who had abandoned the town earlier returned and helped their neighbors as soon as they put their bags into the house.

People who lost their lives to Gilly were mourned with their own private funerals. Despite their bad attitudes, the Hansens and Mrs. Bobby all received attendance from the entire town. Father O'Shannon received a good size as well, but it was Chris and Kierra who attracted the largest audience. Carol Carroll's online article about their sacrifice to save a group of teenagers for the greater good went viral and thousands showed up for the joint funeral that the Ghost of William Shakespeare gladly recited the entirety of *Romeo & Juliet* for as an eulogy.

It's what Chris and Kierra would've wanted.

After the week of mourning, rebuilding, and reorganizing, Mayor Hunter was able to hold his very first festival in celebration of all of their efforts. Various booths and tents lined the streets of Sterbenville, their attendants bundled up against the fresh November winter. Lucy put her camera to her eye and snapped a picture of the Morrisons handing out some hot chocolate to pedestrians.

"It's nice to see Sterben not trying to make money off of a tragedy for once," Natalie asked. "Oops! Sterbenville. Gosh, that's still going to take some getting used to."

"Change always requires an adjustment period," Lucy said, checking the image on her camera screen. "Sterbenville seems to be adjusting nicely though."

"Oh yeah absolutely," Natalie said. "I mean, Gilly had some solid points. Sterben *was* in a pretty rough state." Carol Carroll's voice echoed across the space as she screeched at some kids who got in the way of her photo for the Sterbenville Herald. "It's still pretty rough. But it doesn't deserve to get sent into hell, like Gilly wanted."

"Refusal to accept one's own faults is a bitter poison, and one that can hurt others if left unchecked," Lucy stated. "That being said, I do have to apologize if my honesty makes you uncomfortable or anxious at points. While it's a quality I admire, I can also understand my...blunt attitude can be hurtful. I will work harder to understand the difference between what needs to be said and what should be said."

"Are you seriously apologizing for that?!" Natalie exclaimed with a laugh. "Honesty's a good trait to have, especially with a friend." She stopped laughing with a sigh. "But if we're apologizing for our faults....then I'm sorry for not being able to handle my stress at times."

Lucy made a face. "You have no reason to apologize for that."

"Yeah but I said a lot of hurtful things to you when I was stressed," Natalie said.

"Nothing would be more hurtful than if a poltergeist condemned us to hell," Lucy said. "We were all stressed. We all used unhealthy coping mechanisms to deal with it."

Natalie let out a laugh. "Chase didn't. He took everything super cool."

"Which is why he's the mayor for the most stressful small town in America," Lucy said. When Natalie gave her a look, Lucy rolled her eyes. "*And* his family owns the largest plot of land in Sterbenville, but still. Chase was the best choice."

"Absolutely," Natalie said. "Well, Charlotte would be a great choice too if she wasn't so committed to her current job."

Their conversation was halted by the sound of police sirens. The Sterbenville Police vehicle halted to a screeching stop in front of the girls, the word 'ville' added to the existing Sterben sticker with black Sharpie. Both Lucy and Natalie let out a sigh as the officer climbed out of the window and peered over the top of their cruiser at the young ladies. Then they each faked a smile.

"Hello Officer Hansen!" They said in unison.

Officer Hansen waved her hands excitedly. "Hiya girls!"

Officer Officer Hansen's widow, Susie Hansen, had returned to Sterbenville a couple days ago. While mostly indifferent to her husband's death, possibly because she continued to believe he just ran off, she was more than happy to discover that Georgia decided to stay on as a roommate. Not only that, but when Chase posted a call for a new law enforcement officer for the community, she was the first (and only) person to sign up. Apparently, Susie had watched the same cop shows, if not more, that Officer Hansen watched to train for his job. That, apparently, made her the most qualified for the position.

"Mayor Hunter wants y'all to come on down to this office right away," Officer Hansen said. "He says he's got something important to tell y'all before the ceremony! So get in!"

Lucy and Natalie shared a look before reluctantly climbing into the police cruiser. The good news was that Officer Susie Hansen was a better driver than Officer Officer Hansen. The bad news was that Officer Officer Hansen wasn't that great of a driver to begin with. By the time the girls reached town hall, they each felt a little barfy. But the new officer of the law was trying her best, so they just wished her good-bye and watched her drive into a fire hydrant in silence.

Mayor Chase Hunter met them out on the steps leading to Town Hall. He was wearing a thick wool coat with dress pants and a grey button top underneath. Despite the politician get-up, he was still the ruggedly handsome farm boy they both knew and he smiled widely at them as he approached.

"I'm sorry, y'all," Chase said. "My knee accidentally brushed against the panic button and I felt bad for calling Officer Hansen in on a false alarm so I just had her pick you guys up. Is that okay?"

"Yeah, sure," Natalie said. "We were heading over here anyway!"

"Great!" Chase said. "The new school board will be here any minute and I wanted to hang out with you guys before then."

The three of them all smiled before heading inside to the refurbished town hall. While the main areas remained the same, the mayor's office had been remodeled during the rebuilding campaign. Gilly blasting open the impossibly heavy doors made room for Chase to tear down the wall completely and allowing his separate office to join the larger space. His fancy mayor's desk was positioned closer to the clumps of desks now occupying the area. Georgia currently sat in the second fanciest desk near the front of the office wearing a bright pink blazer and grey business skirt.

Squealing, she stood to her feet and ran over to her friends. "OMG you guys came! I told Chase it was, like, a good idea to just tell Susie to pick you guys up!"

Chase shrugged before walking over to his desk. Natalie and Lucy both smiled at Georgia.

"So, how are you liking the new job?" Natalie asked.

"It's really, really great!" Georgia said. "It turns out I'm like really good at cheering people on and taking messages for them and keeping everything, like, super tidy and organized." She nodded excitedly. "Oh! And party planning! I'm super good at that."

"Congratulations, Georgia," Lucy said. "We knew you would be great at this job."

Beaming, Georgia bounced on her heels in excitement. Chase returned to the girls with four champagne flutes and sparkling cider. Placing a flute in each girls' hand, Chase happily filled their glasses first before filling his own. He then placed the bottle down on a nearby desk before raising his cider to the girls.

"To the best team of advisors a mayor could ever ask for," Chase said. "Thanks for making my first week as mayor a success."

"Aww Chase...." Georgia cooed.

Natalie lifted her flute. "Cheers to our new mayor for being dedicated to the position rather than the title! It makes our job as advisors a lot easier."

"Cheers!" Lucy and Georgia echoed.

They all touched the rims of their flutes together before taking a sip of the apple cider. There was a knock at the door leading to the mayor's office. Georgia put her cider down on her desk and ran to the door. As soon as she opened it, Charlotte barged in followed by the rest of the Hunter family, including James, and a handful of other adults Lucy didn't recognize. There was a bluetooth attached to Charlotte's ear as she poked at her smartphone, only barely glancing up at her son.

"We're slightly ahead of schedule, but I think that's alright." Charlotte finally put the smartphone back into her pocket. "It's important for the new mayor to meet with the new school board, especially since you'll be sharing classes with some of them within the next week."

Paw, Chadron, and Chevron all shared an amused snort.

"He's related to half of us," Paw said.

"The principal's his paw for cryin' out loud," Chadron said.

"Nepotism at its finest," Chevron said.

The other teachers behind the Hunter family snickered. Mayor Hunter put his cider glass on a nearby desk and nodded at them.

"Uh, welcome!" Chase said. "Make yourselves comfortable. There'll be an official meet and greet after the ceremony-"

"Oh they should know!" Georgia exclaimed. "I, like, sent them the full itinerary last night so they could get settled at their own pace."

Natalie and Lucy shared an impressed look with each other before returning to their flutes of cider. As Charlotte and Georgia worked in tandem on giving the new school board a tour of the refurbished mayor's office, Mayor Hunter grabbed his cider again and joined Natalie and Lucy. With a deep exhale, Chase raised his eyebrows at his friends.

"This mayor-ing thing is hard," He confessed. "I'd rather take on another poltergeist than try to fix the Hansen's budget before the new year, honestly."

"We were just discussing that," Lucy said. "You were remarkably calm compared to the rest of us when we fought the spirit. How did you handle your stress so well?"

Chase arched an eyebrow. "Are you kiddin'? My whole life is a stress mess. I've got two older brothers dying to kill me since I came out the womb, one younger brother I've had to protect his whole life, a massive farm to help maintain, and, not only that, but we're Democrats in a state that's been painted red since 1964." He sighed and ran his fingers through his golden hair. "Not to mention, my ACT was only a 30 so Brown waitlisted me so now I gotta decide between taking a gap year for this whole mayor thing or go to K-State and hope for a transfer-"

"Brown?" Natalie interrupted. "You, *you*, Chase Hunter, want to get in-to....*Brown?!*"

"Well you know I found some fliers for it in the science lab so I just thought I'd apply for fun." He made a face at her. "Why? You think it's too ambitious or something?"

Natalie smiled. "No! It's...those were *my* fliers, you know. From last year?"

"Yeah!" Chase said. He rubbed the back of his neck, his cheeks flushing red as he looked at Natalie. "Uh, you know...um, do you, maybe-"

"Natalie and Chase sittin' in a tree!" Chevy sang. The trio jumped at the little brother's sudden appearance at Chase's side. "K-I-S-S-I-"

"Stop it, you little booger butt!" Chase took a swing at his little brother and Chevy ran off. He was laughing as the mayor chased him down, threatening to exile him into Lebenville for treason.

Once Chase was out of listening distance, Lucy turned to her friend with an amused smile. "It appears the Mayor just attempted to ask you out, Miss Hendrix."

"I *know*," Natalie said with a smile. "I mean...I don't know though. Chase's is really nice-"

"And attractive," Lucy said.

"Yes very much so," Natalie said. "But....I don't wanna ruin what we've got going now. Plus, I'm one of his advisors and...I don't know. I'm just not really cut out for this dating thing."

With a shrug, Lucy took another sip of her apple cider. "You can always think about it. At least if you reject him, you know he won't drag the town into hell."

Natalie laughed. "True that. By the way, what happened to Chevy's crush on you?"

"Side effect of Gilly," Lucy said. "Think the bald guy and the ginger girl from Harry Potter."

Natalie whistled. "Ooo good *almost* nerd reference."

"I'm trying my best to learn your language."

Laughing, the girls clinked their flutes together before finishing off their sparkling cider. As they placed their empty glasses down on the table, the door creaked open. Mike Vitalis poked his head in, scanning the room before looking over at Lucy and Natalie. He smiled and walked through the door, straightening out the tie on his suit as he approached the girls.

"Hey Luce, Natalie," Mike said. "How do I look?"

"Like a hero worthy of the inaugural Sterbenville Samaritan Award," Lucy said. "Congrats Dad."

Mike Vitalis smiled widely, not noticing Charlotte Hunter break away from her tour group. She towed a woman in her late-30's behind her, allowing the woman to catch up to her pace as they reached Mike. The woman had a heftier frame with flecks of gray touching the roots of her dusty brown hair. All in all, she was very average looking but held a kind face with a hint of laugh lines at the corners of her eyes.

"Mike! I was hoping you'd be by a little early," Charlotte said. Mike turned to the two women. "This is Alice Patrick. She's the new school counselor, but she's been generous enough to offer her services to those outside of the school system as well. Alice, this is Mike Vitalis. He's the resident paranormal investigator."

"Nice to meet you, Mike!" Alice said, shaking his hand heartily as Charlotte returned to the tour group. "A paranormal investigator, huh? Sounds interesting!"

"Ah...nah," Mike said, shaking his head slightly. "It's more or less like being a glorified ghostbuster but without Bill Murray."

Alice Patrick twisted her face into confusion. "A...ghostbuster? What's a ghostbuster?"

"Like the movie?" Mike asked. When Alice Patrick shook her head, still at a lost for his reference, he lightened up. "Oh. Well. Then. Never mind."

Surprisingly the woman giggled, showing exactly where her laugh lines were. Lucy quietly took a picture of the woman. At the flash of the camera, Alice froze, looking over at Lucy in surprise. Mike cleared his throat.

"Uh, Alice, this is my daughter Lucy," Mike said. "She's a junior at Sterbenville High and an amazing photographer. She's planning a show for next semester about Sterbenville."

"Don't let my presence deter you in your romantic pursuit of my father," Lucy said. "My mother is long gone and I am at an age of self-sufficiency. My father is free to pursue his own independent relationships without my contribution."

Alice stared at Lucy for a long time, unsure of what to make of the girl. Mike only nodded proudly. "She's also very honest. Now, did Charlotte forward you my techniques on post-poltergeist recovery?"

"Oh...yes!" Alice smiled at Lucy. "Nice to meet you, dear. I can't wait to see your photos!" She turned back to Mike. "I was thinking group therapy would be an excellent addition to what you sent me, given the size of people affected by this thing."

The two adults walked off discussing their therapy techniques, leaving Natalie and Lucy alone again. Lucy continued to take photos of the impromptu pre-party that was now going on in the mayor's office as the girls gossiped about the new teachers. Georgia stopped by every now and again to ask a question or share her excitement for her first day of school at Sterbenville High. The mayor even visited as well with no mention or hint of his crush on Natalie. Mike and Alice continued their conversation in a private corner of the office. Lucy was happy to see she had gotten more pictures of the two of them smiling than not.

Finally, it was time for the ceremony. Charlotte kicked everyone out except for Mayor Hunter and Georgia Peaches. Emerging outside, Lucy could see there was a large crowd occupying the folding chairs positioned around the mayor's podium in the center of the block. There was three empty seats in the front row dedicated to her, Natalie, and Mike. As the girls walked to them, the Ghost of William Shakespeare emerged from the side and approached the women.

"Good morrow, sweet ladies!" He announced. "How dost thou fair on such sweet times?"

"Shakespeare?" Natalie asked. "You're still hanging around here?"

"We haven't seen you for the past week," Lucy said. "We assumed you realized Gilly no longer had a hold on you and you could go free."

"Ah but an artist by any other name, would be a fool to remain not," The Ghost of William Shakespeare said. "Howbeit, this land preserves, a dignity of art, a master of stage, and the greatest playwright must remain."

"Lin-Manuel Miranda's here?" Natalie asked.

The Bard furrowed his ghostly eyebrows. "I still know not of who you speak, but the joke perseveres. Much like two lovers, with bounty as boundless as the sea."

Two more ghosts appeared at the Ghost of William Shakespeare's side.

"Ta-da!" Chris and Kierra sang in unison.

Natalie and Lucy both jumped back.

"Chris and Kierra?!" Lucy exclaimed. "You're back?"

"Of course!" Kierra said. "It turns out that we totally didn't deserve to die."

"Yeah two newlyweds with an entire future of happy memories stolen from them? We were like #1 on the list to come back as ghosts," Chris said. "Plus, we made those vows about loving each other beyond death and stuff."

"Yeah that's this guy's fault," Kierra explained, jokingly nudging her ghostly husband. "But we don't mind! It was a *gorgeous* second wedding and it was totally worth it to accidentally commit to spend an undead eternity together."

With a gasp, Chris turned to his spectral wife. "Honey! Do you know what this means?"

As she came to the same realization, Kierra also gasped. "Ghost wedding?!"

"Ghost wedding!" Chris echoed. They embraced, turning into a mass of semi-transparent white for a moment. The Ghost of William Shakespeare sighed.

"For all eternity, I am condemned to these lovers," The Bard said. He shrugged. "Could be a worse fate, for at least my art remains."

"Yeah!" Chris pulled away from Kierra to face the two girls again. "Will and I are gonna do *so* many plays for the theatre program. We're going to have to talk to Chevron and James about it, but there's some potential for some new works of Shakespeare premiering in Sterbenville."

At Lucy and Natalie's wide eyes, The Ghost of William Shakespeare nodded. "'Tis true. Recent events have invoked an inspiration, a catalyst for my survived art."

Natalie nodded. "Well....good luck then. Break a leg!"

Kierra waved at the girls. "We'll be seeing you guys real soon! Come and visit us at our place any time. I'll be sure to have some cookies prepared."

The three ghosts faded away and Natalie immediately turned to Lucy.

"Who knew Sterbenville would be the next Globe Theater?" Natalie asked.

"Chris was determined enough in his life, it probably would have eventually happened," Lucy said. "Although I don't believe anyone outside of this town will believe that the Ghost of William Shakespeare is back."

Natalie and Lucy shared a laugh before taking their seats in the front row. Seeing his daughter had taken her seat, Mike Vitalis excused himself from Alice Patrick and claimed his reserved seat. Lucy smirked as she adjusted her camera for the bright outdoor scenery.

"Did you get her phone number?" Lucy asked.

"Yeah," Mike said. "For...work purposes, you know. Someone might have seen a spirit and she needs help defining the issue or something."

"Sure, Dad," Lucy said, holding a tight smile.

The ceremony was a surprising success. The town of Sterbenville listened attentively to their new mayor. Chase announced the new school board and congratulated the community on their rebuilding efforts. Mike Vitalis was honored with the inaugural Sterbenville Samaritan Award for his work defeating the poltergeist. Lucy, Natalie, and Georgia were also gifted small merit awards as well for their help, but Chase didn't want to appear biased to his public so he kept them to a minimum.

The biggest announcement, and surprise to the community, was the reveal for plans to dedicate a beautiful statue to Chris and Kierra. It would be placed in the town hall center where everyone could honor the couple's sacrifice. Chase announced that it was a symbol of the Sterbenville spirit of perseverance, optimism, and unconditional neighborly love. The announcement and resulting design reveal of Kierra looking badass with her gun and Chris holding a prop sword to the air brought the crowd to a standing ovation.

After the ceremony, while Chase was preoccupied with posing for pictures of breaking the ground for the statue, Natalie, Georgia, and Lucy all found themselves off to the side of everyone. While Natalie and Lucy were desperately trying to convince Georgia that Shakespeare told them he was going to write more plays, there was a small meow that interrupted them. They all turned to see Murasaki holding Okiku in her arms.

"Hello Georgia," Murasaki said. "You looked wonderful up there."

Georgia blushed. "Thanks Mara! We've got a medal for you too." She handed a small golden token to Murasaki who stared at it in her gray palm. "It was really nice of you to show up to the ceremony like this!"

Murasaki attempted a smile. "May we go for a walk? I wish to extend my gratitude for your kindness."

"Sure!" Georgia smiled at her friends. "I'll meet up with you guys later."

Georgia and Murasaki walked off together, Okiku hopping after the two women. All Natalie could do was shake her head. "Do you think she's found out Murasaki's a thousands old undead spirit yet?"

"Absolutely," Lucy said. "But I don't think she cares."

With a shrug, Natalie accepted the answer. "Well I'm going to go find my parents. They probably want to dote over my new medal or whatever. Wanna come?"

"Thank you for the invitation, but I could use a break," Lucy said. "Want me to hold your program for you?"

"Oh! Yeah definitely!" Natalie said. She passed the piece of paper to her friend. "I gotta put it in the scrapbook. I mean, when else are we going to be honored for fighting off a poltergeist from taking over an entire town?"

The girls laughed and made a promise to see each other soon. As soon as Natalie turned to find her parents, Lucy opened her messenger bag and tried to find a safe place to hold onto Natalie's program. Her eyes caught hold of something else instead and she smiled. Trading the program for the new item, Lucy scanned the crowd for her father. He was hanging around near the mayor podium, accepting well wishes from Sterbenville residents.

Lucy skipped to his side and waited patiently for him to finish his conversation. As soon as he was done, Mike turned to his daughter with a happy sigh. "What's up? Are you taking lots of pictures?"

"Yes I am, but I'm visiting you for another reason," Lucy said. "I meant to give this to you earlier...."

Lucy then handed her father the action figure she bought at the Harvest Festival a little under a month ago. Mike examined the figure with the Ghostbuster body and the mis-matching Superman head glued onto it. His eyebrows furrowed as Lucy stared at him with expecting eyes. Finally, he pointed to the doll.

"Is this supposed to be me?" He asked.

"Yes!" Lucy cheered. "Well, to avoid legal issues, they were advertising it as the 'Hero of Sterben', but it's definitely-"

Mike Vitalis interrupted his daughter with a booming laugh. She smiled widely. Tears came to Mike Vitalis's eyes as he continued to laugh at the doll. He then shook it at his daughter.

"This...this is the best thing I've ever seen!" It took another moment for Mike to find his breath after laughing so hard. "Oh...goodness....thanks, Luce. This is too funny."

Lucy beamed. "I thought you would like it."

"Lucy!" Natalie shouted. Lucy turned to the voice to see all of her friends lined up together with Carol Carroll facing her iPhone at them. Natalie waved Lucy over. "Get over here! They want a picture of all of us for the pa-per!"

Deflating, Lucy shook her head. "No thank you! I don't like presenting myself in photographs."

All of her friends protested in their own way. Georgia was using her puppy dog eyes, Chase offered kind reasoning for it, and Natalie kept insisting it was just "one picture". With sad eyes, Lucy looked to her father for support. He shrugged.

"It's just one picture, Luce," Mike said. "I understand if you don't want to, but I think your friends would really appreciate it."

With a deep sigh, Lucy nodded. "Alright. One picture then."

Her friends cheered as she approached them, removing her camera from her neck as she did so. Carol Carroll smiled and repositioned herself to fit Lucy into the shot. "Okay everyone! Ready? Three, two-"

"Wait!" Lucy stepped forward. "Use my camera. It's a better quality. I already have the settings calibrated."

Letting her jaw slack in shock, Carol Carroll accepted Lucy's camera with two hands. "Uh...thank you! How do you-"

"It's really easy," Lucy said. "Just give the button a half-tap to focus the image and then a full tap to capture the shot. Follow the rule of thirds, use plenty of white space on both sides, and it should capture an excellent image."

Carol Carroll nodded slowly. "Okay...yeah, that sounds easy. Okay."

With an encouraging half-smile, Lucy joined her friends. Chase posed happily with his shovel. Natalie and Georgia matched his enthusiasm with their own bright smiles. Despite the happy situation, Lucy could only manage an awkward grimace that she hoped would be mistaken for a smile. When the picture was finally taken, Lucy was quick to grab her camera back from Carol Carroll.

Her friends were lost in their own joyful conversations about the ceremony and Chase's new role as mayor to notice Lucy walk off to the side, desperately flipping through the pictures on her camera. Finally she found the one they just took. Her friends looked fine. She knew they would look fine. It was the image of herself that she was worried about.

For there was a secret, a secret Lucy uncovered when she first took a picture of herself, that she never told anyone about. She kept it from her mother, from her father, from all of her friends, and, for the most part, she hid it from herself most days as well. But in every picture of herself, Lucy Vitalis had a shadow behind her. Not a shadow she could claim, but something else. It was a dark shade with unnaturally hollow eyes that looked down at her with rage, with envy, as if it were waiting for the day to consume her soul. Every picture she took of herself, the more vivid the shadow became. She didn't know where it came from and she wasn't prepared to find out.

Lucy looked down at the picture and, as soon as she recognized the familiar shadow, she checked behind herself. When it was clear the shadow had yet to manifest itself into a physical form, she turned back to the camera and deleted the image.

Acknowledgements

OH WOW. I HAVE A BOOK out in the world now. This has been a dream of mine since I was six years old and now it's here. Wow. This is absolutely unbelievable and could not have been done without the wonderful support system in my life who have been nothing but encouraging and supportive throughout this entire process.

First, a HUGE special thank you to my best enemy, Kierra. This book literally could not have happened without her "encouragement" (see Stephen King's *Misery*) to not only put her character into a novel, but to finish said novel as well. So a special thanks for not only allowing me to use her likeness in my silly book, but for answering every text message about the book, reading and editing it WHILE in nursing school, and for continuing to be a great teammate long after we stopped playing softball. You're the best, #41.

Then, of course, my best friend Julie also deserves a special shoutout for reading and editing this book out of the kindness and generosity of her heart, even when I was cruel enough to set an impossible deadline against her. She also answered every nervous text message even when she didn't know the answer and she's also just the best. Always. <3

My family was also crucial to the development of this novel. Thank you to my mom for being the very first reader EVER for this book, even when I said she didn't have to read it right away, and offering her own critiques that improved this book immensely. Thank you to my dad for always supporting my dreams no matter how far-fetched they are/seem to be and always leaving some coffee in the pot for me in the mornings. Thank you to Nate for contributing ideas and encouragement in his own special way. Sorry that the name "Chate" didn't make the final cut. Also thank you to Scout, the best unofficial writing partner in the world who sat on my lap while I wrote.

Thank you to my cheerleading squad: Levi, Harmony, Dyrani, Haley, Danny, Mitch, Grecia, Christa, and all of my Moonfighters on YouTube. You guys are the most supportive bunch of people I've ever been fortunate to meet both online and off and I'm so grateful for our friendship! I also wish to thank the Schusters, the Jacksons, the Murphys, the towns of Axtell, Kansas & Hastings, Nebraska, and St. Joseph Catholic School for their (mostly unknowing) support.

A very, *very* special thank you to Colwell. Thank you for taking a chance on the awkward, never-published freshman who walked into your pub room after school hours and asked to write a story for your award-winning paper. Thank you for continuing to nurture her love for writing over the next four years with patience and encouragement. Without your guidance, I never would've had the courage to pursue writing as a career. Thank you.

Finally, a thank you to *you*, whoever picked up this book. You're the reason six year old me wanted to be a writer and you're the reason why I continue to write. Thank you for reading my silly book.

Enjoy the book?

Please review it!

Reviews are essential to indie authors and small publishers. They allow new readers to discover the book and, depending on the platform, increase the likelihood of the book appearing eslewhere on the site. So if you really enjoyed this novel and want others to read it, we would appreciate it if you reviewed the book on your platform of choice!

Follow our social media to keep track of future books!

www.dalygoodmedia.com
Twitter/Instagram: @dalygoodmedia
dalygoodbusiness@gmail.com

About the Author

Maddie Gudenkauf is also the author of the young adult paranormal comedy *How to Survive a Ghost Story*. She previously ran the variety YouTube channel known as "TheMaddness22" with over 2,300 subscribers and 500,000 views. Maddie currently lives in Colorado with her dog Mollie and overfilled bookcases in every room.

Read more at https://maddiegudenkauf.com/.